THE FAR LOVERS

"Ken," she says. Her hand touches the scanner. His comes in answer. They stand with light years between their fingertips.

We can measure, but cannot imagine, how far. If Sol let go of Earth and the planet whipped into space like a stone from a sling, it would get here in a thousand centuries.-Twenty times the length of our history since first in Sumer they scratched in stone what they knew of the stars...

"Becky," he says. "How're you doing, lass?"

"Lonely," she says. "But I'm glad to see you again!"

THE DARK BETWEEN THE STARS

Poul Anderson

Berkley Books by Poul Anderson

THE AVATAR
THE CORRIDORS OF TIME
THE DARK BETWEEN THE STARS
THE EARTH BOOK OF STORMGATE
THE ENEMY STARS
THE HIGH CRUSADE
HOMEWARD AND BEYOND
MIRKHEIM
OPERATION CHAOS
SATAN'S WORLD
THE STAR FOX
STAR PRINCE CHARLIE (with Gordon Dickson)
TAU ZERO
THREE HEARTS AND THREE LIONS
TIME AND STARS
TRADER TO THE STARS
THE TROUBLE TWISTERS
VAULT OF THE AGES

POUL ANDERSON

THE DARK BETWEEN THE STARS

BERKLEY BOOKS, NEW YORK

THE DARK BETWEEN THE STARS

A Berkley Book / published by arrangement with the author

PRINTING HISTORY
Berkley edition / December 1981

Cover illustration by David Egge.

For information address: Berkley Publishing Corporation, 200 Madison Avenue, New York, New York 10016

ISBN: 0-425-04291-X

A BERKLEY BOOK ® TM 757, 375
PRINTED IN THE UNITED STATES OF AMERICA

Acknowledgments

These stories were originally published as follows:

"The Sharing of Flesh," *Galaxy*, December 1968, copyright © 1968 by Galaxy Publishing Corp.
"Fortune Hunter," *Infinity Four*, copyright © 1972 by Lancer Books, Inc.
"Eutopia," *Dangerous Visions*, copyright © 1967 by Harlan Ellison.
"The Pugilist," *The Magazine of Fantasy and Science Fiction*, November 1973, copyright © 1973 by Mercury Press, Inc.
"Night Piece," *The Magazine of Fantasy and Science Fiction*, July 1961, copyright © 1961 by Mercury Press, Inc.
"The Voortrekkers," in *Final Stage*, copyright © 1974 by Edward L. Ferman and Barry N. Malzberg.
"Gibraltar Falls," *The Magazine of Fantasy and Science Fiction*, October 1975, copyright © 1975 by Mercury Press, Inc.
"Windmill," in *Saving Worlds*, copyright © 1973 by Roger Elwood and Virginia Kidd.
"Call Me Joe," in *Astounding Science Fiction*, April 1957, copyright © 1957 by Street & Smith Publications, Inc.

To Alva Rogers

Contents

Foreword

If science fiction today shows an enormous variety of themes and treatments, that is only in part due to the considerable number of different writers, some of them with very considerable gifts, who are creating it. More important, I think, is its orientation toward reality, the inspiration it draws from that source; for the variety of the universe is infinite. I hope this book will provide an example.

At first glance, the claim looks absurd. Included here are stories involving such ideas as telepathy, parallel space-times, travel faster than light, and time travel—all of them scientifically disreputable, or worse. Though other tales stay closer to home and involve nothing that a physicist could say is impossible in principle, nevertheless, they are set in future years: which is to say that their settings are totally imaginary.

And yet . . . Well, it would seem profoundly unscientific to claim that we will never come upon natural phenomena unknown to us now, never have to revise our physics from the ground up, as has been necessary two or three times in the past. In fact, today work is going on at the frontiers of knowledge (yes, even in general relativity) with results which suggest that those heterodox concepts may not be so preposterous after all.

More important to my point is the observation that, no matter if occasional far-out postulates have been made for the sake of narrative, at its core each of these stories derives from something existent. "Fortune Hunter," "The Pugilist," and "Windmill" reflect certain of our contemporary concerns. "The Sharing of Flesh" was suggested by an entomological research report in *Science*. "Eutopia" draws on history, "Gibraltar Falls" on geology, "Night Piece" on psychology, "The Voortrekkers" on current developments in astronautics, cybernetics, and biology. "Call Me Joe," the oldest and perhaps best-known of the lot, is based on planetary astronomy as of the time it was written. Later discoveries have vastly modified our image of Jupiter and its moons; but that kind of obsolescence is inevitable as long as science continues to advance, and has not caused other tales in the same plight to be discarded.

Besides these specific topics, of course, the stories deal with people. All fiction must, one way or another, and therefore never quite gets away from reality.

Lest the foregoing seem pretentious, let me close with the simple wish that you will enjoy what you find here.

Poul Anderson

THE DARK BETWEEN THE STARS

The Sharing of Flesh

Moru understood about guns. At least, the tall strangers had demonstrated to their guides what the things that each of them carried at his hip could do in a flash and a flameburst. But he did not realize that the small objects they often moved about in their hands, while talking in their own language, were audiovisual transmitters. Probably he thought they were fetishes.

Thus, when he killed Donli Sairn, he did so in full view of Donli's wife.

That was happenstance. Except for prearranged times, morning and evening of the planet's twenty-eight-hour day, the biologist, like his fellows, sent only to his computer. But because they had not been married long, and were helplessly happy, Evalyth received his 'casts whenever she could get away from her own duties.

The coincidence that she was tuned in at that one moment was not great. There was little for her to do. As militech of the expedition—she being from a half barbaric part of Kraken where the sexes had equal opportunities to learn of combat suitable to primitive environments—she had overseen the building of a compound; and she kept the routines of guarding it under a close eye. However, the inhabitants of Lokon were as cooperative with the visitors from heaven as mutual mysteriousness allowed. Every instinct and experience assured Evalyth Sairn that their reticence masked nothing except awe, with perhaps a wistful hope of friendship. Captain Jonafer agreed. Her position having thus become rather a sinecure, she was trying to learn enough about Donli's work to be a useful assistant after he returned from the lowlands.

Also, a medical test had lately confirmed that she was pregnant. She wouldn't tell him, she decided; not yet, over all those hundreds of kilometers, but when they lay again together. Meanwhile, the knowledge that they had begun a new life made him a lodestar to her.

On the afternoon of his death she entered the biolab whistling. Outside, sunlight struck fierce and brass-colored on dusty ground, on prefab shacks huddled about the boat which had brought everyone and everything down from the orbit where *New Dawn* circled, on the parked flitters and gravsleds that took men around the big island that was the only habitable land on this globe, on the men and the women themselves. Beyond the stockade, plumy treetops, a glimpse of mud-brick buildings, a murmur of voices and mutter of footfalls, a drift of bitter woodsmoke, showed that a town of several thousand people sprawled between here and Lake Zelo.

The biolab occupied more than half the structure where the Sairns lived. Comforts were few, when ships from a handful of cultures struggling back to civilization ranged across the ruins of empire. For Evalyth, though, it sufficed that this was their home. She was used to austerity anyway. One thing that had first attracted her to Donli, meeting him on Kraken, was the cheerfulness with which he, a man from Atheia, which was supposed to have retained or regained almost as many amenities as Old Earth knew in its glory, had accepted life in her gaunt grim country.

The gravity field here was 0.77 standard, less than two-thirds of what she had grown up in. Her gait was easy through the clutter of apparatus and specimens. She was a big young woman, good-looking in the body, a shade too strong in the features for most men's taste outside her own folk. She had their blondness and, on legs and forearms, their intricate tattoos; the blaster at her waist had come down through many generations. Otherwise she had abandoned Krakener costume for the plain coveralls of the expedition.

How cool and dim the shack was! She sighed with pleasure, sat down, and activated the receiver. As the image formed, three-dimensional in the air, and Donli's voice spoke, her heart sprang a little.

"—appears to be descended from a clover."

The image was of plants with green trilobate leaves, scattered low among the reddish native pseudo-grasses. It swelled as Donli brought the transmitter near, so that the computer might record details for later analysis. Evalyth frowned, trying to recall what . . . oh, yes. Clover was another of those life forms that man had brought with him from Old Earth, to more planets than anyone now remembered, before the Long Night fell. Often they were virtually unrecognizable; over thousands of years, evolution had fitted them to alien conditions, or mutation and genetic drift had acted on small initial populations in a nearly random fashion. No one on Kraken had known that pines and gulls and rhizobacteria were altered immigrants, until Donli's crew arrived and identified them. Not that he, or anybody from this part of the galaxy, had yet made it back to the mother world. But the Atheian data banks were packed with information, and so was Donli's dear curly head—

And there was his hand, huge in the field of view, gathering specimens. She wanted to kiss it. *Patience, patience,* the officer part of her reminded the bride. *We're to work. We've discovered one more lost colony, the most wretched one so far, sunken back to utter primitivism. Our duty is to advise the Board whether a civilizing mission is worthwhile, or whether the slender resources that the Allied Planets can spare had better be used elsewhere, leaving these people in their misery for another two or three hundred years. To make an honest report, we must study them, their cultures, their world. That's why I'm in the barbarian highlands and he's down in the jungle among out-and-out savages.*

Please finish soon, darling.

She heard Donli speak in the lowland dialect. It was a debased form of Lokonese, which in turn was remotely descended from Anglic. The expedition's linguists had unraveled the language in a few intensive weeks. Then all personnel took a brain-feed in it. Nonetheless, she admired how quickly her man had become fluent in the woodsrunners' version, after mere days of conversation with them.

"Are we not coming to the place, Moru? You said the thing was close by our camp."

"We are nearly arrived, man-from-the-clouds."

A tiny alarm struck within Evalyth. What was going on? Donli hadn't left his companions to strike off alone with a native, had he? Rogar of Lokon had warned them to beware of treachery in those parts. But, to be sure, only yesterday the guides had rescued Haimie Fiell when he tumbled into a swift-running river... at some risk to themselves....

The view bobbed as the transmitter swung in Donli's grasp. It made Evalyth a bit dizzy. From time to time she got glimpses of the broader setting. Forest crowded about a game trail, rust-colored leafage, brown trunks and branches, shadows beyond, the occasional harsh call of something unseen. She could practically feel the heat and dank weight of the atmosphere, smell the unpleasant pungencies. This world (which no longer had a name, except World, because the dwellers upon it had forgotten what the stars really were) was ill suited to colonization. The life it had spawned was often poisonous, always nutritionally deficient. With the help of species they had brought along, men survived marginally. The original settlers doubtless meant to improve matters. But then the breakdown came—evidence was that their single town had been missiled out of existence, a majority of the people with it—and resources were lacking to rebuild, and the miracle was that anything human remained except bones.

"Now here, man-from-the-clouds."

The swaying scene grew steady. Silence hummed from jungle to cabin. "I do not see anything," Donli said at length.

"Follow me. I show."

Donli put his transmitter in the fork of a tree. It scanned him and Moru while they moved across a meadow. The guide looked childish beside the space traveler, barely up to his shoulder: an old child, though, near-naked body seamed with scars and lame in the right foot from some injury of the past, face wizened in a great black bush of hair and beard. He, who could not hunt, could only fish and trap to support his family, was even more impoverished than his fellows. He must have been happy indeed when the flitter landed near their village and the strangers offered fabulous trade goods for a week or two of being shown around the countryside. Donli had projected the image of Moru's straw hut for Evalyth, the pitiful few possessions, the woman already worn out with toil, the two surviving sons who, at ages said to be about seven or eight, which would equal twelve or thirteen standard years, were shriveled gnomes.

Rogar had seemed to declare—the Lokonese tongue was by no means perfectly understood yet—that the lowlanders would be less poor if they weren't such a vicious lot, tribe forever at war with tribe. *But really,* Evalyth thought, *what possible menace can they be?*

Moru's gear consisted of a loinstrap, a cord around his body for preparing snares, an obsidian knife, and a knapsack so woven and greased that it could hold liquids at need. The other men of his group, being able to pursue game and to win a share of booty by taking part in battles, were noticeably better off. They didn't look much different in person, however. Without room for expansion, the island populace must be highly inbred.

The dwarfish man squatted, parting a shrub with his hands. "Here," he grunted, and stood up again.

Evalyth knew well the eagerness that kindled in Donli. Nevertheless he turned around, smiled straight into the transmitter, and said in Atheian: "Maybe you're watching, dearest, If so, I'd like to share this with you. It may be a bird's nest."

She remembered vaguely that the existence of birds would be an ecologically significant datum. What mattered was what he had just said to her. "Oh yes, oh yes!" she wanted to cry. But his group had only two receivers with them, and he wasn't carrying either.

She saw him kneel in the long, ill-colored vegetation. She saw him reach with the gentleness she also knew, into the shrub, easing its branches aside, holding his breath lest he—

She saw Moru leap upon his back. The savage wrapped legs about Donli's middle. His left hand seized Donli's hair and pulled the head back. The knife flew in his right.

Blood spurted from beneath Donli's jaw. He couldn't shout, not with his throat gaping open, he could only bubble and croak while Moru haggled the wound wider. He reached blindly for his gun. Moru dropped the knife and caught his arms, they rolled over in that embrace, Donli threshed and flopped in the spouting of his own blood, Moru hung on, the brush trembled around them and hid them, until Moru rose red and dripping, painted, panting, and Evalyth screamed into the transmitter beside her, into the universe, and she kept on screaming and fought them when they tried to take her away from the scene in the meadow where Moru went about his butcher's work, until something stung her with coolness and she toppled into the bottom of the universe whose stars had all gone out forever.

Haimie Fiell said through white lips: "No, of course we didn't know till you alerted us. He and that—creature—were several kilometers from our camp. *Why* didn't you let us go after him right away?"

"Because of what we'd seen on the transmission," Captain Jonafer replied. "Sairn was irretrievably dead. You could've been ambushed, arrows in the back or something, pushing down those narrow trails. Best you stay where you were, guarding each other, till we got a vehicle to you."

Fiell looked past the big gray-haired man, out of the door of the command hut, to the stockade and the unpitying noon sky. "But what that little monster was doing meanwhile—" Abruptly he closed his mouth.

With equal haste, Jonafer said: "The other guides ran away, you've told me, as soon as they sensed you were angry. I've just had a report from Kallaman. His team flitted to the village. It's deserted. The whole tribe's pulled up stakes. Afraid of our revenge, evidently. Though it's no large chore to move, when you can carry your household goods on your back and weave yourself a new house in a day."

Evalyth leaned forward. "Stop evading me," she said. "What did Moru do with Donli that you might have prevented if you'd arrived in time?"

Fiell continued to look past her. Sweat gleamed in droplets on his forehead. "Nothing, really," he mumbled. "Nothing that mattered . . . once the murder itself had been committed."

"I meant to ask you what kind of services you want for him, Lieutenant Sairn," Jonafer said to her. "Should the ashes be buried here, or scattered in space after we leave, or brought home?"

Evalyth turned her gaze full upon him. "I never authorized that he be cremated, Captain," she said slowly.

"No, but— Well, be realistic. You were first under anaesthesia, then heavy sedation, while we recovered the body. Time had passed. We've no facilities for, um, cosmetic repair, nor any extra refrigeration space, and in this heat—"

Since she had been let out of sickbay, there had been a kind of numbness in Evalyth. She could not entirely comprehend the fact that Donli was gone. It seemed as if at any instant yonder doorway would fill with him, sunlight across his shoulders, and he would call to her, laughing, and console her for a meaningless nightmare she had had. That was the effect of the psychodrugs, she knew, and damned the kindliness of the medic.

She was almost glad to feel a slow rising of anger. It meant the drugs were wearing off. By evening she would be able to weep.

"Captain," she said, "I saw him killed. I've seen deaths before, some of them quite as messy. We don't mask the truth on Kraken. You've cheated me of my right to lay my man out and close his eyes. You will not cheat me of my right to obtain justice. I demand to know exactly what happened."

Jonafer's fists knotted on his desktop. "I can hardly stand to tell you."

"But you shall, Captain."

"All right! All right!" Jonafer shouted. The words leaped out like bullets. "We saw the thing transmitted. He stripped Donli, hung him up by the heels from a tree, bled him into that knapsack. He cut off the genitals and threw them in with the blood. He opened the body and took heart, lungs, liver, kidneys, thyroid, prostate, pancreas, and loaded them up too, and ran off into the woods. Do you wonder why we didn't let you see what was left?"

"The Lokonese warned us against the jungle dwellers," Fiell said dully. "We should have listened. But they seemed like pathetic dwarfs. And they did rescue me from the river. When Donli asked about birds—described them, you know, and asked if anything like that was known—Moru said yes, but they were rare and shy; our gang would scare them off; but if one man would come along with him, he could find a nest and they might see the bird. A 'house', he called it, but Donli thought he meant a nest. Or so he told us. It'd been a talk with Moru when they happened to be a ways offside, in sight but out of earshot. Maybe that should have alerted us, maybe we should have asked the other tribesmen. But we didn't see any reason to—I mean, Donli was bigger, stronger, armed with a blaster, what savage would dare attack him, and anyway, they *had* been friendly, downright frolicsome after they got over their initial fear of us, and they'd shown as much eagerness for further contact as anybody here in Lokon has, and—" His voice trailed off.

"Did he steal tools or weapons?" Evalyth asked.

"No," Jonafer said. "I have everything your husband was carrying, ready to give you."

Fiell said: "I don't think it was an act of hatred. Moru must have had some superstitious reason."

Jonafer nodded. "We can't judge him by our standards."

"By whose, then?" Evalyth retorted. Supertranquillizer or no, she was surprised at the evenness of her own tone. "I'm from Kraken, remember. I'll not let Donli's child be born and grow up knowing he was murdered and no one tried to get justice for him."

"You can't take revenge on an entire tribe," Jonafer said.

"I don't mean to. But—Captain, the personnel of this expedition are from several different planets, each with its characteristic societies. The articles specifically state that the essential mores of every member shall be respected. I want to be relieved of my regular duties until I have arrested the killer of my husband and done justice upon him."

Jonafer bent his head. "I have to grant that," he said low.

Evalyth rose. "Thank you, gentlemen," she said. "If you will excuse me, I'll commence my investigation at once."

—while she was still a machine, before the drugs wore off.

In the drier, cooler uplands, agriculture had remained possible after the colony otherwise lost civilization. Fields and orchards, painstakingly cultivated with neolithic tools, supported a scattering of villages and the capital town Lokon.

Its people bore a family resemblance to the forest dwellers. Few settlers indeed could have survived to become the ancestors of this world's humanity. But the highlanders were better nourished, bigger, straighter. They wore gaily dyed tunics and sandals. The well-to-do added jewelry of gold and silver. Hair was braided, chins kept shaven. Folk walked boldly, without the savages' constant fear of ambush, and talked merrily.

To be sure, this was only strictly true of the free. While *New Dawn*'s anthropologists had scarcely begun to unravel the ins and outs of the culture, it had been obvious from the first that Lokon kept a large slave class. Some were sleek household servants. More toiled meek and naked in the fields, the quarries, the mines, under the lash of overseers and the guard of soldiers whose spearheads and swords were of ancient Imperial metal. But none of the space travelers were unduly shocked. They had seen worse elsewhere. Historical data banks described places in olden time called Athens, India, America.

Evalyth strode down twisted, dusty streets, between the gaudily painted walls of cubical, windowless adobe houses. Commoners going about their tasks made respectful salutes. Although no one feared any longer that the strangers meant harm, she did tower above the tallest man, her hair was colored like metal and her eyes like the sky, she bore lightning at her waist and none knew what other godlike powers.

Today soldiers and noblemen also genuflected, while slaves went on their faces. Where she appeared, the chatter and clatter of everyday life vanished; the business of the market plaza halted when she passed the booths; children ceased their games and fled; she moved in a silence akin to the silence in her soul. Under the sun and the snowcone of Mount Burus, horror brooded. For by now Lokon knew that a man from the stars had been slain by a lowland brute; and what would come of that?

Word must have gone ahead to Rogar, though, since he awaited her in his house by Lake Zelo next to the Sacred Place. He was not king or council president or high priest, but he was something of all three, and he it was who dealt most with the strangers.

His dwelling was the usual kind, larger than average but dwarfed by the adjacent walls. Those enclosed a huge compound, filled with buildings, where none of the outworlders had been admitted. Guards in scarlet robes and grotesquely carved wooden helmets stood always at its gates. Today their numbers were doubled, and others flanked Rogar's door. The lake shone like polished steel at their backs. The trees along the shore looked equally rigid.

Rogar's majordomo, a fat elderly slave, prostrated himself in the entrance as Evalyth neared. "If the heaven-borne will deign to follow this unworthy one, *Klev* Rogar is within—" The guards dipped their spears to her. Their eyes were wide and frightened.

Like the other houses, this turned inward. Rogar sat on a dais in a room opening on a courtyard. It seemed doubly cool and dim by contrast with the glare outside. She could scarcely discern the frescos on the walls or the patterns on the carpet; they were crude art anyway. Her attention focused on Rogar. He did not rise, that not being a sign of respect here. Instead, he bowed his grizzled head above folded hands. The majordomo offered her a bench and Rogar's chief wife set a bombilla of herb tea by her before vanishing into the women's quarters.

"Be greeted, *Klev,*" Evalyth said formally.

"Be greeted, heaven-borne." Alone now, shadowed from the cruel sun, they observed a ritual period of silence.

Then: "This is terrible what has happened, heaven-borne," Rogar said. "Perhaps you do not know that my white robe and bare feet signify mourning as for one of my own blood."

"That is well done," Evalyth said. "We shall remember."

The man's dignity faltered. "You understand that none of us have anything to do with the evil, do you not? The savages are our enemies too. They are vermin. Our ancestors caught some and made them slaves, but they are good for nothing else. I warned your friends not to go down among those we have not tamed."

"Their wish was to do so," Evalyth replied. "Now my wish is to get revenge for my man." She didn't know if this language included a word for justice. No matter. Because of the drugs, which heightened the logical faculties while they muffled the emotions, she was speaking Lokonese quite well enough for her purposes.

"We can gather soldiers and help you kill as many as you choose," Rogar offered.

"Not needful. With this weapon at my side I alone can destroy more than your army might. I want your counsel and help in a different matter. How can I find him who slew my man?"

Rogar frowned. "The savages can vanish into trackless jungles, heaven-borne."

"Can they vanish from other savages, though?"

"Ah! Shrewdly thought, heaven-borne. Those tribes are endlessly at each other's throats. If we can make contact with one, its hunters will soon learn for you where the killer's people have taken themselves." His scowl deepened. "But he may have gone from them, to hide until you have departed our land. A single man might be impossible to find. Lowlanders are good at hiding, of necessity."

"What do you mean by necessity?"

Rogar showed surprise at her failure to grasp what was obvious to him. "Why, consider a man out hunting," he said. "He cannot go with companions after every kind of game, or the noise and scent would frighten it away. So he is often alone in the jungle. Someone from another tribe may well set upon him. A man stalked and killed is just as useful as one slain in open war."

"Why this incessant fighting?"

Rogar's look of bafflement grew stronger. "How else shall they get human flesh?"

"But they do not live on that!"

"No, surely not, except as needed. But that need comes many times, as you know. Their wars are their chief way of taking men; booty is good too, but not the main reason to fight. He who slays, owns the corpse, and naturally divides it solely among his close kin. Not everyone is lucky in battle. Therefore those who did not chance to kill in a war may well go hunting on their own, two or three of them together hoping to find a single man from a different tribe. And that is why a lowlander must be skilful at hiding."

Evalyth did not move or speak. Rogar drew a long breath and continued trying to explain: "Heaven-borne, when I heard the evil news, I spoke long with men from your company. They told me what they had seen from afar by the wonderful means you command. Thus it is clear to me what happened. This guide, what is his name, yes, Moru, he is a cripple. He had no hope of killing himself a man except by treachery. When he saw that chance, he took it."

He ventured a smile. "That would never happen in the highlands," he declared. "We do not fight wars, save when we are attacked, nor do we hunt our fellow men as if they were animals. Like yours, ours is a civilized race." His lips drew back from startlingly white teeth. "But heaven-borne, your man was slain. I propose we take vengeance, not simply on the killer if we catch him, but on his tribe, which we can certainly find as you suggested. That will teach all the savages to beware of their betters. Afterward we can share the flesh, half to your people, half to mine."

Evalyth could only know an intellectual astonishment. Yet she had the feeling somehow of having walked off a cliff. She stared through the shadows, into the grave old face, and after a long time she heard herself whisper: "You . . . also . . . here . . . eat men?"

"Slaves," Rogar said. "No more than required. One of them will do for four boys."

Her hand dropped to her gun. Rogar sprang up in alarm.

"Heaven-borne," he exclaimed, "I told you we are civilized! Never fear attack from any of us! We—we—"

She rose too, high above him. Did he read judgment in her gaze? Was the terror that snatched him on behalf of his whole people? He cowered from her, sweating and shuddering. "Heaven-borne, believe me, you have no quarrel with Lokon—no, now, let me show you, let me take you into the Sacred Place, even if, if you are no initiate . . . for surely you are akin to the gods, surely the gods will not be offended— Come, let me show you how it is, let me prove we have no will and no *need* to be your enemies—"

There was the gate that Rogar opened for her in that massive wall. There were the shocked countenances of the guards and loud promises of many sacrifices to appease the Powers. There was the stone pavement beyond, hot and hollowly resounding underfoot. There were the idols grinning around a central temple. There was the house of the acolytes who did the work and who shrank in fear when they saw their master conduct a foreigner in. There were the slave barracks.

"See, heaven-borne, they are well-treated, are they not? We do have to crush their hands and feet when we choose them as children for this service. Think how dangerous it would be otherwise, hundreds of boys and young men in here. But we treat them kindly unless they misbehave. Are they not fat? Their own Holy Food is especially honorable, bodies of men of all degree who have died in their full strength. We teach them that they will live on in those for whom they are slain. Most are content with that, believe me, heaven-borne. Ask them yourself . . . though remember, they grow dull-witted, with nothing to do year after year. We slay them quickly, cleanly, at the beginning of each summer—no more than we must for that year's crop of boys entering into manhood, one slave for four boys, no more than that. And it is a most beautiful rite, with days of feasting and merrymaking afterward. Do you understand now, heaven-borne? You have nothing to fear from us. We are not savages, warring and raiding and skulking to get our man-flesh. We are civilized—not godlike in your fashion, no, I dare not claim that, do not be angry—but civilized—surely worthy of your friendship, are we not, are we not, heaven-borne?"

Chena Darnard, who headed the cultural anthropology team, told her computer to scan its data bank. Like the others, it was a portable, its memory housed in *New Dawn*. At the moment the spaceship was above the opposite hemisphere, and perceptible time passed while beams went back and forth along the strung-out relay units.

Chena leaned back and studied Evalyth across her desk. The Krakener girl sat so quietly. It seemed unnatural, despite the drugs in her bloodstream retaining some power. To be sure, Evalyth was of aristocratic descent in a warlike society. Furthermore, hereditary psychological as well as physiological differences might exist on the different worlds. Not much was known about that, apart from extreme cases like Gwydion (or this planet?). Regardless, Chena thought, it would be better if Evalyth gave way to simple shock and grief.

"Are you quite certain of your facts, dear?" the anthropologist asked as gently as possible. "I mean, while this island alone is habitable, it's large, the topography is rugged, communications are primitive, my group has already identified scores of distinct cultures."

"I questioned Rogar for more than an hour," Evalyth replied in the same flat voice, as before. "I know interrogation techniques, and he was badly rattled. He talked.

"The Lokonese themselves are not as backward as their technology. They've lived for centuries with savages threatening their borderlands. It's made them develop a good intelligence network. Rogar described its functioning to me in detail. It can't help but keep them reasonably well-informed about everything that goes on. And, while tribal customs do vary tremendously, the cannibalism is universal. That's why none of the Lokonese thought to mention it to us. They took for granted that we had our own ways of providing human meat."

"People have, m-m-m, latitude in those methods?"

"Oh yes. Here they breed slaves for the purpose. But most lowlanders have too skimpy an economy for that. Some of them use war and murder. Among others, men past a certain age draw lots for who shall die. Among still others, they settle it within the tribe by annual combats. Or— Who cares? The fact is that, everywhere in this country, in whatever fashion it may be, the boys undergo a puberty rite that involves eating an adult male."

Chena bit her lip. "What in the name of chaos might have started—? Computer! Have you scanned?"

"Yes," said the machine voice out of the case on her desk. "Data on cannibalism in man are comparatively sparse, because it is a rarity. On all planets hitherto known to us it is banned, and has been throughout their history, although it is sometimes considered forgivable as an emergency measure when no alternative means of preserving life is available. Very limited forms of what might be called ceremonial cannibalism have occurred, as for example the drinking of minute amounts of each other's blood in pledging oath brotherhood among the Falkens of Lochlanna—"

"Never mind that," Chena said. A tautness in her throat thickened her tone. "Only here, it seems, have they degenerated so far that— Or is it degeneracy? Reversion, perhaps? What about Old Earth?"

"Information is fragmentary. Aside from what was lost during the Long Night, knowledge is under the handicap that the last primitive societies there vanished before interstellar travel began. But certain data collected by ancient historians and scientists remain.

"Cannibalism was an occasional part of human sacrifice. As a rule, victims were left uneaten. But in a minority of religions, the bodies, or selected portions of them, were consumed, either by a special class, or by the community as a whole. Generally this was regarded as theophagy. Thus, the Aztecs of Mexico offered thousands of individuals annually to their gods. The requirement of doing this forced them to provoke wars and rebellions, which in turn made it easy for the eventual European conqueror to get native allies. The majority of prisoners were simply slaughtered, their hearts given directly to the idols. But in at least one cult the body was divided among the worshippers.

"Cannibalism could be a form of magic, too. By eating a person, one supposedly acquired his virtues. This was the principal motive of the cannibals of Africa and Polynesia. Contemporary observers did report that the meals were relished, but that is easy to understand, especially in protein-poor areas.

"The sole recorded instance of systematic non-ceremonial cannibalism was among the Carib Indians of America. They ate man because they preferred man. They were especially fond of babies, and used to capture women from other tribes for breeding stock. Male children of these slaves were generally gelded to make them docile and tender. In large part because of strong aversion to such practices, the Europeans exterminated the Caribs to the last man.''

The report stopped. Chena grimaced. ''I can sympathize with the Europeans,'' she said.

Evalyth might once have raised her brows; but her face stayed as wooden as her speech. ''Aren't you supposed to be an objective scientist?''

''Yes. Yes. Still, there is such a thing as value judgment. And they did kill Donli.''

''Not they. One of them. I shall find him.''

''He's nothing but a creature of his culture, dear, sick with his whole race.'' Chena drew a breath, struggling for calm. ''Obviously, the sickness has become a behavioral basic,'' she said. ''I daresay it originated in Lokon. Cultural radiation is practically always from the more to the less advanced peoples. And on a single island, after centuries, no tribe has escaped the infection. The Lokonese later elaborated and rationalized the practice. The savages left its cruelty naked. But highlander or lowlander, their way of life is founded on that particular human sacrifice.''

''Can they be taught differently?'' Evalyth asked without real interest.

''Yes. In time. In theory. But—well, I do know enough about what happened on Old Earth, and elsewhere, when advanced societies undertook to reform primitive ones. The entire structure was destroyed. It had to be.

''Think of the result, if we told these people to desist from their puberty rite. They wouldn't listen. They couldn't. They *must* have grandchildren. They *know* a boy won't become a man unless he has eaten part of a man. We'd have to conquer them, kill most, make sullen prisoners of the rest. And when the next crop of boys did in fact mature without the magic food . . . what then? Can you imagine the demoralization, the sense of utter inferiority, the loss of that tradition which is the core of every personal identity? It might be kinder to bomb this island sterile.''

Chena shook her head. ''No,'' she said harshly, ''the single decent way for us to proceed would be gradually. We could send missionaries. By their precept and example, we could start the natives phasing out their custom after two or three generations . . . And we can't afford such an effort. Not for a long time to come. Not with so many other worlds in the galaxy, so much worthier of what little help we can give. I am going to recommend we depart as soon as possible. When we get home,

I will recommend this planet be left alone."

Evalyth considered her for a moment before asking: "Isn't that partly because of your own reaction?"

"Yes," Chena admitted. "I can't overcome my disgust. And I, as you pointed out, am supposed to be professionally broad-minded. So even if the Board tried to recruit missionaries, I doubt they'd succeed." She hesitated. "You yourself, Evalyth—"

The Krakener rose. "My emotions don't matter," she said. "My duty does. Thank you for your help." She turned on her heel and went with military strides out of the cabin.

The chemical barriers were crumbling. Evalyth stood for a moment before the little building that had been hers and Donli's, afraid to enter. The sun was low, so that the compound was filling with shadows. A thing, leathery-winged and serpentine, cruised silently overhead. From outside the stockade drifted sounds of feet, foreign voices, the whine of a wooden flute. The air was cooling. She shivered. Their home would be too hollow.

Someone approached. She recognized the person glimpse-wise, Alsabeta Mondain from Nuevamerica. Listening to her well-meant foolish condolences would be worse than going inside. Evalyth took the last three steps and slid the door shut behind her.

Donli will not be here again. Eternally.

But the cabin proved not to be empty of him. Rather, it was too full. That chair where he used to sit, reading that worn volume of poetry which she could not understand and teased him about, that table across which he had toasted her and tossed kisses, that closet where his clothes hung, that scuffed pair of slippers, that bed, it screamed of him. Evalyth went fast into the laboratory section and drew the curtain that separated it from the living quarters. Rings rattled along the rod. The noise was monstrous in twilight.

She closed her eyes and fists and stood breathing hard. *I will not go soft,* she declared. *You always said you loved me for my strength (among numerous other desirable features, you'd add with your slow grin, but I won't remember that yet), and I don't aim to let slip anything you loved.*

I've got to get busy, she told Donli's child. *The expedition command is pretty sure to act on Chena's urging and haul mass for home. We've not many days to avenge your father.*

Her eyes snapped open. *What am I doing,* she thought, bewildered, *talking to a dead man and an embryo?*

She turned on the overhead fluoro and went to the computer. It was made no differently from the other portables. Donli had used it. But she could look away from the unique scratches and bumps on that square case, as she could not escape his microscope, chemanalysers, chromosome tracer, biological specimens . . . She seated herself. A drink would have been very welcome, except that she needed clarity. "Activate!" she ordered.

The On light glowed yellow. Evalyth tugged her chin, searching for words. "The objective," she said at length, "is to trace a lowlander who has consumed several kilos of flesh and blood from one of this party, and afterward vanished into the jungle. The killing took place about sixty hours ago. How can he be found?"

The least hum answered her. She imagined the links: to the maser in the ferry, up past the sky to the nearest orbiting relay unit, to the next, to the next, around the bloated belly of the planet, by ogre sun and inhuman stars, until the pulses reached the mother ship; then down to an unliving brain that routed the question to the appropriate data bank; then to the scanners, whose resonating energies flew from molecule to distorted molecule, identifying more bits of information than it made sense to number, data garnered from hundreds or thousands of entire words, data preserved through the wreck of Empire and the dark ages that followed, data going back to an Old Earth that perhaps no longer existed. She shied from the thought and wished herself back on dear stern Kraken. *We will go there,* she promised Donli's child. *You will dwell apart from these too many machines and grow up as the gods meant you should.*

"Query," said the artificial voice. "Of what origin was the victim of this assault?"

Evalyth must wet her lips before she could reply: "Atheian. He was Donli Sairn, your master."

"In that event, the possibility of tracking the desired local inhabitant may exist. The odds will now be computed. In the interim, do you wish to know the basis of the possibility?"

"Y-yes."

"Native Atheian biochemistry developed in a manner quite parallel to Earth's," said the voice, "and the early colonists had no difficulty in introducing terrestrial species. Thus they enjoyed a friendly environment, where the population soon grew sufficiently large to obviate the danger of racial change through mutation and/or genetic drift. In addition, no selection pressure tended to force change. Hence the modern Atheian human is little different from his ancestors of Earth, on which account his physiology and biochemistry are known in detail.

"This has been essentially the case on most colonized planets for which records are available. Where different breeds of men have arisen, it has generally been because the original settlers were highly selected groups. Randomness, and evolutionary adaptation to new conditions, have seldom produced radical changes in biotype. For example, the robustness of the average Krakener is a response to comparatively high gravity, his size aids him in resisting cold, his fair complexion is helpful beneath a sun poor in ultraviolet. But his ancestors were people who already had the natural endowments for such a world. His deviations from their norm are not extreme. They do not preclude his living on more Earth-like planets or interbreeding with the inhabitants of these.

"Occasionally, however, larger variations have occurred. They appear to be due to a small original population or to unterrestroid conditions or both. The population may have been small because the planet could not support more, or have become small as the result of hostile action when the Empire fell. In the former case, genetic accidents had a chance to be significant; in the latter, radiation produced a high rate of mutant births among survivors. The variations are less apt to be in gross anatomy than in subtle endocrine and enzymatic qualities, which affect the physiology and psychology. Well-known cases include the reaction of the Gwydiona to nicotine and certain indoles, and the requirement of the Ifrians for trace amounts of lead. Sometimes the inhabitants of two planets are actually intersterile because of their differences.

"While this world has hitherto received the sketchiest of examinations—" Evalyth was yanked out of a reverie into which the lecture had led her—"certain facts are clear. Few terrestrial species have flourished; no doubt others were introduced originally, but died off after the technology to maintain them was lost. Man has thus been forced to depend on autochthonous life for the major part of his food. This life is deficient in various elements of human nutrition. For example, the only Vitamin C appears to be in immigrant plants; Sairn observed that the people consume large amounts of grass and leaves from those species, and that fluoroscopic pictures indicate this practice has measurably modified the digestive tract. No one would supply skin, blood, sputum, or similar samples, not even from corpses." *Afraid of magic,* Evalyth thought drearily, *yes, they're back to that too.* "But intensive analysis of the usual meat animals shows these to be undersupplied with three essential amino acids, and human adaptation to this must have involved considerable change on the cellular and sub-cellular levels. The probable type and extent of such change are computable.

"The calculations are now complete." Evalyth gripped the arms of her chair and could not breathe. "While the answer is subject to error for lack of precise data, it indicates a fair probability of success. In effect, Atheian flesh is alien here. It can be metabolized, but the body of the local consumer will excrete certain compounds and these will impart a characteristic odor to skin and breath as well as to urine and feces. The chance is good that it will be detectable by neo-Freeholder technique at distances of several kilometers, after sixty or seventy hours. But since the molecules in question are steadily being degraded and dissipated, speed of action is recommended."

I am going to find Donli's murderer. Darkness roared around Evalyth.

"Shall the organisms be ordered for you and given the appropriate search program?" asked the voice. "They can be on hand in an estimated three hours."

"Yes," she stammered. "Oh, please— Have you any other . . . other . . . advice?"

"The man ought not to be killed out of hand, but brought here for examination: if for no other reason, then in order that the scientific ends of the expedition may be served."

That's a machine talking, Evalyth cried. *It's designed to help research. Nothing more. But it was his.* And its answer was so altogether Donli that she could no longer hold back her tears.

The single big moon rose nearly full, shortly after sundown. It drowned most stars; the jungle beneath was cobbled with silver and dappled with black; the snowcone of Mount Burus floated unreal at the unseen edge of the world. Wind slid around Evalyth where she crouched on her gravsled; it was full of wet acrid odors, and felt cold though it was not, and chuckled at her back. Somewhere something screeched, every few minutes, and something else cawed reply.

She scowled at her position indicators, aglow on the control panel. Curses and chaos, Moru had to be in this area! He couldn't have escaped from the valley on foot in the time available, and her search pattern had practically covered it. If she ran out of bugs before she found him, must she assume he was dead? They ought to be able to find his body regardless, ought they not? Unless it was buried deep— Here. She brought the sled to hover, took the next phial off the rack, and stood up to open it.

The bugs came out many and tiny, like smoke in the moonlight. Their cloud whirled, began to break apart. Evalyth felt a nausea. Another failure?

No! Wait! Were not those motes dancing back together, into a streak barely visible under the moon, and vanishing downward? Heart thuttering, she turned to the indicator. Its neurodetector antenna was not aimlessly wobbling but pointed straight west-northwest, declination thirty-two degrees below horizontal. Only a concentration of the bugs could make it behave like that. And only the particular mixture of molecules to which the bugs had been presensitized, in several parts per million or better, would make them converge on the source.

"Ya-a-a-ah!" She couldn't help the one hawk-yell. But thereafter she bit her lips shut—blood trickled unnoticed down her chin—and drove the sled in silence.

The distance was a mere few kilometers. She came to a halt above an opening in the forest. Pools of scummy water gleamed in its rank growth. The trees made a solid-seeming wall around. Evalyth clapped her night goggles down off her helmet and over her eyes. A lean-to became visible. It was hastily woven from vines and withes, huddled against a pair of the largest trees to let their branches hide it from the sky. The bugs were entering.

Evalyth lowered her sled to a meter off the ground and got to her feet again. A stun pistol slid from its sheath into her right hand. Her left rested on the blaster.

Moru's two sons groped from the shelter. The bugs whirled around them, a mist that blurred their outlines. *Of course,* Evalyth realized, nonetheless shocked into a higher hatred, *I should have known, they did the actual devouring*. More than ever did they resemble gnomes—skinny limbs, big heads, the pot bellies of undernourishment. Krakener boys of their age would have twice their bulk and be noticeably on the way to becoming men. These nude bodies belonged to children, except that they had the grotesqueness of eld.

The parents followed them, ignored by the entranced bugs. The mother wailed. Evalyth identified a few words, "What is the matter, what are those things—oh, help—" but her gaze was locked upon Moru.

Limping out of the hutch, stooped to clear its entrance, he made her think of some huge beetle crawling from an offal heap. But she would know that bushy head though her brain were coming apart. He carried a stone blade, surely the one that hacked up Donli. *I will take it away from him, and the hand with it,* Evalyth wept. *I will keep him alive while I dismantle him with these my own hands, and in between times he can watch me flay those repulsive spawn of his.*

The wife's scream broke through. She had seen the metal thing, and the giant that stood on its platform, with skull and eyes shimmering beneath the moon.

"I have come for you who killed my man," Evalyth said.

The mother screamed anew and cast herself before the boys. The father tried to run around in front of her, but his lame foot twisted under him and he fell into a pool. As he struggled out of its muck, Evalyth shot the woman. No sound was heard; she folded and lay moveless. "Run!" Moru shouted. He tried to charge the sled. Evalyth twisted a control stick. Her vehicle whipped in a circle, heading off the boys. She shot them from above, where Moru couldn't quite reach her.

He knelt beside the nearest, took the body in his arms and looked upward. The moonlight poured relentlessly across him. "What can you now do to me?" he called.

She stunned him too, landed, got off and quickly hogtied the four of them. Loading them aboard, she found them lighter than she had expected.

Sweat had sprung forth upon her, until her coverall stuck dripping to her skin. She began to shake, as if with fever. Her ears buzzed. "I would have destroyed you," she said. Her voice sounded remote and unfamiliar. A still more distant part wondered why she bothered speaking to the unconscious, in her own tongue at that. "I wish you hadn't acted the way you did. That made me remember what the computer said, about Donli's friends needing you for study.

"You're too good a chance, I suppose. After your doings, we have the right under Allied rules to make prisoners of you, and none of his friends are likely to get maudlin about your feelings.

"Oh, they won't be inhumane. A few cell samples, a lot of tests, anaesthesia where necessary, nothing harmful, nothing but a clinical examination as thorough as facilities allow. No doubt you'll be better fed than at any time before, and no doubt the medics will find some pathologies they can cure for you. In the end, Moru, they'll release your wife and children."

She stared into his horrible face. "I am pleased," she said, "that to you, who won't comprehend what is going on, it will be a bad experience. And when they are finished, Moru, I will insist on having you, at least, back. They can't deny me that. Why, your tribe itself has, in effect, cast you out. Right? My colleagues won't let me do more than kill you, I'm afraid, but on this I will insist."

She gunned the engine and started toward Lokon, as fast as possible, to arrive while she felt able to be satisfied with that much.

And the days without him and the days without him.

The nights were welcome. If she had not worked herself quite to exhaustion, she could take a pill. He rarely returned in her dreams. But she had to get through each day, and would not drown him in drugs.

Luckily, there was a good deal of work involved in preparing to depart, when the expedition was short-handed and on short notice. Gear must be dismantled, packed, ferried to the ship, and stowed. *New Dawn* herself must be readied, numerous systems recommissioned and tested. Her militechnic training qualified Evalyth to double as mechanic, boat jockey, or loading gang boss. In addition, she kept up the routines of defense in the compound.

Captain Jonafer objected mildly to this. "Why bother, Lieutenant? The locals are scared blue of us. They've heard what you did—and this coming and going through the sky, robots and heavy machinery in action, floodlights after dark—I'm having trouble persuading them not to abandon their town!"

"Let them," she snapped. "Who cares?"

"We did not come here to ruin them, Lieutenant."

"No. In my judgment, though, Captain, they'll be glad to ruin us if we present the least opportunity. Imagine what special virtues *your* body must have."

Jonafer sighed and gave in. But when she refused to receive Rogar the next time she was planetside, he ordered her to do so and to be civil.

The *Klev* entered the biolab section—she would not have him in her living quarters—with a gift held in both hands, a sword of Imperial metal. She shrugged; no doubt a museum would be pleased to get the thing. "Lay it on the floor," she told him.

Because she occupied the single chair, he stood. He looked little and old in his robe. "I came," he whispered, "to say how we of Lokon rejoice that the heaven-borne has won her revenge."

"Is winning it," she corrected.

He could not meet her eyes. She stared moodily at his faded hair. "Since the heaven-borne could . . . easily . . . find those she wished . . . she knows the truth in the hearts of us of Lokon, that we never intended harm to her folk."

That didn't seem to call for an answer.

His fingers twisted together. "Then why do you forsake us?" he went on. "When first you came, when we had come to know you and you spoke our speech, you said you would stay for many moons, and after you would come others to teach and trade. Our hearts rejoiced. It was not alone the goods you might someday let us buy, nor that your wisemen talked of ways to end hunger, sickness, danger, and sorrow. No, our jubilation and thankfulness were most for the wonders you opened. Suddenly the world was made great, that had been so narrow. And now you are going away. I have asked, when I dared, and those of your men who will speak to me say none will return. How have we offended you, and how may it be made right, heaven-borne?"

"You can stop treating your fellow men like animals," Evalyth got past her teeth.

"I have gathered . . . somewhat . . . that you from the stars say it is wrong what happens in the Sacred Place. But we only do it once in our lifetimes, heaven-borne, and because we must!"

"You have no need."

Rogar went on his hands and knees before her. "Perhaps the heaven-borne are thus," he pleaded, "but we are merely men. If our sons do not get the manhood, they will never beget children of their own, and the last of us will die alone in a world of death, with none to crack his skull and let the soul out—" He dared glance up at her. What he saw made him whimper and crawl backwards into the sun-glare.

Later Chena Darnard sought Evalyth. They had a drink and talked around the subject for a while, until the anthropologist plunged in: "You were pretty hard on the sachem, weren't you?"

"How'd you— Oh." The Krakener remembered that the interview had been taped, as was done whenever possible for later study. "What was I supposed to do, kiss his man-eating mouth?"

"No." Chena winced. "I suppose not."

"Your signature heads the list, on the official recommendation that we quit this planet."

"Yes. But— Now I don't know. I was repelled. I am. However— I've been observing the medical team working on those prisoners of yours. Have you?"

"No."

"You should. The way they cringe, and shriek, and reach to each other when they're strapped down in the lab, and cling together afterward in their cell."

"They aren't suffering any pain or mutilation, are they?"

"Of course not. But can they believe it when their captors say they won't? They can't be tranquillized while under study, you know, if the results are to be valid. Their fear of the absolutely unknown— Well, Evalyth, I had to stop observing. I couldn't take any more." Chena gave the other a long stare. "You might, though."

Evalyth shook her head. "I don't gloat. I'll shoot the murderer because my family honor demands it. The rest can go free, even the boys, even in spite of what they ate." She poured herself a stiff draught and tossed it off in a gulp. The liquor burned on the way down.

"I wish you wouldn't," Chena said. "Donli wouldn't have liked it. He had a proverb that he claimed was very ancient—he was from my city, don't forget, and I have known . . . I did know him longer than you, dear—I heard him say, twice or thrice, *Do I not destroy my enemies if I make them my friends?*"

"Think of a venomous insect," Evalyth replied. "You don't make friends with it. You put it under your heel."

"But a man does what he does because of what he is, what his society has made him." Chena's voice grew urgent; she leaned forward to grip Evalyth's hand, which did not respond. "What is one man, one lifetime, against all who live around him and all who have gone before? Cannibalism wouldn't be found everywhere over this island, in every one of these otherwise altogether different groupings, if it weren't the most deeply rooted cultural imperative this race has got."

Evalyth grinned around a rising anger. "And what kind of race are they to acquire it? And how about according me the privilege of operating on my own cultural imperatives? I'm bound home, to raise Donli's child away from your gutless civilization. He will not grow up disgraced because his mother was too weak to exact justice for his father. Now if you'll excuse me, I have to get up early and take another boatload to the ship and get it inboard."

That task required a while. Evalyth came back toward sunset the next day. She felt a little more tired than usual, a little more peaceful. The raw edge of what had happened was healing over. The thought crossed her mind, abstract but not shocking, not disloyal: *I'm young. One year another man will come. I won't love you the less, darling.*

Dust scuffed under her boots. The compound was half stripped already, a corresponding number of personnel berthed in the ship. The evening reached quiet beneath a yellowing sky. Only a few of the expedition stirred among the machines and remaining cabins. Lokon lay as hushed as it had lately become. She welcomed the thud of her footfalls on the steps into Jonafer's office.

He sat waiting for her, big and unmoving behind his desk. "Assignment completed without incident," she reported.

"Sit down," he said.

She obeyed. The silence grew. At last he said, out of a stiff face: "The clinical team has finished with the prisoners."

Somehow it was a shock. Evalyth groped for words: "Isn't that too soon? I mean, well, we don't have a lot of equipment, and just a couple of men who can use the advanced stuff, and then without Donli for an expert on Earth biology— Wouldn't a good study, down to the chromosomal level if not further—something that the physical anthropologists could use—wouldn't it take longer?"

"That's correct," Jonafer said. "Nothing of major importance was found. Perhaps something would have been, if Uden's team had any inkling of what to look for. Given that, they could have made hypotheses, and tested them in a whole-organism context, and come to some understanding of their subjects as functioning beings. You're right, Donli Sairn had the kind of professional intuition that might have guided them. Lacking that, and with no particular clues, and no cooperation from those ignorant, terrified savages, they had to grope and probe almost at random. They did establish a few digestive peculiarities—nothing that couldn't have been predicted on the basis of ambient ecology."

"Then why have they stopped? We won't be leaving for another week at the earliest."

"They did so on my orders, after Uden had shown me what was going on and said he'd quit regardless of what I wanted."

"What—? Oh." Scorn lifted Evalyth's head. "You mean the psychological torture."

"Yes. I saw that scrawny woman secured to a table. Her head, her body were covered with leads to the meters that clustered around her and clicked and hummed and flickered. She didn't see me; her eyes were blind with fear. I suppose she imagined her soul was being pumped out. Or maybe the process was worse for being something she couldn't put a name to. I saw her kids in a cell, holding hands. Nothing else left for them to hold onto, in their total universe. They're just at puberty; what'll this do to their psychosexual development? I saw their father lying drugged beside them, after he'd tried to batter his way straight through the wall. Uden and his helpers told me how they'd tried to make friends and failed. Because naturally the prisoners know they're in the power of those who hate them with a hate that goes beyond the grave."

Jonafer paused. "There are decent limits to everything, Lieutenant," he ended, "including science and punishment. Especially when, after all, the chance of discovering anything else unusual is slight. I ordered the investigation terminated. The boys and their mother will be flown to their home area and released tomorrow."

"Why not today?" Evalyth asked, foreseeing his reply.

"I hoped," Jonafer said, "that you'd agree to let the man go with them."

"No."

"In the name of God—"

"Your God." Evalyth looked away from him. "I won't enjoy it, Captain. I'm beginning to wish I didn't have to. But it's not as if Donli'd been killed in an honest war or feud or— He was slaughtered like a pig. That's the evil in cannibalism; it makes a man nothing but another meat animal. I won't bring him back, but I will somehow even things, by making the cannibal nothing but a dangerous animal that needs shooting."

"I see." Jonafer too stared long out of the window. In the

sunset light his face became a mask of brass. "Well," he said finally, coldly, "under the Charter of the Alliance and the articles of this expedition, you leave me no choice. But we will not have any ghoulish ceremonies, and you will not deputize what you want done. The prisoner will be brought to your place privately after dark. You will dispose of him at once and assist in cremating the remains."

Evalyth's palms grew wet. *I never killed a helpless man before!*

But he *did,* it answered. "Understood, Captain," she said.

"Very good, Lieutenant. You may go clean up and join the mess for dinner if you wish. No announcements to anyone. The business will be scheduled for—" Jonafer glanced at his watch, set to local rotation—"2600 hours."

Evalyth swallowed around a clump of dryness. "Isn't that rather late?"

"On purpose," he told her. "I want the camp asleep." His glance struck hers. "And want you to have time to reconsider."

"No!" She sprang erect and went for the door.

His voice pursued her: "Donli would have asked you for that."

Night came in and filled the room. Evalyth didn't rise to turn on the light. It was as if this chair, which had been Donli's favourite, wouldn't let her go.

Finally she remembered the psychodrugs. She had a few tablets left. One of them would make the execution easy to perform. No doubt Jonafer would direct that Moru be tranquilized—now, at last—before they brought him here. So why should she not give herself calmness?

It wouldn't be right.

Why not?

I don't know. I don't understand anything any longer.

Who does? Moru alone. He knows why he murdered and butchered a man who trusted him. Evalyth found herself smiling wearily into the darkness. *He has superstition for his sure guide. He's actually seen his children display the first signs of maturity. That ought to console him a little.*

Odd, that the glandular upheaval of adolescence should have commenced under frightful stress. One would have expected a delay instead. True, the captives had been getting a balanced diet for a change, and medicine had probably eliminated various chronic low-level infections. Nonetheless the fact was odd. Besides, normal children under normal conditions would not develop the outward signs beyond mistaking in this short a time. Donli would have puzzled over the matter. She could almost see him, frowning, rubbing his forehead, grinning one-sidedly with the pleasure of a problem.

"I'd like to have a go at this myself," she heard him telling Uden over a beer and a smoke. "Might turn up an angle."

"How?" the medic would have replied. "You're a general biologist. No reflection on you, but detailed human physiology is out of your line."

"Um-m-m . . . yes and no. My main job is studying species of terrestrial origin and how they've adapted to new planets. By a remarkable coincidence, man is included among them."

But Donli was gone, and no one else was competent to do his work—to be any part of him, but she fled from that thought and from the thought of what she must presently do. She held her mind tightly to the realization that none of Uden's team had tried to apply Donli's knowledge. As Jonafer remarked, a living Donli might well have suggested an idea, unorthodox and insightful, that would have led to the discovery of whatever was there to be discovered, if anything was. Uden and his assistants were routineers. They hadn't even thought to make Donli's computer ransack its data banks for possibly relevant information. Why should they, when they saw their problem as strictly medical? And, to be sure, they were not cruel. The anguish they were inflicting had made them avoid whatever might lead to ideas demanding further research. Donli would have approached the entire business differently from the outset.

Suddenly the gloom thickened. Evalyth fought for breath. Too hot and silent here; too long a wait; she must do something or her will would desert her and she would be unable to squeeze the trigger.

She stumbled to her feet and into the lab. The fluoro blinded her for a moment when she turned it on. She went to his computer and said: "Activate!"

Nothing responded but the indicator light. The windows were totally black. Clouds outside shut off moon and stars.

"What—" The sound was a curious croak. But that brought a releasing gall: *Take hold of yourself, you blubbering idiot, or you're not fit to mother the child you're carrying*. She could then ask her question. "What explanations in terms of biology can be devised for the behavior of the people on this planet?"

"Matters of that nature are presumably best explained in terms of psychology and cultural anthropology,'' said the voice.

''M-m-maybe,'' Evalyth said. ''And maybe not.'' She marshalled a few thoughts and stood them firm amidst the others roiling in her skull. ''The inhabitants could be degenerate somehow, not really human.'' *I want Moru to be.* ''Scan every fact recorded about them, including the detailed clinical observations made on four of them in the past several days. Compare with basic terrestrial data. Give me whatever hypotheses look reasonable.'' She hesitated. ''Correction. I mean possible hypotheses—anything that doesn't flatly contradict established facts. We've used up the reasonable ideas already.''

The machine hummed. Evalyth closed her eyes and clung to the edge of the desk. *Donli, please help me.*

At the other end of forever, the voice came to her:

''The sole behavioral element which appears to be not easily explicable by postulates concerning environment and accidental historical developments, is the cannibalistic puberty rite. According to the anthropological computer, this might well have originated as a form of human sacrifice. But that computer notes certain illogicalities in the idea, as follows.

''On Old Earth, sacrificial religion was normally associated with agricultural societies, which were more vitally dependent on continued fertility and good weather than hunters. Even for them, the offering of humans proved disadvantageous in the long run, as the Aztec example most clearly demonstrates. Lokon has rationalized the practice to a degree, making it part of the slavery system and thus minimizing its impact on the generality. But for the lowlanders it is a powerful evil, a source of perpetual danger, a diversion of effort and resources that are badly needed for survival. It is not plausible that the custom, if ever imitated from Lokon, should persist among every one of those tribes. Nevertheless it does. Therefore it must have some value and the problem is to find what.

''The method of obtaining victims varies widely, but the requirement always appears to be the same. According to the Lokonese, one adult male body is necessary and sufficient for the maturation of four boys. The killer of Donli Sairn was unable to carry off the entire corpse. What he did take of it is suggestive.

''Hence a dipteroid phenomenon may have appeared in man on this planet. Such a thing is unknown among higher animals elsewhere, but is conceivable. A modification of the Y chromosome would produce it. The test for that modification, and thus the test of the hypothesis, is easily made."

The voice stopped. Evalyth heard the blood slugging in her veins. "What are you talking about?"

"The phenomenon is found among lower animals on several worlds," the computer told her. "It is uncommon and so is not widely known. The name derives from the Diptera, a type of dung fly on Old Earth."

Lightning flickered: "Dung fly—good, yes!"

The machine went on to explain.

Jonafer came alone with Moru. The savage's hands were tied behind his back, and the spaceman loomed enormous over him. Despite that and the bruises he had inflicted on himself, he hobbled along steadily. The clouds were breaking and the moon shone ice-white. Where Evalyth waited, outside her door, she saw the compound reach bare to the saw-topped stockade and a crane stand above like a gibbet. The air was growing cold—the planet spinning toward an autumn—and a small wind had arisen to whimper behind the dust devils that stirred across the earth. Jonafer's footfalls rang loud.

He noticed her and stopped. Moru did likewise. "What did they learn?" she asked.

The captain nodded. "Uden got right to work when you called," he said. "The test is more complicated than your computer suggested—but then, it's for Donli's kind of skill, not Uden's. He'd never have thought of it unassisted. Yes, the notion is true."

"How?"

Moru stood waiting while the language he did not understand went to and fro around him.

"I'm no medic." Jonafer kept his tone altogether colorless. "But from what Uden told me, the chromosome defect means that the male gonads here can't mature spontaneously. They need an extra supply of hormones—he mentioned testosterone and androsterone, I forget what else—to start off the series of changes which bring on puberty. Lacking that, you'll get eunuchism. Uden thinks the surviving population was tiny after the colony was bombed out, and so poor that it resorted to cannibalism for bare survival, the first generation or two. Under those circumstances, a mutation that would otherwise have eliminated itself got established and spread to every descendant."

Evalyth nodded. "I see."

"You understand what this means, I suppose," Jonafer said. "There'll be no problem to ending the practice. We'll simply tell them we have a new and better Holy Food, and prove it with a few pills. Terrestrial-type meat animals can be reintroduced later and supply what's necessary. In the end, no doubt our geneticists can repair that faulty Y chromosome."

He could not stay contained any longer. His mouth opened, a gash across his half-seen face, and he rasped: "I should praise you for saving a whole people. I can't. Get your business over with, will you?"

Evalyth trod forward to stand before Moru. He shivered but met her eyes. Astonished, she said: "You haven't drugged him."

"No," Jonafer said. "I wouldn't help you." He spat.

"Well, I'm glad." She addressed Moru in his own language: "You killed my man. Is it right that I should kill you?"

"It is right," he answered, almost as levelly as she. "I thank you that my woman and my sons are to go free." He was quiet for a second or two. "I have heard that your folk can preserve food for years without it rotting. I would be glad if you kept my body to give your sons."

"Mine will not need it," Evalyth said. "Nor will the sons of your sons."

Anxiety tinged his words: "Do you know why I slew your man? He was kind to me, and like a god. But I am lame. I saw no other way to get what my sons must have; and they must have it soon, or it would be too late and they could never become men."

"He taught me," Evalyth said, "how much it is to be a man."

She turned to Jonafer, who stood tense and puzzled. "I had my revenge," she said in Donli's tongue.

"What?" His question was a reflexive noise.

"After I learned about the dipteroid phenomenon," she said. "All that was necessary was for me to keep silent. Moru, his children, his entire race would go on being prey for centuries, maybe forever. I sat for half an hour, I think, having my revenge."

"And then?" Jonafer asked.

"I was satisfied, and could start thinking about justice," Evalyth said.

She drew a knife. Moru straightened his back. She stepped behind him and cut his bonds. "Go home," she said. "Remember him."

Fortune Hunter

After cleaning up indoors, I stepped outside for a look at the evening. I'd only moved here a few days ago. Before, I'd been down in the woods. Now I was above timberline, and there'd just been time to make my body at home—reassemble the cabin and its furnishings, explore the area, deploy the pickups, let lungs acquire a taste for thinner air. My soul was still busy settling in.

I missed sun-flecks spattered like gold on soft shadow-brown duff, male ruggedness and woman-sweet odor of pines and their green that speared into heaven, a brook that glittered and sang, bird calls, a splendidly antlered wapiti who'd become my friend and took food from my hand. (He was especially fond of cucumber peels. I dubbed him Charlie.) You don't live six months in a place, from the blaze of autumn through the iron and white of winter, being reborn with the land when spring breathes over it—you don't do this and not keep some of that place ever afterward inside your bones.

Nevertheless, I'd kept remembering high country, and when Jo Modzeleski said she'd failed to get my time extended further, I decided to go up for what remained of it. That was part of my plan; she loved the whole wilderness as much as I did, but she kept her heart on its peaks and they ought to help make her mood right. However, I myself was happy to return.

And as I walked out of the cabin, past my skeletal flitter, so that nothing human-made was between me and the world, suddenly the whole of me was again altogether belonging where I was.

This base stood on an alpine meadow. Grass grew thick and moist, springy underfoot, daisy-starred. Here and there bulked boulders the size of houses, grayness scored by a glacier which had once gouged out the little lake rippling and sparkling not far away: a sign to me that I also was included in eternity. Everywhere around, the Wind River Mountains lifted snow crowns and the darker blues of their rock, into a dizzyingly tall heaven where an eagle hovered. He caught on his wings the sunlight which slanted out of the west. Those beams seemed to fill the chilliness, turning it somehow molten; and the heights were alive with shadows.

I smelled growth, more austere than in the forest but not the less strong. A fish leaped, I saw the brief gleam and an instant later, very faintly through quietness, heard the water clink. Though there was no real breeze, my face felt the air kiss it.

I buttoned my mackinaw, reached for smoking gear, and peered about. A couple of times already, I'd spied a bear. I knew better than to try a Charlie-type relationship with such a beast, but surely we could share the territory amicably, and if I could learn enough of his ways to plant pickups where they could record his life—or hers, in which case she'd be having cubs—

No. You're bound back to civilization at the end of this week. Remember?

Oh, but I may be returning.

As if in answer to my thought, I heard a whirr aloft. It grew, till another flitter hove into sight. Jo was taking me up on my invitation at an earlier hour than I'd expected when I said, "Come for dinner about sundown." Earlier than I'd hoped? My heart knocked. I stuck pipe and tobacco pouch back in my pockets and walked fast to greet her.

She landed and sprang out of the bubble before the airpad

motors were silent. She always had been quick and graceful on her feet. Otherwise she wasn't much to look at: short, stocky, pug nose, pale round eyes under close-cropped black hair. For this occasion she'd left off the ranger's uniform in favor of an iridescent clingsuit; but it couldn't have done a lot for her even if she had known how to wear it.

"Welcome," I said, took both her hands and gave her my biggest smile.

"Hi." She sounded breathless. Color came and went across her cheeks. "How are you?"

"Okay. Sad at leaving, naturally." I turned the smile wry, so as not to seem self-pitiful.

She glanced away. "You'll be going back to your wife, though."

Don't push too hard. "You're ahead of yourself, Jo. I meant to have drinks and snacks ready in advance. Now you'll have to come in and watch me work."

"I'll help."

"Never, when you're my guest. Sit down, relax." I took her arm and guided her toward the cabin.

She uttered an uncertain laugh. "Are you afraid I'll get in your way, Pete? No worries. I know these knockdown units—I'd better, after three years—"

I was here for four, and that followed half a dozen years in and out of other wildernesses, before I decided that this was the one I wanted to record in depth, it being for me the loveliest of the lovely.

"—and they only have one practical place to stow any given kind of thing," she was saying. Then she stopped, which made me do likewise, turned her head from side to side, drank deep of air and sun-glow. "Please, don't let me hurry you. This is such a beautiful evening. You were out to enjoy it."

Unspoken: And you haven't many left, Pete. The documentation project ended officially last year. You're the last of the very few mediamen who got special permission to stay on and finish their sequences; and now, no more stalling, no more extra time, the word is Everybody Out.

My unspoken reply: Except you rangers. A handful of you, holding degrees in ecology and soil biotics and whatnot—a handful who won in competition against a horde—does that give you the right to lord it over all this?

"Well, yes," I said, and segued to: "I'll enjoy it especially in present company."

"Thank you, kind sir." She failed to sound cheery.

I squeezed her arm. "You know, I am going to miss you, Jo. Miss you like hell." This past year, as my plan grew within me, I'd been cultivating her. Not just card games and long conversations over the sensiphone; no, in-the-flesh get-togethers for hikes, rambles, picnics, fishing, birdwatching, deerwatching, starwatching. A mediaman gets good at the cultivation of people, and although this past decade had given me scant need to use that skill, it hadn't died. As easy as breathing, I could show interest in her rather banal remarks, her rather sappy-sentimental opinions. . . . "Come see me when you get a vacation."

"Oh, I'll—I'll call you up . . . now and then . . . if Marie won't . . . mind."

"I mean come in person. Holographic image, stereo sound, even scent and temperature and every other kind of circuit a person might pay for the use of—a phone isn't the same as having a friend right there."

She winced. "You'll be in the city."

"It isn't so bad," I said in my bravest style. "Pretty fair-sized apartment, a lot bigger than that plastic shack yonder. Soundproofed. Filtered and conditioned air. The whole conurb fully screened and policed. Armored vehicles available when you sally forth."

"And a mask for my nose and mouth!" She nearly gagged.

"No, no, that hasn't been needed for a long while. They've gotten the dust, monoxide, and carcinogens down to a level, at least in my city, which—"

"The stinks. The tastes. No, Pete, I'm sorry, I'm no delicate flower but the visits to Boswash I make in line of duty are the limit of what I can take . . . after getting to know this land."

"I'm thinking of moving into the country myself," I said. "Rent a cottage in an agrarea, do most of my business by phone, no need to go downtown except when I get an assignment to document something there."

She grimaced. "I often think the agrareas are worse than any 'tropolis."

"Huh?" It surprised me that she could still surprise me.

"Oh, cleaner, quieter, less dangerous, residents not jammed elbow to elbow, true," she admitted. "But at least those snarling, grasping, frenetic city folk have a certain freedom, a certain . . . *life* to them. It may be the life of a ratpack, but it's real, it has a bit of structure and spontaneity and— In the hinterlands, not only nature is regimented. The people are.''

Well, I don't know how else you could organize things to feed a world population of fifteen billion.

''All right,'' I said. ''I understand. But this is a depressing subject. Let's saunter for a while. I've found some gentian blooming.''

''So early in the season? Is it in walking distance? I'd like to see.''

''Too far for now, I'm afraid. I've been tramping some mighty long days. However, let me show you the local blueberry patch. It should be well worth a visit, come late summer.''

As I took her arm again, she said, in her awkward fashion, ''You've become an expert, haven't you, Pete?''

''Hard to avoid that,'' I grunted. ''Ten years, collecting sensie material on the Wilderness System.''

''Ten years. . . . I was in high school when you began. I only knew the regular parks, where we stood in line on a paved path to see a redwood or a geyser, and we reserved swimming rights a month in advance. While you—'' Her fingers closed around mine, hard and warm. ''It doesn't seem fair to end your stay.''

''Life never was fair.''

Too damn much human life. Too little of any other kind. And we have to keep a few wildernesses, a necessary reserve for what's left of the planet's ecology; a source of knowledge for researchers who're trying to learn enough about that ecology to shore it up before it collapses altogether; never mentioned, but present in every thinking head, the fact that if collapse does come, the wildernesses will be Earth's last seedbeds of hope.

''I mean,'' Jo plodded, ''of course areas like this were being destroyed by crowds—loved to death, as somebody wrote—so the only thing to do was close them to everybody except a few caretakers and scientists, and that was politically impossible unless 'everybody' meant *everybody*.'' Ah, yes, she was back to her habit of thumbing smooth-worn clichés. ''And after all, the sensie documentaries that artists like you have been making, they'll be available and—'' The smoothness vanished. ''*You* can't come back, Pete! Not ever again!''

Her fingers remembered where they were and let go of me.

Mine followed them and squeezed, a measured gentleness. Meanwhile my pulse fluttered. It was as well that words didn't seem indicated at the moment, because my mouth was dry.

A mediaman should be more confident. But such a God damn lot was riding on this particular bet. I'd gotten Jo to care about me, not just in the benevolent way of her colleagues, isolated from mankind so they can afford benevolence, but about me, this Pete-atom that wanted to spend the rest of its flickering days in the Wind River Mountains. Only how deeply did she care?

We walked around the lake. The sun dropped under the peaks—for minutes, the eastern snows were afire—and shadows welled up. I heard an owl hoot to his love. In royal blue, Venus kindled. The air sharpened, making blood run faster.

"Br-r-r!" Jo laughed. "Now I do want that drink."

I couldn't see her features through the dusk. The first stars stood forth infinitely clear. But Jo was a blur, a warmth, a solidness, no more. She might almost have been Marie.

If she had been! Marie was beautiful and bright and sexy and—Sure, she took lovers while I was gone for months on end; we'd agreed that the reserves were my mistresses. She'd had no thought for them on my returns. . . . Oh, if only we could have shared it all!

Soon the sky would hold more stars than darkness, the Milky Way would be a white cataract, the lake would lie aglow with them, and when Jupiter rose there would be a perfect glade across the water. I'd stayed out half of last night to watch that.

Already the shining was such that we didn't need a penflash to find the entrance to my cabin. The insulation layer yielded under my touch. We stepped through, I zipped the door and closed the main switch, fluoros awoke as softly as the ventilation.

Jo was correct: those portables don't lend themselves to individuality. (She had a permanent cabin, built of wood and full of things dear to her.) Except for a few books and the like, my one room was strictly functional. True, the phone could bring me the illusion of almost anything or anybody, anywhere in the world, that I might want. We city folk learn to travel light. This interior was well-proportioned, pleasingly tinted, snug; a step outside was that alpine meadow. What more did I need?

Out of hard-earned habit, I checked the nucleo gauge—ample power—before taking dinner from the freezer and setting it to cook. Thereafter I fetched nibblies, rum, and fruit juice, and mixed drinks the way Jo liked them. She didn't try to help after all, but settled back into the airchair. Neither of us had said much while we walked. I'd expected chatter out of her—a bit nervous, a bit too fast and blithe—once we were here. Instead, her stocky frame hunched in its mother-of-pearl suit that wasn't meant for it, and she stared at the hands in her lap.

No longer cold, I shucked my mackinaw and carried her drink over to her. "Revelry, not reverie!" I ordered. She took it. I clinked glasses. My other hand being then free, I reached thumb and forefinger to twitch her lips at the corners. "Hey, you, smile. This is supposed to be a jolly party."

"Is it?" The eyes she raised to me were afloat in tears.

"Sure, I hate to go—"

"Where's Marie's picture?"

That rocked me back. I hadn't expected so blunt a question. "Why, uh—" *Okay. Events are moving faster than you'd planned on, Peter. Move with them.* I took a swallow, squared my shoulders, and said manfully: "I didn't want to unload my troubles on you, Jo. The fact is, Marie and I have broken up. Nothing's left but the formalities."

"What?"

Her mouth is open, her look lost in mine; she spills some of her drink and doesn't notice— Have I really got it made? This soon?

I shrugged. "Yeah. The notice of intent to dissolve relationship arrived yesterday. I'd seen it coming, of course. She'd grown tired of waiting around."

"Oh, Pete!" She reached for me.

I was totally aware—walls, crowded shelves, night in a window, murmur and warm gusting from the heat unit, monitor lamp on the radionic oven and meat fragrances seeping out of it, this woman whom I must learn to desire—and thought quickly that at the present stage of things, I'd better pretend not to notice her gesture. "No sympathy cards," I said in a flat tone. "To be quite honest, I'm more relieved than otherwise."

"I thought—" she whispered. "I thought you two were happy."

Which we have been, my dear, Marie and I: though a sophisticated mediaman does suspect that considerable of our happiness, as opposed to contentment, has been due to my long absences this past decade. They've added spice. That's something you'll always lack, whatever happens, Jo. Yet a man can't live only on spices.

"It didn't last," I said as per plan. "She's found someone more compatible. I'm glad of that."

"You, Pete?"

"I'll manage. C'mon, drink your drink. I insist that we be merry."

She gulped. "I'll try."

After a minute: "You haven't even anyone to come home to!"

"'Home' doesn't mean a lot to a city man, Jo. One apartment is like another; and we move through a big total of 'em in a lifetime." The liquor must have touched me a bit, since I rushed matters: "Quite different from, say, these mountains. Each patch of them is absolutely unique. A man could spend all his years getting to know a single one, growing into it— Well."

I touched a switch and the airchair expanded, making room for me to settle down beside her. "Care for some background music?" I asked.

"No." Her gaze dropped—she had stubby lashes—and she blushed—blotchily—but she got her words out with a stubbornness I had come to admire. Somebody who had that kind of guts wouldn't be too bad a partner. "At least, I'd not hear it. This is just about my last chance to talk . . . really talk . . . to you, Pete. Isn't it?"

"I hope not." *More passion in that voice, boy.* "Lord, I hope not!"

"We have had awfully good times together. My colleagues are fine, you know, but—" She blinked hard. "You've been special."

"Same as you to me."

She was shivering a bit, meeting my eyes now, lips a bare few centimeters away. Since she seldom drank alcohol, I guessed that what I'd more or less forced on her had gotten a good strong hold, under these circumstances. *Remember, she's no urbanite who'll hop into bed and scarcely remember it two days later. She went directly from a small town to a tough university to here, and may actually be a virgin. However, you've worked toward this moment for months, Pete, old chum. Get started!*

It was the gentlest kiss I think I have ever taken.

"I've been, well, afraid to speak," I murmured into her hair, which held an upland sunniness. "Maybe I still am. Only I don't, don't, don't want to lose you, Jo."

Half crying, half laughing, she came back to my mouth. She

didn't really know how, but she held herself hard against me, and I thought: *May she end up sleeping with me, already this night?*

No matter, either way. What does count is, the Wilderness Administration allows qualified husband-and-wife teams to live together on the job; and she's a ranger and I, being skilled in using monitoring devices, would be an acceptable research assistant.

And then-n-n:

I didn't know, I don't know to this day what went wrong. We'd had two or three more drinks, and a good deal of joyous tussling, and her clothes were partly off her and dinner was beginning to scorch in the oven when

I was too hasty

she was too awkward and/or backward-holding, and I got impatient and she felt it

I breathed out one of those special words which people say to each other only, and she being a bit terrified anyway decided it wasn't mere habit-accident but I was pretending she was Marie because in fact my eyes were shut

she wasn't as naive as she, quite innocently, had led me to believe, and in one of those moments which (contrary to fantasy) are forever coming upon lovers, asked herself, "Hey, what the hell is really going on?"

or whatever. It makes no difference. Suddenly she wanted to phone Marie.

"If, if, if things are as you say, Pete, she'll be glad to learn—"

"Wait a minute! Wait one damn minute! Don't you trust me?"

"Oh, Pete, darling, of course I do, but—"

"But nothing." I drew apart to register offense.

Instead of coming after me, she asked, as quietly as the night outside: "Don't you trust *me?*"

Never mind. A person can't answer a question like that. We both tried, and shouldn't have. All I truly remember is seeing her out the door. A smell of charred meat pursued us. Beyond the cabin, the air was cold and altogether pure, sky wild with stars, peaks aglow. I watched her stumble to her flitter. The galaxy lit her path. She cried the whole way. But she went.

However disappointed, I felt some relief, too. It would have been a shabby trick to play on Marie, who had considerable love invested in me. And our apartment is quite pleasant, once it's battened down against the surroundings; I belong to the fortunate small minority. We had an appropriate reunion. She even babbled about applying for a childbearing permit. I kept enough sense to switch that kind of talk off immediately.

Next evening there was a rally which we couldn't well get out of attending. The commissioners may be right as far as most citizens go. "A sensiphone, regardless of how many circuits are tuned in, is no substitute for the physical togetherness of human beings uniting under their leaders for our glorious mass purposes." We, though, didn't get anything out of it except headaches, ears ringing from the cadenced cheers, lungs full of air that had passed through thousands of other lungs, and skins which felt greasy as well as gritty. Homebound, we encountered smog so thick it confused our vehicle. Thus we got stopped on the fringes of a riot and saw a machine gun cut a man in two before the militia let us move on. It was a huge relief to pass security check at our conurb and take a transporter which didn't fail even once, up and across to our own place.

There we shared a shower, using an extravagant percentage of our monthly water ration, and dried each other off, and I slipped into a robe and Marie into something filmy; we had a drink and a toke while Haydn lilted, and got relaxed to the point where she shook her long tresses over her shoulders and her whisper tickled my ear: "Aw, c'mon, hero, the computers've got to've edited your last year's coverage by now. I've looked forward all this while."

I thought fleetingly of Jo. Well, she wouldn't appear in a strictly wilderness-experience public-record documentary; and I myself was curious about what I had actually produced, and didn't think a revisit in an electronic dream would pain me, even this soon afterward.

I was wrong.

What hurt most was the shoddiness. Oh, yes, decent reproduction of a primrose nodding in the breeze, a hawk a-swoop, spuming whiteness and earthquake rumble of a distant avalanche, fallen leaves brown and baking under the sun, their smell and crackle, the laughter of a gust which flirted with my hair, suppleness incarnate in a snake or a cougar, flamboyance at sunset and shyness at dawn—a competent show. Yet it wasn't real, it wasn't what I had loved.

Marie said, slowly, in the darkness where we sat, "You did better before. Kruger, Matto Grosso, Baikal, your earlier stays in this region—I almost felt I was at your side. You weren't a recorder there, you were an artist, a great artist. Why is this different?"

"I don't know," I mumbled. "My presentation is kind of mechanical, I admit. I suppose I was tired."

"In that case—" she sat very straight, half a meter from me, fingers gripped together— "you didn't have to stay on. You could have come home to me long before you did."

But I wasn't tired, rammed through my head. *No, now is when I'm drained; then, there, life flowed* into *me.*

That gentian Jo wanted to see . . . it grows where the land suddenly drops. Right at the cliff edge those flowers grow, oh, blue, blue, blue against grass green and daisy white and the strong gray of stone; a streamlet runs past, leaps downward, ringing, cold, tasting of glaciers, rocks, turf, the air which also blows everywhere around me, around the high and holy peaks beyond. . . .

"Lay off!" I yelled. My fist struck the chair arm. The fabric clung and cloyed. A shade calmer, I said, "Okay, maybe I got too taken up in the reality and lost the necessary degree of detachment." *I lie, Marie, I lie like Judas. My mind was never busier, planning how to use Jo and discard you.* "Darling, those sensies, I'll have nothing but them for the rest of my life." *And none of the gentians. I was too busy with my scheme to bother with anything small and gentle and blue.* "Isn't that penalty enough?"

"No. You did have the reality. And you did not bring it back." Her voice was like a wind across the snows of upland winter.

Eutopia

"Gif thit nafn!"

The Danska words barked from the car radio as a jet whine cut across the hum of motor and tires. "Identify yourself!" Iason Philippou cast a look skyward through the bubbletop. He saw a strip of blue between two ragged green walls where pine forest lined the road. Sunlight struck off the flanks of the killer machine up there. It wailed, came about, and made a circle over him.

Sweat started cold from his armpits and ran down his ribs. *I must not panic*, he thought in a corner of his brain. *May the God help me now*. But it was his training he invoked. Psychosomatics: control the symptoms, keep the breath steady, command the pulse to slow, and the fear of death becomes something you can handle. He was young, and thus had much to lose. But the philosophers of Eutopia schooled well the children given into their care. You will be a man, they had told him, and the pride of humanity is that we are not bound by instinct and reflex; we are free because we can master ourselves.

He couldn't pass as an ordinary citizen (no, they said mootman here) of Norland. If nothing else, his Hellenic accent was too strong. But he might fool yonder pilot, for just a few minutes, into believing he was from some other domain of this history. He roughened his tone, as a partial disguise, and assumed the expected arrogance.

"Who are you? What do you want?"

"Runolf Einarsson, captain in the hird of Ottar Thorkelsson, the Lawman of Norland. I pursue one who has brought feud on his own head. Give me your name."

Runolf, Iason thought. *Why, yes, I remember you well, dark and erect with the Tyrker side of your heritage, but you have blue eyes that came long ago from Thule.* In that detached part of him which stood aside watching: *No, here I scramble my histories. I would call the autochthons Erythrai, and you call the country of your European ancestors Danarik.*

"I hight Xipec, a trader from Meyaco," he said. He did not slow down. The border was not many stadia away, so furiously had he driven through the night since he escaped from the Lawman's castle. He had small hope of getting that far, but each turn of the wheels brought him nearer. The forest was blurred with his speed.

"If so be, of course I am sorry to halt you," Runolf's voice crackled. "Call the Lawman and he will send swift gild for the overtreading of your rights. Yet I must have you stop and leave your car, so I may turn the farseer on your face."

"Why?" Another second or two gained.

"There was a visitor from Homeland"—Europe—"who came to Ernvik. Ottar Thorkelsson guested him freely. In return, he did a thing that only his death can make clean again. Rather than meet Ottar on the Valfield, he stole a car, the same make as yours, and fled."

"Would it not serve to call him a nithing before the folk?" *I have learned this much of their barbaric customs, anyhow!*

"Now that is a strange thing for a Meyacan to say. Stop at once and get out, or I open fire."

Iason realized his teeth were clenched till they hurt. How in

Hades could a man remember the hundreds of little regions, each with its own ways, into which the continent lay divided? Westfall was a more fantastic jumble than all Earth in that history where they called the place America. *Well,* he thought, *now we discover what the odds are of my hearing it named Eutopia again.*

"Very well," he said. "You leave me no choice. But I shall indeed want compensation for this insult."

He braked as slowly as he dared. The road was a hard black ribbon before him, slashed through an immensity of trees. He didn't know if these woods had ever been logged. Perhaps so, when white men first sailed through the Pentalimne (calling them the Five Seas) to found Ernvik where Duluth stood in America and Lykopolis in Eutopia. In those days Norland had spread mightily across the lake country. But then came wars with Dakotas and Magyars, to set a limit; and the development of trade—more recently of synthetics—enabled the people to use their hinterland for the hunting they so savagely loved. Three hundred years could re-establish a climax forest.

Sharply before him stood the vision of this area as he had known it at home: ordered groves and gardens, villages planned for beauty as well as use, lithe brown bodies on the athletic fields, music under moonlight . . . Even America the dreadful was more human than a wilderness.

They were gone, lost in the multiple dimensions of space-time, he was alone and death walked the sky. *And no self-pity, you idiot! Spend energy for survival.*

The car stopped, hard by the road edge. Iason gathered his thews, opened the door, and sprang.

Perhaps the radio behind him uttered a curse. The jet slewed around and stooped like a hawk. Bullets sleeted at his heels.

Then he was in among the trees. They roofed him with sun-speckled shadow. Their trunks stood in massive masculine strength, their branches breathed fragrance a woman might envy. Fallen needles softened his foot-thud, a thrush warbled, a light wind cooled his cheeks. He threw himself beneath the shelter of one bole and lay in a gasping and heartbeat which all but drowned the sinister whistle above.

Presently it went away. Runolf must have called back to his lord. Ottar would fly horses and hounds to this place, the only way of pursuit. But Iason had a few hours' grace.

After that— He rallied his training, sat up and thought. If

Socrates, feeling the hemlock's chill, could speak wisdom to the young men of Athens, Iason Philippou could assess his own chances. For he wasn't dead yet.

He numbered his assets. A pistol of the local slug-throwing type; a compass; a pocketful of gold and silver coins; a cloak that might double as a blanket, above the tunic-trousers-boots costume of central Westfall. And himself, the ultimate instrument. His body was tall and broad—together with fair hair and short nose, an inheritance from Gallic ancestors—and had been trained by men who won wreaths at the Olympeion. His mind, his entire nervous system, counted for still more. The pedagogues of Eutopia had made logic, semantic consciousness, perspective as natural to him as breathing; his memory was under such control that he had no need of a map; despite one calamitous mistake, he knew he was trained to deal with the most outlandish manifestations of the human spirit.

And, yes, before all else, he had reason to live. It went beyond any blind wish to continue an identity; that was only something the DNA molecule had elaborated in order to make more DNA molecules. He had his beloved to return to. He had his country: Eutopia, the Good Land, which his people had founded two thousand years ago on a new continent, leaving behind the hatreds and horrors of Europe, taking along the work of Aristotle, and writing at last in their Syntagma, "The national purpose is the attainment of universal sanity."

Iason Philippou was bound home.

He rose and started walking south

That was on Tetrade, which his hunters called Onsdag. Some thirty-six hours later, he knew he was not in Pentade but near sunset of Thorsdag. For he lurched through the wood, mouth filled with mummy dust, belly a cavern of emptiness, knees shaking beneath him, flies a thundercloud about the sweat dried on his skin, and heard the distant belling of hounds.

A horn responded, long brazen snarl through the leaf arches. They had gotten his scent, he could not outrun horsemen and he would not see the stars again.

One hand dropped to his gun. *I'll take a couple of them with me. . . . No.* He was still a Hellene, who did not kill uselessly, not even barbarians who meant to slay him because he had broken a taboo of theirs. *I will stand under an open sky, take their bullets, and go down into darkness remembering Eutopia and all my friends and Niki whom I love.*

Realization came, dimly, that he had left the pine forest and was in a second growth of beeches. Light gilded their leaves and caressed the slim white trunks. And what was that growl up ahead?

He stopped. A portal might remain. He had driven himself near collapse; but the organism has a reserve which the fully integrated man may call upon. From consciousness he abolished the sound of dogs, every ache and exhaustion. He drew breath after breath of air, noting its calm and purity, visualizing the oxygen atoms that poured through his starved tissues. He made the heartbeat quit racketing, go over to a deep slow pulse; he tensed and relaxed muscles until each functioned smoothly again; pain ceased to feed on itself and died away; despair gave place to calm and calculation. He trod forth.

Plowlands rolled southward before him, their young grain vivid in the light that slanted gold from the west. Not far off stood a cluster of farm buildings, long, low, and peak-roofed. Chimney smoke stained heaven. But his eyes went first to the man closer by. The fellow was cultivating with a tractor. Though the dielectric motor had been invented in this world, its use had not yet spread this far north, and gasoline fumes caught at Iason's nostrils. He had thought that stench one of the worst abominations in America—that hogpen they called Los Angeles!—but now it came to him clean and strong, for it was his hope.

The driver saw him, halted, and unshipped a rifle. Iason approached with palms held forward in token of peace. The driver relaxed. He was a typical Magyar: burly, high in the cheekbones, his beard braided, his tunic colorfully embroidered. *So I did cross the border!* Iason exulted. *I'm out of Norland and into the Voivodate of Dakoty.*

Before they sent him here, the anthropologists of the Parachronic Research Institute had of course given him an electrochemical inculcation in the principal languages of Westfall. (Pity they hadn't been more thorough about teaching him the mores. But then, he had been hastily recruited for the Norland post after Megasthenes' accidental death; and it was assumed that his experience in America gave him special qualifications for this history, which was also non-Alexandrine; and, to be sure, the whole object of missions like his was to learn just how societies on the different Earths did vary.) He formed the Ural-Altaic words with ease:

"Greeting to you. I come as a supplicant."

The farmer sat quiet, tense, looking down on him and listening to the dogs far off in the forest. His rifle stayed ready. "Are you an outlaw?" he asked.

"Not in this realm, freeman." (Still another name and concept for "citizen"!) "I was a peaceful trader from Homeland, visiting Lawman Ottar Thorkelsson in Ernvik. His anger fell upon me, so great that he broke sacred hospitality and sought the life of me, his guest. Now his hunters are on my trail. You hear them yonder."

"Norlanders? But this is Dakoty."

Iason nodded. He let his teeth show, in the grime and stubble of his face. "Right. They've entered your country without so much as a by-your-leave. If you stand idle, they'll ride onto your freehold and slay me, who asks your help."

The farmer hefted his gun. "How do I know you speak truth?"

"Take me to the Voivode," Iason said. "Thus you keep both the law and your honor." Very carefully, he unholstered his pistol and offered it butt foremost. "I am forever your debtor."

Doubt, fear and anger pursued each other across the face of the man on the tractor. He did not take the weapon. Iason waited. *If I've read him correctly, I've gained some hours of life. Perhaps more. That will depend on the Voivode. My whole chance lies in using their own barbarism—their division into petty states, their crazy idea of honor, their fetish of property and privacy—to harness them.*

If I fail, then I shall die like a civilized man. That they cannot take away from me.

"The hounds have winded you. They'll be here before we can escape," said the Magyar uneasily.

Relief made Iason dizzy. He fought down the reaction and said: "We can take care of them for a time. Let me have some gasoline."

"Ah . . . thus!" The other man chuckled and jumped to earth. "Good thinking, stranger. And thanks, by the way. Life has been dull hereabouts for too many years."

He had a spare can of fuel on his machine. They lugged it back along Iason's trail for a considerable distance, dousing soil and trees. If that didn't throw the pack off, nothing would.

"Now, hurry!" The Magyar led the way at a trot.

His farmstead was built around an open courtyard. Sweet scents of hay and livestock came from the barns. Several children ran forth to gape. The wife shooed them back inside, took her husband's rifle, and mounted guard at the door with small change of expression.

Their house was solid, roomy, aesthetically pleasing if you could accept the unrestrained tapestries and painted pillars. Above the fireplace was a niche for a family altar. Though most people in Westfall had left myth long behind them, these peasants still seemed to adore the Triple God Odin-Attila-Manitou. But the man went to a sophisticated radiophone. "I don't have an aircraft myself," he said, "but I can get one."

Iason sat down to wait. A girl neared him shyly with a beaker of beer and a slab of cheese on coarse dark bread. "Be you guest-holy," she said.

"May my blood be yours," Iason answered by rote. He managed to take the refreshment not quite like a wolf.

The farmer came back. "A few more minutes," he said. "I am Arpad, son of Kalman."

"Iason Philippou." It seemed wrong to give a false name. The hand he clasped was hard and warm.

"What made you fall afoul of old Ottar?" Arpad inquired.

"I was lured," Iason said bitterly. "Seeing how free the unwed women were—"

"Ah, indeed. They're a lickerish lot, those Danskar. Nigh as shameless as Tyrkers." Arpad got pipe and tobacco pouch off a shelf. "Smoke?"

"No, thank you." *We don't degrade ourselves with drugs in Eutopia.*

The hounds drew close. Their chant broke into confused yelps. Horns shrilled. Arpad stuffed his pipe as coolly as if this were a show. "How they must be swearing!" he grinned. "I'll give the Danskar credit for being poets, also in their oaths. And brave men, to be sure. I was up that way ten years back, when Voivode Bela sent people to help them after the floods they'd suffered. I saw them laugh as they fought the wild water. And then, their sort gave us a hard time in the old wars."

"Do you think there will ever be wars again?" Iason asked. Mostly he wanted to avoid speaking further of his troubles. He wasn't sure how his host might react.

"Not in Westfall. Too much work to do. If young blood isn't cooled enough by a duel now and then, why, there're wars to hire out for, among the barbarians overseas. Or else the planets. My oldest boy champs to go there."

Iason recalled that several realms further south were pooling their resources for astronautical work. Being approximately at the technological level of the American history, and not required to maintain huge military or social programs, they had put a base on the moon and sent expeditions to Ares. In time, he supposed, they would do what the Hellenes had done a thousand years ago, and make Aphrodite into a new Earth. But would they have a true civilization—be rational men in a rationally planned society—by then? Wearily, he doubted it.

A roar outside brought Arpad to his feet. "There's your wagon," he said, "Best you go. Red Horse will fly you to Varady."

"The Danskar will surely come here soon," Iason worried.

"Let them," Arpad shrugged. "I'll alert the neighborhood, and they're not so stupid that they won't know I have. We'll hold a slanging match, and then I'll order them off my land. Farewell, guest."

"I . . . I wish I could repay your kindness."

"Bah! Was fun. Also, a chance to be a man before my sons."

Iason went out. The aircraft was a helicopter—they hadn't discovered gravitics here—piloted by a taciturn young autochthon. He explained that he was a stockbreeder, and that he was conveying the stranger less as a favor to Arpad than as an answer to the Norlander impudence of entering Dakoty unbidden. Iason was just as happy to be free of conversation.

The machine whirred aloft. As it drove south he saw clustered hamlets, the occasional hall of some magnate, otherwise only rich undulant plains. They kept the population within bounds in Westfall as in Eutopia. But not because they knew that men need space and clean air, Iason thought. No, they acted from greed on behalf of the reified family. A father did not wish to divide his possessions among many children.

The sun went down and a nearly full moon climbed huge and pumpkin-colored over the eastern rim of the world. Iason sat back, feeling the engine's throb in his bones, almost savoring his fatigue, and watched. No sign of the lunar base was visible. He must return home before he could see the moon glitter with cities.

And home was more than infinitely remote. He could travel to the farthest of those stars which had begun twinkling forth against purple dusk—were it possible to exceed the speed of light—and not find Eutopia. It lay sundered from him by dimensions and destiny. Nothing but the warpfields of a parachronion might take him across the time lines to his own.

He wondered about the why. That was an empty speculation, but his tired brain found relief in childishness. Why had the God willed that time branch and rebranch, enormous, shadowy, bearing universes like the Yggdrasil of Danskar legend? Was it so that man could realize every potentiality there was in him?

Surely not. So many of them were utter horror.

Suppose Alexander the Conqueror had not recovered from the fever that smote him in Babylon. Suppose, instead of being chastened thereby, so that he spent the rest of a long life making firm the foundations of his empire—suppose he had died?

Well, it *did* happen, and probably in more histories than not. There the empire went down in mad-dog wars of succession. Hellas and the Orient broke apart. Nascent science withered away into metaphysics, eventually outright mysticism. A convulsed Mediterranean world was swept up piecemeal by the Romans: cold, cruel, uncreative, claiming to be the heirs of Hellas even as they destroyed Corinth. A heretical Jewish prophet founded a mystery cult which took root everywhere, for men despaired of this life. And that cult knew not the name of tolerance. Its priests denied all but one of the manifold ways in which the God is seen; they cut down the holy groves, took from the house its humble idols, and martyred the last men whose souls were free.

Oh yes, Iason thought, *in time they lost their grip. Science could be born, almost two millennia later than ours. But the poison remained: the idea that men must conform not only in behavior but in belief. Now, in America, they call it totalitarianism. And because of it, the nuclear rockets have had their nightmare hatching.*

I hated that history, its filth, its waste, its ugliness, its restriction, its hypocrisy, its insanity. I will never have a harder task than when I pretended to be an American that I might see from within how they thought they were ordering their lives. But tonight . . . I pity you, poor raped world. I do not know whether to wish you soon dead, as you likeliest will be, or hope that one day your descendants can struggle to what we achieved an age ago.

They were luckier here. I must admit that. Christendom fell before the onslaught of Arab, Viking, and Magyar. Afterward the Islamic Empire killed itself in civil wars and the barbarians of Europe could go their own way. When they crossed the Atlantic, a thousand years back, they had not the power to commit genocide on the natives; they must come to terms. They had not the industry, then, to gut the hemisphere; perforce they grew into the land slowly, taking it as a man takes his bride.

But those vast dark forests, mournful plains, unpeopled deserts and mountains where the wild goats run . . . those entered their souls. They will always, inwardly, be savages.

He sighed, settled down, and made himself sleep. Niki haunted his dreams.

Where a waterfall marked the head of navigation on that great river known variously as the Zeus, Mississippi, and Longflood, a basically agricultural people who had not developed air transport as far as in Eutopia were sure to build a city. Trade and military power brought with them government, art, science and education. Varady housed a hundred thousand or so—they didn't take censuses in Westfall—whose inward-turning homes surrounded the castle towers of the Voivode. Waking, Iason walked out on his balcony and heard the traffic rumble. Beyond roofs lay the defensive outworks. He wondered if a peace founded on the balance of power between statelets could endure.

But the morning was too cool and bright for such musings. He was here, safe, cleansed and rested. There had been little talk when he arrived. Seeing the condition of the fugitive who sought him, Bela Zsolt's son had given him dinner and sent him to bed.

Soon we'll confer, Iason understood, *and I'll have to be most careful if I'm to live.* But the health which had been restored to him glowed so strong that he felt no need to suppress worry.

A bell chimed within. He re-entered the room, which was spacious and airy however overornamented. Recalling that custom disapproved of nudity, he threw on a robe, not without wincing at its zigzag pattern. "Be welcome," he called in Magyar.

The door opened and a young woman wheeled in his breakfast. "Good luck to you, guest," she said with an accent; she was a Tyrker, and even wore the beaded and fringed dress of her people. "Did you sleep well?"

"Like Coyote after a prank," he laughed.

She smiled back, pleased at his reference, and set a table. She joined him too. Guests did not eat alone. He found venison a rather strong dish this early in the day, but the coffee was delicious and the girl chattered charmingly. She was employed as a maid, she told him, and saving her money for a marriage portion when she returned to Cherokee land.

"Will the Voivode see me?" Iason asked after they had finished.

"He awaits your pleasure." Her lashes fluttered. "But we have no haste." She began to untie her belt.

Hospitality so lavish must be the result of customal superimposition, the easygoing Danskar and still freer Tyrker mores influencing the austere Magyars. Iason felt almost as if he were now home, in a world where individuals found delight in each other as they saw fit. He was tempted, too—that broad smooth brow reminded him of Niki. But no. He had little time. Unless he established his position unbreakably firm before Ottar thought to call Bela, he was trapped.

He leaned across the table and patted one small hand. "I thank you, lovely," he said, "but I am under vow."

She took the answer as naturally as she had posed the question. This world, which had the means to unify, chose as if deliberately to remain in shards of separate culture. Something of his alienation came back to him as he watched her sway out the door. For he had only glimpsed a small liberty. Life in Westfall remained a labyrinth of tradition, manner, law and taboo.

Which had well-nigh cost him his life, he reflected; and might yet. Best hurry!

He tumbled into the clothes laid out for him and made his way down long stone halls. Another servant directed him to the Voivode's seat. Several people waited outside to have complaints heard or disputes adjudicated. But when he announced himself, Iason was passed through immediately.

The room beyond was the most ancient part of the building. Age-cracked timber columns, grotesquely carved with gods and heroes, upheld a low roof. A fire pit in the floor curled smoke toward a hole; enough stayed behind for Iason's eyes to sting. They could easily have given their chief magistrate a modern office, he thought—but no, because his ancestors had judged in this kennel, so must he.

Light filtering through slit windows touched the craggy features of Bela and lost itself in shadow. The Voivode was thickset and gray-haired; his features bespoke a considerable admixture of Tyrker chromosomes. He sat a wooden throne, his body wrapped in a blanket, horns and feathers on his head. His left hand bore a horse-tailed staff and a drawn saber was laid across his lap.

"Greeting, Iason Philippou," he said gravely. He gestured at a stool. "Be seated."

"I thank my lord." The Eutopian remembered how his own people had outgrown titles.

"Are you prepared to speak truth?"

"Yes."

"Good." Abruptly the figure relaxed, crossed legs, and extracted a cigar from beneath the blanket. "Smoke? No? Well, I will." A smile meshed the leathery face in wrinkles. "You being a foreigner, I needn't keep up this damned ceremony."

Iason tried to reply in kind. "That's a relief. We haven't much in the Peloponnesian Republic."

"Your home country, eh? I hear things aren't going so well there."

"No. Homeland grows old. We look to Westfall for our tomorrows."

"You said last night that you came to Norland as a trader."

"To negotiate a commercial agreement." Iason was staying as near his cover story as possible. You couldn't tell different histories that the Hellenes had invented the parachronion. Besides changing the very conditions that were being studied, it would be too cruel to let men know that other men lived in perfection. "My country is interested in buying lumber and furs."

"Hm. So Ottar invited you to stay with him. I can grasp why. We don't see many Homelanders. But one day he was after your blood. What happened?"

Iason might have claimed privacy, but that wouldn't have sat well. And an outright lie was dangerous; before this throne, one was automatically under oath. "To a degree, no doubt, the fault was mine," he said. "One of his family, almost grown, was attracted to me and—I had been long away from my wife, and everyone had told me the Danskar hold with freedom before marriage, and—well, I meant no harm. I merely encouraged—But Ottar found out, and challenged me."

"Why did you not meet him?"

No use to say that a civilized man did not engage in violence when any alternative existed. "Consider, my lord," Iason said. "If I lost, I'd be dead. If I won, that would be the end of my company's project. The Ottarssons would never have taken weregild, would they? No, at the bare least they'd ban us all from their land. And Peloponnesus needs that timber. I thought I'd do best to escape. Later my associates could disown me before Norland."

"M-m . . . strange reasoning. But you're loyal, anyhow. What do you ask of me?"

"Only safe conduct to—Steinvik." Iason almost said, "Neathenai." He checked his eagerness. "We have a factory there, and a ship."

Bela streamed smoke from his mouth and scowled at the glowing cigar end. "I'd like to know why Ottar grew wrathful. Doesn't sound like him. Though I suppose, when a man's daughter is involved, he doesn't feel so lenient." He hunched forward. "For me," he said harshly, "the important thing is that armed Norlanders crossed my border without asking."

"A grievous violation of your rights, true."

Bela uttered a horseman's obscenity. "You don't understand, you. Borders aren't sacred because Attila wills it, whatever the shamans prate. They're sacred because that's the only way to keep the peace. If I don't openly resent this crossing, and punish Ottar for it, some hothead might well someday be tempted; and now everyone has nuclear weapons."

"I don't want war on my account!" Iason exclaimed, appalled. "Send me back to him first!"

"Oh no, no such nonsense. Ottar's punishment shall be that I deny him his revenge, regardless of the rights and wrongs of your case. He'll swallow that."

Bela rose. He put his cigar in an ashtray, lifted the saber, and all at once he was transfigured. A heathen god might have spoken: "Henceforward, Iason Philippou, you are peace-holy in Dakoty. While you remain beneath our shield, ill done you is ill done me, my house and my people. So help me the Three!"

Self-command broke down. Iason went on his knees and gasped his thanks.

"Enough," Bela grunted. "Let's arrange for your transportation as fast as may be. I'll send you by air, with a military squadron. But of course I'll need permission from the realms you'll cross. That will take time. Go back, relax, I'll have you called when everything's ready."

Iason left, still shivering.

He spent a pleasant couple of hours adrift in the castle and its courtyards. Thc young men of Bela's retinue were eager to show off before a Homelander. He had to grant the picturesqueness of their riding, wrestling, shooting, and riddling contests; something stirred in him as he listened to tales of faring over the plains and into the forests and by river to Unnborg's fabled metropolis; the chant of a bard awakened glories which went deeper than the history told, down to the instincts of man the killer ape.

But these are precisely the bright temptations that we have turned our backs on in Eutopia. For we deny that we are apes. We are men who can reason. In that lies our manhood.

I am going home. I am going home. I am going home.

A servant tapped his arm. "The Voivode wants you." It was a frightened voice.

Iason hastened back. What had gone wrong? He was not taken to the room of the high seat. Instead, Bela awaited him on a parapet. Two men-at-arms stood at attention behind, faces blank under the plumed helmets.

The day and the breeze were mocked by Bela's look. He spat on Iason's feet. "Ottar has called me," he said.

"I— Did he say—"

"And I thought you were only trying to bed a girl. Not seeking to destroy the house that befriended you!"

"My lord—"

"Have no fears. You sucked my oath out of me. Now I must spend years trying to make amends to Ottar for cheating him."

"But—" *Calm! Calm! You might have expected this.*

"You will not ride in a warcraft. You'll have your escort, yes. But the machine that carries you must be burned afterward. Now go wait by the stables, next to the dung heap, till we're ready."

"I meant no harm," Iason protested. "I did not know."

"Take him away before I kill him," Bela ordered.

Steinvik was old. These narrow cobbled streets, these gaunt houses, had seen dragon ships. But the same wind blew off the Atlantic, salt and fresh, to drive from Iason the last hurt of that sullenness which had ridden here with him. He pushed whistling through the crowds.

A man of Westfall, or America, would have slunk back. Had he not failed? Must he not be replaced by someone whose cover story bore no hint of Hellas? But they saw with clear eyes in Eutopia. His failure was due to an honest mistake: a mistake he would not have made had they taught him more carefully before sending him out. One learns by error.

The memory of people in Ernvik and Varady—gusty, generous people whose friendship he would have liked to keep—had nagged him awhile. But he put that aside too. There were other worlds, an endlessness of them.

A signboard creaked in the wind. The Brotherhood of Hunyadi and Ivar, Shipfolk. Good camouflage, that, in a town where every second enterprise was bent seaward. He ran to the second floor. The stairs clattered under his boots.

He spread his palm before a chart on the wall. A hidden scanner identified his fingerpatterns and a hidden door opened. The room beyond was wainscoted in local fashion. But its clean proportions spoke of home; and a Nike statuette spread wings on a shelf.

Nike . . . Niki . . . I'm coming back to you! The heart leaped in him.

Daimonax Aristides looked up from his desk. Iason sometimes wondered if anything could rock the calm of that man. "Rejoice!" the deep voice boomed. "What brings you here?"

"Bad news, I'm afraid."

"So? Your attitude suggests the matter isn't catastrophic." Daimonax's big frame left his chair, went to the wine cabinet, filled a pair of chaste and beautiful goblets, and relaxed on a couch. "Come, tell me."

Iason joined him. "Unknowingly," he said, "I violated what appears to be a prime taboo. I was lucky to get away alive."

"Eh." Daimonax stroked his iron-gray beard. "Not the first such turn, or the last. We fumble our way toward knowledge, but reality will always surprise us. . . . Well, congratulations on your whole skin. I'd have hated to mourn you."

Solemnly, they poured a libation before they drank. The rational man recognizes his own need for ceremony; and why not draw it from otherwise outgrown myth? Besides, the floor was stainproof.

"Do you feel ready to report?" Daimonax asked.

"Yes, I ordered the data in my head on the way here."

Daimonax switched on a recorder, spoke a few cataloguing words and said, "Proceed."

Iason flattered himself that his statement was well arranged: clear, frank and full. But as he spoke, against his will experience came back to him, not in the brain but in the guts. He saw waves sparkle on the greatest of the Pentalimne; he walked the halls of Ernvik castle with eager and wondering young Leif; he faced an Ottar become beast; he stole from the keep and overpowered a guard and by-passed the controls of a car with shaking fingers; he fled down an empty road and stumbled through an empty forest; Bela spat and his triumph was suddenly ashen. At the end, he could not refrain:

"Why wasn't I informed? I'd have taken care. But they said this was a free and healthy folk, before marriage anyway. How could I know?"

"An oversight," Daimonax agreed. "But we haven't been in this business so long that we don't still tend to take too much for granted."

"Why are we here? What have we to learn from these barbarians? With infinity to explore, why are we wasting ourselves on the second most ghastly world we've found?"

Daimonax turned off the recorder. For a time there was silence between the men. Wheels trundled outside, laughter and a snatch of song drifted through the window, the ocean blazed under a low sun.

"You do not know?" Daimonax asked at last, softly.

"Well... scientific interest, of course—" Iason swallowed. "I'm sorry. The Institute works for sound reasons. In the American history we're observing ways that man can go wrong. I suppose here also."

Daimonax shook his head. "No."

"What?"

"We are learning something far too precious to give up," Daimonax said. "The lesson is humbling, but our smug Eutopia will be the better for some humility. You weren't aware of it, because to date we haven't sufficient hard facts to publish any conclusions. And then, you are new in the profession, and your first assignment was elsewhen. But you see, we have excellent reason to believe that Westfall is also the Good Land."

"Impossible," Iason whispered.

Daimonax smiled and took a sip of wine. "Think," he said. "What does man require? First, the biological necessities, food, shelter, medicine, sex, a healthful and reasonably safe environment in which to raise his children. Second, the special human need to strive, learn, create. Well, don't they have these things here?"

"One could say the same for any Stone Age tribe. You can't equate contentment with happiness."

"Of course not. And if anything, is not ordered, unified, planned Eutopia the country of the cows? We have ended every conflict, to the very conflict of man with his own soul; we have mastered the planets; the stars are too distant; were the God not so good as to make possible the parachronion, what would be left for us?"

"Do you mean—" Iason groped after words. He reminded himself that it was not sane to take umbrage at any mere statement, however outrageous. "Without fighting, clannishness, superstition, ritual and taboo . . . man has nothing?"

"More or less that. Society must have structure and meaning. But nature does not dictate what structure or what meaning. Our rationalism is a non-rational choice. Our leashing of the purely animal within us is simply another taboo. We may love as we please, but not hate as we please. So are we more free than men in Westfall?"

"But surely some cultures are better than others!"

"I do not deny that," Daimonax said; "I only point out that each has its price. For what we enjoy at home, we pay dearly. We do not allow ourselves a single unthinking, merely felt impulse. By excluding danger and hardship, by eliminating distinctions between men, we leave no hopes of victory. Worst, perhaps, is this: that we have become pure individuals. We belong to no one. Our sole obligation is negative, not to compel any other individual. The state—an engineered organization, a faceless undemanding mechanism—takes care of each need and each hurt. Where is loyalty unto death? Where is the intimacy of an entire shared lifetime? We play at ceremonies, but because we know they are arbitrary gestures, what is their value? Because we have made our world one, where are color and contrast, where is pride in being peculiarly ourselves?

"Now these Westfall people, with all their faults, do know who they are, what they are, what they belong to and what belongs to them. Tradition is not buried in books but is part of life; and so their dead remain with them in loving memory. Their problems are real; hence their successes are real. They believe in their rites. The family, the kingdom, the race is something to live and die for. They use their brains less, perhaps—though even that I am not certain of—but they use nerves, glands, muscles more. So they know an aspect of being human which our careful world has denied itself.

"If they have kept this while creating science and machine technology, should we not try to learn from them?"

Iason had no answer.

Eventually Daimonax said he might as well return to Eutopia. After a vacation, he could be reassigned to some history he might find more congenial. They parted in friendly wise.

The parachronion hummed. Energies pulsed between the universes. The gate opened and Iason stepped through.

He entered a glazed colonnade. White Neathenai swept in grace and serenity down to the water. The man who received him was a philosopher. Decent tunic and sandals hung ready to be donned. From somewhere resounded a lyre.

Joy trembled in Iason. Leif Ottarsson fell out of memory. He had only been tempted in his loneliness by a chance resemblance to his beloved. Now he was home. And Niki waited for him, Nikias Demostheneou, most beautiful and enchanting of boys.

The Pugilist

They hadn't risked putting me in the base hospital or any other regular medical facility. Besides, the operation was very simple. Needed beforehand: a knife, an anesthetic, and a supply of coagulant and enzyme to promote healing inside a week. Needed afterward: drugs and skillful talking to, till I got over being dangerous to myself or my surroundings. The windows of my room were barred, I was brought soft plastic utensils with my meals, my clothes were pajamas and paper slippers, and two husky men sat in the hall near my open door. Probably I was also monitored on closed-circuit TV.

There was stuff to read, especially magazines which carried stories about the regeneration center in Moscow. Those articles bore down on the work being still largely experimental. A structure as complicated as a hand, a leg, or an eye wouldn't yet grow back right, though surgery helped. However, results were excellent with the more basic tissues and organs. I saw pics of a girl whose original liver got mercury poisoning, a man who'd had most of his skin burned off in an accident, beaming from the pages as good as new—or so the text claimed.

Mannix must have gone to some trouble to find those issues. The latest was from months ago. You didn't see much now that wasn't related to the war.

Near the end of that week my male nurse gave me a letter from Bonnie. It was addressed to me right here, John Reed A.F.B., Willits, California 95491, in her own slanty-rounded handwriting, and according to the postmark—when I remembered to check that several hours later—had doubtless been mailed from our place, not thirty kilometers away. The envelope was stamped EXAMINED, but I didn't think the letter had been dictated. It was too her. About how the kids and the roses were doing, and the co-op where she worked was hoping the Recreation Bureau would okay its employees vacationing at Lake Pillsbury this year, and hamburger had been available day before yesterday and she'd spent three hours with her grandmother's old cookbook deciding how to fix it "and if only you'd been across the table, you and your funny slow smile; oh, do finish soon, Jim-Jim, and c'mon home!"

I read slowly, the first few times. My hands shook so much. Later I crawled into bed and pulled the sheet over my face against bugeyes.

Mannix arrived next morning. He was small and chipper, always in the neatest of civvies, his round red face always amiable—almost always—under a fluff of white hair. "Well, how are you, Colonel Dowling?" he exclaimed as he bounced in. The door didn't close behind him at once. My guards would watch a while. I stand 190 centimeters in my bare feet and black belt.

I didn't rise from my armchair, though. Wasn't sure I could. It was as if that scalpel had, actually, teased the bones out of me. The windows stood open to a cool breeze and a bright sky. Beyond the neat buildings and electric fence of the base, I could see hills green with forest roll up and up toward the blueness of the sierra. It felt like painted scenery. Bonnie acts in civic theater.

Mannix settled on the edge of my bed. "Dr. Arneson tells me you can be discharged anytime, fit for any duty," he said. "Congratulations."

"Yeah," I managed to say, though I could hear how feeble

the sarcasm was. "You'll send me right back to my office."

"Or to your family? You have a charming wife."

I stirred and made a noise. The guard in the entrance looked uneasy and dropped a hand to his stunner. Mannix lifted a palm. "If you please," he chirped. "I'm not baiting you. Your case presents certain difficulties, as you well know."

I'd imagined I was calm, but numb. I was wrong, Blackness took me in a wave that roared. "Why, why, why?" I felt rip my throat. "Why not just shoot me and be done?"

Mannix waited till I sank back. The wind whined in and out of me. Sweat plastered the pajamas to my skin. It reeked.

He offered me a cigarette. At first I ignored him, then accepted both it and the flare of his lighter, and dragged my lungs full of acridness. Mannix said mildly, "The surgical procedure was necessary, Colonel. You were told that. Diagnosis showed cancer."

"The f-f-f—the hell it did," I croaked.

"I believe the removed part is still in alcohol in the laboratory," Mannix said. "Would you like to see it?"

I touched the hot end of the cigarette to the back of my hand. "No," I answered.

"And," Mannix said, "regeneration is possible."

"In Moscow."

"True, the Lomonosov institute has the world's only such capability to date. I daresay you've been reading about that." He nodded at the gay-colored covers on the end table. "The idea was to give you hope. Still . . . you are an intelligent, technically educated man. You realize it isn't simple to make the adult DNA repeat what it did in the fetus; and not repeat identically, either. Not only are chemicals, catalysts, synthevirus required; the whole process must be monitored and computer-controlled. No wonder they concentrate on research and save clinical treatment for the most urgent cases." He paused. "Or the most deserving."

"I saw this coming," I mumbled.

Mannix shrugged. "Well, when you are charged with treasonable conspiracy against the People's Republic of the United States—" That was one phrase he had to roll out in full every time.

"You haven't proved anything," I said mechanically.

"The fact of your immunity to the usual interrogation techniques is, shall we say, indicative." He grew arch again. "Consider your own self-interest. Let the war in the Soviet Union break into uncontrolled violence, and where is Moscow? Where's the Institute? The matter is quite vital, Colonel."

"What can I do?" I asked out of hollowness.

Mannix chuckled. "Depends on what you know, what you are. Tell me and we'll lay plans. Eh?" He cocked his head. Bonnie, who knew him merely as a political officer, to be invited to dinner now and then on that account, liked him. She said he ought to play the reformed Scrooge, except he'd be no good as the earlier, capitalist Scrooge, before the Spirits of the New Year visited him.

"I've been studying your file personally," he went on, "and I'm blessed if I can see why you should have gotten involved in this unsavory business. A fine young man who's galloped through his promotions at the rate you have. It's not as if your background held anything unAmerican. How did you ever get sucked in?"

He bore down a little on the word "sucked." That broke me.

I'd never guessed how delicious it is to let go, to admit—fully admit and take into you—the fact that you're whipped. It was like, well, like the nightly surrender to Bonnie. I wanted to laugh and cry and kiss the old man's hands. Instead, stupidly, all I could say was, "I don't know."

The answer must lie deep in my past.

I was a country boy, raised in the backwoods of Georgia, red earth, gaunt murky-green pines, cardinals and mockingbirds and a secret fishing hole. The government had tried to modernize our area before I was born, but it didn't lend itself to collectives. So mostly we were allowed to keep our small farms, stores, sawmills, and repair shops on leasehold. The schools got taped lectures on history, ideology, and the rest. However, this isn't the same as having trained political educators in the flesh. Likewise, our local scoutmaster was lax about everything except woodcraft. And, while my grandfather mumbled a little about damn niggers everywhere like nothing since Reconstruction, he used to play poker with black Sheriff Jackson. Sometimes he, Granddad that is, would take on a bit too much moon and rant about how poor, decent Joe Jackson was being used. My parents saw to it that no outsiders heard him.

All in all, we lived in a pretty archaic fashion. I understand the section has since been brought up to date.

Now patriotism is as Southern as hominy grits. They have

trouble realizing this further north. They harp on the Confederate Rebellion, though actually—as our teachers explained to us—folks in those days were resisting Yankee capitalism and the slaveholders were a minority who milked the common man's love for his land. True, when the People's Republic was proclaimed, there was some hothead talk, even some shooting. But there was never any need for the heavy concentration of marshals and deputies they sent down to our states. Damn it, we still belonged.

We were the topmost rejoicers when word came: the Treaty of Berlin was amended, the United States could maintain armed forces well above police level, and was welcomed to the solid front of peace-loving nations against the Sino-Japanese revisionists.

Granddad turned into a wild man in a stiff jacket. He'd fought for the imperialist regime once, when it tried to suppress the Mekong Revolution, though he never said a lot about that. Who would? (I suppose Dad was lucky, just ten years old at the time of the Sacred War, which thus to him was like a hurricane or some other natural spasm. Of course, the hungry years afterward stunted his growth.) "This's the first step!" Granddad cried to us. "The first step back! You hear?" He stood outdoors waving his cane, autumn sumac a shout of red behind him, and the wind shouted, too, till I imagined old bugles blowing again at Valley Forge and Shiloh and Omaha Beach. Maybe that was when I first thought I might make the Army a career.

A year later, units of the new service held maneuvers beneath Stone Mountain. Granddad had been tirelessly reading and watching news, writing letters, making phone calls from the village booth, keeping in touch. Hence he knew about the event well in advance, knew the public would be invited to watch from certain areas, and saved his money and his travel allowance till he could not only go himself but take me along.

And it was exciting, oh, yes, really beautiful when the troops went by in ground-effect carriers like magic boats, the dinosaur tanks rumbling past, the superjets screaming low overhead, while the Star and Stripes waved before those riders carved in the face of the mountain.

Except—the artillery opened up. Granddad and I were quite a ways off, the guns were toys in our eyes, we'd see a needle-thin flash, a puff where the shell exploded; long, long afterward, distance-shrunken thunder reached us. The monument was slow to crumble away. That night, in the tourist dorm, I heard a speech about how destroying that symbol of oppression marked the dawn of our glorious new day. I didn't pay much attention. I kept seeing Granddad, there under the Georgia sky, suddenly withered and old.

Nobody proposed I go home to Bonnie. Least of all myself. Whether or not I could have made an excuse for . . . not revealing to her what had happened . . . I couldn't have endured it. I did say, over and over, that she had no idea I was in the Stephen Decatur Society. This was true. Not that she would have betrayed me had she known, Bonnie whose heart was as bright as her hair. I was already too far in to back out when first we met, too weak and selfish to run from her; but I was never guilty of giving her guilty knowledge.

"She and your children must have had indications," Mannix murmured. "If only subliminal. They might be in need of correctional instruction."

I whimpered before him. There are camps and camps, of course, but La Pasionara is the usual one for West Coast offenders. I've met a few of those who've been released from it. They are terribly obedient, hard-working, and close-mouthed. Most lack teeth. Rumor says conditions can make young girls go directly from puberty to menopause. I have a daughter.

Mannix smiled. "At ease, Jim. Your family's departure would tip off the Society."

I blubbered my thanks.

"And, to be sure, you may be granted a chance to win pardon, if we can find a proper way," he soothed me. "Suggestions?"

"I-I-I can tell you . . . what I know—"

"An unimaginative minimum. Let us explore you for a start. Maybe we'll hit on a unique deed you can do." Mannix drummed his desktop.

We had moved to his office, which was lush enough that the portraits of Lenin and the President looked startlingly austere. I sat snug and warm in a water chair, cigarets, coffee, brandy at hand, nobody before me or behind me except this kindly white-haired man and his recorder. But I was still gulping, sniffing, choking, and shivering, still too dazed to think. My lips tingled and my body felt slack and heavy.

"What brought you into the gang, Jim?" he asked as if in simple curiosity.

I gaped at him. I'd told him I didn't know. But maybe I did.

Slowly I groped around in my head. The roots of everything go back to before you were born.

I'd inquired about the origins of the organization, in my early days with it. Nobody knew much except that it hadn't been important before Sotomayor took the leadership—whoever, wherever he was. Until him, it was a spontaneous thing.

Probably it hadn't begun right after the Sacred War. Americans had done little except pick up pieces, those first years. They were too stunned when the Soviet missiles knocked out their second-strike capability and all at once their cities were hostages for the good behavior of their politicians and submarines. They were too relieved when no occupation followed, aside from inspectors and White House advisors who made sure the treaty limitations on armaments were observed. (Oh, several generals and the like were hanged as war criminals.) True, the Soviets had taken a beating from what U.S. nukes did get through, sufficient that they couldn't control China or, later, a China-sponsored Japanese S.S.R. The leniency shown Americans was not the less welcome for being due to a shortage of troops.

Oath-brothers had told me how they were attracted by the mutterings of friends and presently recruited, after Moscow informed Washington that John Halper would be an unacceptable candidate for President in the next election. Others joined in reaction against a collectivist sentiment whose growth was hothouse-forced by government, schools, and universities.

I remember how Granddad growled, on a day when we were alone in the woods and I'd asked him about that period.

"The old order was blamed for the war and the war's consequences, Jimmy. Militarists, capitalists, imperialists, racists, bourgeoisie. Nobody heard any different any more. Those who'd've argued weren't gettin' published or on the air, nothin'." He drew on his pipe. Muscles bunched in the angle of his jaw. "Yeah, everybody was bein' blamed—except the liberals who'd worked to lower our guard so their snug dreams wouldn't be interrupted, the conservatives who helped 'em so's to save a few wretched tax dollars, the radicals who disrupted the country, the copouts who lifted no finger—" The bit snapped between his teeth. He stooped for the bowl and squinted at it ruefully while his heel ground out the scattered ashes. At last he sighed. "Don't forget what I've told you, Jimmy. But bury it deep, like a seed."

I can't say if he was correct. My life was not his. I wasn't born when the Constitutional Convention proclaimed the People's Republic. Nor did I ever take a strong interest in politics.

In fact, my recruitment was glacier gradual. At West Point I discovered step by step that my best friends were those who wanted us to become a first-class power again, not conquer anybody else, merely cut the Russian apron strings. . . . Clandestine bitching sessions, winked at by our officers, slowly turned into clandestine meetings which hinted at eventual action. An illegal newsletter circulated. . . . After graduation and assignment, I did trivial favors, covering up for this or that comrade who might otherwise be in trouble, supplying bits of classified information to fellows who said they were blocked from what they needed by stupid bureaucrats, hearing till I believed it that the proscribed and abhorred Stephen Decatur Society was not counterrevolutionary, not fascist, simply patriotic and misunderstood. . . .

The final commitment to something like that is when you make an excuse to disappear for a month—in my case, a backpacking trip with a couple of guys, though my C.O. warned me that asocial furloughs might hurt my career—and you get flitted to an unspecified place where they induct you. One of the psychotechs there explained that the treatment, drugs, sleep deprivation, shock conditioning, the whole damnable works, meant more than installing a set of reflexes. Those guarantee you can't be made to blab involuntarily under serum or torture. But the suffering has a positive effect, too: it's a rite of passage. Afterward you can't likely be bribed either.

Likely. The figures may change on a man's price tag, but he never loses it.

I don't yet know how I was detected. A Decaturist courier had cautioned my cell about microminiature listeners which can be slipped a man in his food, operate off body heat, and take days to be eliminated. With my work load, both official on account of the crisis and after hours in preparing for our coup, I must have gotten careless.

Presumably, though, I was caught by luck rather than suspicion, in a spot check. If the political police had identified any fair-sized number of conspirators, Mannix wouldn't be as anxious to use me as he was.

Jarred, I realized I hadn't responded to his last inquiry. "Sir," I begged, "honest, I'm no traitor. I wish our country had more voice in its own affairs. Nothing else."

"A Titoist." Recognizing my glance of dull surprise at the new word, he waved it off. "Never mind. I forgot they've reimproved the history texts since I was young. Let's stick to practical matters, then."

"I, I can . . . identify for you—those in my cell." Jack whose wife was pregnant, Bill who never spared everyday helpfulness, Tim . . . "B-but there must be others on the base and in the area, and, well, some of them must know *I* belong."

"Right." Mannix nodded. "We'll stay our hand as regards those you have met. Mustn't alert the organization. It does seem to be efficient. That devil Sotomayor—well, let's get on."

He was patient. Hours went by before I could talk coherently.

At that time he had occasion to turn harsh. Leaning across his desk—the window behind framed him in night—he snapped: "You considered yourself a patriot. Nevertheless you plotted mutiny."

I cringed. "No, sir. Really. I mean, the idea—was—"

"Was what?" In his apple face stood the eyes of Old Scrooge.

"Sir, when civil war breaks out in the Motherland—those Vasiliev and Kunin factions—"

"Party versus Army."

"What?" I don't know why I tried to argue. "Sir, last I heard, Vasiliev's got everything west of the, uh, Yenisei . . . millions of men under arms, effective control of West Europe—"

"You do not understand how to interpret events. The essential struggle is between those who are loyal to the principles of the Party, and those who would substitute military dictatorship." His finger jabbed. "Like you, Dowling."

We had told each other in our secret meetings, we Decatur folk, better government by colonels than commissioners.

"No, sir, no, sir," I protested. "Look, I'm only a soldier. But I see . . . I smell the factions here, too . . . the air's rotten with plotting . . . and what about in Washington? I mean, do we *know* what orders we'll get, any day now? And what is the situation in Siberia?"

"You have repeatedly been informed—the front is stabilized and relatively quiet."

My wits weren't so shorted out that I hinted the official media might ever shade the truth. I did reply: "Sir, I'm a missileman. In the, uh, the opinion of every colleague I've talked with—most of them loyal, I'm certain—what stability the front has got is due to the fact both sides have ample rockets, lasers, the works. If they both cut loose, there'd be mutual wipeout. Unless we Americans . . . we hold the balance." Breath shuddered into me. "Who's going to order our birds targeted where?"

Mannix sat for a while that grew very quiet. I sat listening to my heart stutter. Weariness filled me like water fills a sponge. I wanted to crawl off and curl up in darkness, alone, more than I wanted Bonnie or my children or tomorrow's sunrise or that which had been taken from me. But I had to keep answering.

At last he asked, softly, almost mildly, "Is this your honest evaluation? Is this why you were in a conspiracy to seize control of the big weapons?"

"Yes, sir." A vacuum passed through me. I shook myself free of it. "Yes, sir. I think my belief—the belief of most men involved—is, uh, if a, uh, a responsible group, led by experts, takes over the missile bases for the time being . . . those birds won't get misused. Like by, say, the wrong side in Washington pulling a coup—" I jerked my head upright.

"Your superiors in the cabal have claimed to you that the object is to keep the birds in their nests, keep America out of the war," Mannix said. "How do you know they've told you the truth?"

I thought I did. Did I? Was I? Big soft waves came rolling.

"Jim," Mannix said earnestly, "they've tricked you through your whole adult life. Nevertheless, what we've learned shows me you're important to them. You're slated for commander here at Reed, once the mutiny begins. I wouldn't be surprised but what they've been grooming you for years and that's how come your rapid rise in the service. Clues there—but as for now, you must have ways to get in touch with higher echelons."

"Uh-huh," I said. "Uh-huh. Uh-huh."

Mannix grew genial. "Let's discuss that, shall we?"

I don't remember being conducted to bed. What stands before me is how I woke, gasping for air, nothing in my eyes except night and nothing in the hand that grabbed at my groin.

I rolled over on my belly, clutched the pillow, and crammed it into my mouth. Bonnie, Bonnie, I said, they've left me this one way back to you. I pledge allegiance to you, Bonnie, and to the Chuck and Joanlet you have mothered, and *screw* the rest of the world!

("Even for a man in his thirties," said a hundred teachers,

intellectuals, officials, entertainers out of my years, "or even for an adolescent, romantic atavism is downright unpatriotic. The most important thing in man's existence is his duty to the people and the molding of their future." The echoes went on and on.)

I've been a rat, I said to my three, to risk—and lose—the few things which counted, all of which were ours. Bonnie, it's no excuse for my staying with the Decaturists, that I'd see you turn white at this restriction or that command to volunteer service or yonder midnight vanishing of a neighbor. No excuse, nothing but a rationalization. I've led us down my rathole, and now my duty is to get us out in whatever way I am able.

("There should be little bloodshed," the liaison man told our cell; we were not shown his face. "The war is expected to remain stalemated for the several weeks we need. When the moment is right, our folk will rise, disarm and expel everybody who isn't with us, and dig in. We can hope to seize most of the rocket bases. Given the quick retargetability of every modern bird, we will then be in a position to hit any point on Earth and practically anything in orbit. However, we won't. The threat—plus the short-range weapons—should protect us from counterattack. We will sit tight, and thus realize our objective: to keep the blood of possibly millions off American hands, while giving America the self-determination that once was hers.")

Turn the Decaturists over to the Communists. Let all the ists kill each other off and leave human beings in peace.

("My friend, my friend," Mannix sighed, "you cannot be naïve enough to suppose the Asians have no hand in this. You yourself, I find, were involved in our rocket-scattering of munitions across the rebellious parts of India. Have they not been advising, subsidizing, equipping, infiltrating the upper leadership of your oh-so-patriotic Decatur Society? Let the Soviet Union ruin itself—which is the likeliest outcome if America doesn't intervene—let that happen, and, yes, America could probably become the boss of the Western Hemisphere. But we're not equipped to conquer the Eastern. You're aware of that. The gooks would inherit. The Russians may gripe you. You may consider our native leaders their puppets. But at least they're white; at least they share a tradition with us. Why, they helped us back on our feet, Jim, after the war. They let us rearm, they aided it, precisely so we could cover each other's backs, they in the Old World, we in the New. . . . Can you prove your Society isn't a Jappochink tool?")

No, but I can prove we have rockets here so we'll draw some

of the Jappochink fire in the event of a big war. They're working on suicide regardless of what I do, Bonnie. America would already have declared for one splinter or the other, if America weren't likewise divided. Remember your Shakespeare? Well, Caesar has conquered the available world and is dead; Anthony and Octavian are disputing his loot. What paralyzes America is—has to be—a silent struggle in Washington. Maybe not altogether silent; I get word of troop movements, "military exercises" under separate commands, throughout the Atlantic states. . . . Where can we hide, Bonnie?

("We have reason to believe," said the political lecturer to us at assembly, "that the conflict was instigated, to a considerable degree at least, by *agents provocateurs* of the Asian deviationists, who spent the past twenty years or more posing as Soviet citizens and worming their way close to the top. With our whole hearts we trust the dispute can be settled peacefully. Failing that, gentlemen, your duty will be to strike as ordered by your government to end this war before irrevocable damage has been done the Motherland.")

There is no place to hide, Bonnie Brighteyes. Nor can we bravely join the side of the angels. There are no angels either.

("Yeah, sure, I've heard the same," said Jack who belonged to my cell. "If we grab those bases and refuse to join this fight, peace'll have to be negotiated, lives and cultural treasures 'ull be spared, the balance of power 'ull be preserved, yeah, yeah. Think, man. What do you suppose Sotomayor and the rest really want? Isn't it for the war to grow hot—incandescent? Never mind who tries the first strike! The Kuninists might, thinking they'd better take advantage of a U.S. junta fairly sympathetic to them before it's overthrown. Or the Vasilievists might, they being Party types who can't well afford a compromise. Either way, no matter who comes out on top, the Soviets overnight turn themselves into the junior member of our partnership. Then *we* tell *them* what to do for a change.")

Not that I am altogether cynical, Bonnie. I don't choose to believe we've brought Chuck and Joan into a world of wolves and jackals—when you've said you wish for a couple more children. No, I've simply had demonstrated to me that our best chance—mankind's best chance—lies with the legitimate government of the United States as established by the People's Constitutional Convention.

* * *

Next day Mannix turned me over to his interrogation specialists, who asked me more questions than I'd known I had answers for. A trankstim pill kept me alert but unemotional, as if I were operating myself by remote control.

Among other items, I showed them how a Decaturist who had access to the right equipment made contact with fellows elsewhere, whom he'd probably never met, or with high-ups whom he definitely hadn't. The method had been considered by political police technicians, but they'd failed to devise any means of coping.

Problem: How do you maintain a network of illicit communications?

In practice you mostly use the old-fashioned mail drop. It's unfeasible to read the entire mails. The authorities must settle for watching the correspondence of suspicious individuals and these may have ways of posting and collecting letters unobserved.

Yet sometimes you need to send a message fast. The telephone's no good, of course, since computers became able to monitor every conversation continuously. However, those same machines, or their cousins, can be your carriers.

Remember, we have millions of computers around these days, nationally interconnected. They do drudge work like record-keeping and billing; they operate automated plants; they calculate for governmental planners and R & D workers; they integrate organizations; they keep day-by-day track of each citizen, etc. Still more than in the case of the mails, the volume of data transmissions would swamp human overseers.

Given suitable codes, programmers and other technicians can send practically anything practically anywhere. The printout is just another string of numbers to those who can't read it. Once it has been read, the card is recycled and the electronic traces are wiped as per routine. That message leaves the office in a single skull.

Naturally, you save this capability for your highest-priority calls. I'd used it a few times, attracting no attention since my job on base frequently required me to prepare or receive top-secret calculations.

I couldn't give Mannix's men any code except the latest that had been given me. Every such message was recoded en route, according to self-changing programs buried deep down in the banks of the machines concerned. I could, though, put him in touch with somebody close to Sotomayor. Or, rather, I could put myself in touch.

What would happen thereafter was uncertain. We couldn't develop an exact plan. My directive was to do my best and if my best was good enough I'd be pardoned and rewarded.

I was rehearsed in my cover story till I was letter perfect, and given a few items like phone numbers to learn. Simulators and reinforcement techniques made this quick.

Perhaps my oath-brothers would cut my throat immediately, as a regrettable precaution. That didn't seem to matter. The drug left me no particular emotion except a desire to get the business done.

At a minimum, I was sure to be interrogated, strip-searched, encephalogrammed, x-rayed, checked for metal and radioactivity. Perhaps blood, saliva, urine, and spinal fluid would be sampled. Agents have used pharmaceuticals and implants for too many years.

Nevertheless Mannix's outfit had a weapon prepared for me. It was not one the Army had been told about. I wondered what else the political police labs were working on. I also wondered if various prominent men, who might have been awkward to denounce, had really died of strokes or heart attacks.

"I can't tell you details," said a technician. "With your education, you can figure out the general idea for yourself. It's a micro-version of the fission gun, enclosed in lead to baffle detectors. You squeeze—you'll be shown how—and the system opens; a radioactive substance bombards another material which releases neutrons which touch off the fissionable atoms in one of ten successive chambers."

Despite my chemical coolness, awe drew a whistle from me. Given the right isotopes, configurations, and shielding, critical mass gets down to grams and you can direct the energy through a minilaser. I'd known that. In this system, the lower limit must be milligrams; and the efficiency must approach 100 percent if you could operate it right out of your own body.

Still... "You do have components that'll register if I'm checked very closely," I said.

The technician grinned. "I doubt you will be, where we have in mind. They'll load you tomorrow morning."

Because I'd need practice in the weapon, I wasn't drugged then. I'd expected to be embarrassed. But when I entered an instrument-crammed concrete room after being unable to eat breakfast, I suddenly began shaking.

Two P.P. men I hadn't met before waited for me. One wore a lab coat, one a medic's tunic. My escort said, "Dowling," closed the door, and left me alone with them.

Lab Coat was thin, bald, and sourpussed. "Okay, peel down and let's get started," he snapped.

Medic, who was a fattish blond, laughed—giggled, I thought in a gust of wanting to kill him. "Short-arm inspection," he said.

Bonnie, I reminded myself, and dropped my clothes on a chair. Their eyes went to my crotch. Mine couldn't. I bit jaws and fists together and stared at the wall beyond them.

Medic sat down. "Over here," he ordered. I obeyed, stood before him, felt him finger what was left. "Ah," he chuckled. "Balls but no musket, eh?"

"Shut up, funny man," Lab Coat said and handed him a pair of calipers. I felt him measure the stump.

"They should've left more," Lab Coat complained. "At least two centimeters more."

"This glue could stick it straight onto his bellybutton," Medic said.

"Yeah, but the gadgets aren't rechargeable," Lab Coat retorted. "He'll go through four or five today before the final one and nothing but elastic collars holding 'em in place. What a clot of a time I'll have fitting *them*." He shuffled over to a workbench and got busy.

"Take a look at your new tool," Medic invited me. "Generous, eh? Be the envy of the neighborhood. And what a jolt for your wife."

The wave was red, not black, and tasted of blood. I lunged, laid fingers around his throat, and bawled—I can't remember—maybe, "Be quiet, you filthy fairy, before I kill you."

He squealed, then gurgled. I shook him till his teeth rattled. Lab Coat came on the run. "Stop that!" he barked. "Stop or I'll call a guard!"

I let go, sank down on the floor—its chill flowed into my buttocks, up my spine, out along my ribcage—and struggled not to weep.

"You bastard," Medic chattered. "I'm gonna file charges. I am."

"You are not. Another peep and I'll report you." Lab Coat hunkered beside me, laid an arm around my shoulder, and said, "I understand, Dowling. It was heroic of you to volunteer. You'll get the real thing back when you're finished. Never forget that."

Volunteer?

Laughter exploded. I whooped, I howled, I rolled around and beat my fists on the concrete; my muscles ached from laughing when finally I won back to silence.

After that, and a short rest, I was calm—cold, even—and functioned well. My aim improved fast, till I could hole the center circle at every shot.

"You've ten charges," Lab Coat reminded me. "No more. The beam being narrow, the head's your best target. If the apparatus gets detected after all, or if you're in Dutch for some other reason and your ammo won't last, press inward from the end—like this—and it'll self-destruct. You'll be blown apart and escape a bad time. Understand? Repeat."

He didn't bother bidding me good-bye at the end of the session. (Medic was too sulky for words.) No doubt he'd figured what sympathy to administer earlier. Efficiency is the P.P. ideal. Mannix, or somebody, must have ordered my gun prepared almost at the moment I was arrested, or likelier before.

My escort had waited, stolid, throughout those hours. Though I recognized it was a practical matter of security, I felt hand-lickingly grateful to Mannix that this fellow—that very few people—knew what I was.

The day after, I placed my call to the Decaturists. It was brief. I had news of supreme importance—the fact I'd vanished for almost a month made this plausible—and would stand by for transportation at such-and-such different rendezvous, such-and-such different times.

Just before the first of these, I swallowed a stim with a hint of trank, in one of those capsules which attach to the stomach wall and spend the next hundred hours dissolving. No one expected I'd need more time before the metabolic price had to be paid. A blood test would show its presence, but if I was carrying a vital message, would I not have sneaked me a supercharger?

I was not met, and went back to my room and waited. A side effect, when every cell worked at peak, was longing for Bonnie. Nothing sentimental; I loved her, I wanted her, I had to keep thrusting away memories of eyes, lips, breasts beneath my hand till my hand traveled downward. . . . In the course of hours, I learned how to be a machine.

* * *

They came for me at the second spot on my list, a trifle past midnight. The place was a bar in a village of shops and rec centers near the base. It wasn't the sleek, state-owned New West, where I'd be recognized by officers, engineers, and Party functionaries who could afford to patronize. This was a dim and dingy shack, run by a couple of workers on their own time, at the tough end of town. Music, mostly dirty songs, blared from a taper, ear-hurtingly loud, and the booze was rotgut served in glasses which seldom got washed. Nevertheless I had to push through the crowd and, practically, the smoke—pot as well as tobacco. The air also smelled of sweat and urine.

You see more of this kind of thing every year. I imagine the government only deplores the trend officially. People need some unorganized pleasure. Or, as the old joke goes, "What is the stage between socialism and communism called? Alcoholism."

A girl in a skimpy dress made me a business offer. She wasn't bad-looking, in a sleazy fashion, and last month, I'd merely have said no, thanks. As was, the drug in me didn't stop me from screaming, "Get away, you whore!" Scared, she backed off, and I drew looks from the men around. In cheap civvies, I was supposed to be inconspicuous. Jim Dowling, officer, rocketeer, triple agent, boy wonder, ha! I elbowed my way onward to the bar. Two quick shots eased my shakes and the crowd around forgot me.

I'd almost decided to leave when a finger tapped my arm. A completely forgettable little man stood there. "Excuse me," he said. "Aren't you Sam Chalmers?"

"Uh, no, I'm his brother Roy." Beneath the once more cold surface, my pulse knocked harder.

"Well, well," he said. "Your father's told me a lot about you both. My name's Ralph Wagner."

"Yes, he's mentioned you. Glad to meet you, Comrade Wagner."

We shook hands and ad-libbed conversation a while. The counter-signs we'd used were doubtless obsolete, but he'd allowed for my having been out of touch. Presently we left.

A car bearing Department of Security insignia was perched on the curb. Two much larger men, uniformed, waited inside. We joined them, the blowers whirred, and we were off. One man touched a button. A steel plate slid down and cut us three in the rear seat off from the driver. The windows I could see turned opaque. I had no need to know where we were bound. I did estimate our acceleration and thus our cruising speed. About three hundred K.P.H. Going some, even for a security vehicle!

From what Granddad had told me, this would have been lunacy before the war. Automobiles were so thick then that often they could barely crawl along. Among my earliest memories is that the government was still congratulating itself on having solved that problem.

Wind hooted around the shell. A slight vibration thrummed through my bones. The overhead light was singularly bleak. The big man on my left and the small man on my right crowded me.

"Okay," said the big man, "what happened?"

"I'll handle this," said he who named himself Wagner. The bruiser snapped his mouth shut and settled back. He was probably the one who'd kill me if that was deemed needful, but he was not the boss.

"We've been alarmed about you." Wagner spoke as gently as Mannix. In an acid way I liked the fact that he didn't smile.

I attempted humor in my loneliness: "I'd be alarmed if you hadn't been."

"Well?"

"I was called in for top-secret conferences. They've flitted me in and out—to Europe and back—under maximum security."

The big man formed an oath. Wagner waited.

"They've gotten wind of our project," I said.

"I don't know of any other vanishments than yours," Wagner answered, flat-voiced.

"Would you?" I challenged.

He shrugged. "Perhaps not."

"Actually," I continued, "I wasn't told about arrests and there may have been none. What they discussed was the Society, the Asians—they have a fixed idea the Peking-Tokyo Axis has taken over the Society—and what they called 'open indications.' The legal or semi-legal talk you hear about 'socialist lawfulness,' 'American socialism,' and the rest. Roger Mannix—he turns out to be high in the P.P., by the way, and a shrewd man; I recommend we try to knock him off—Mannix takes these signs more seriously than I'd imagined anybody in the government did." I cleared my throat. "Details at your convenience. The upshot is, the authorities decided there is a definite risk of a cabal seizing the rocket bases. Never mind whether they have the data to make that a completely logical conclusion. What counts is that it *is* their conclusion."

"And right, Goddamn it, right," muttered the big man. He slammed a fist on his knee.

"What do they propose to do?" Wagner asked, as if I'd revealed the government was considering a reduced egg ration.

"That was a . . . tough question." I stared at the blank, enclosing panel. "They dare not shut down the installations, under guard of P.P. who don't know a mass ratio from a hole in the ground. Nor dare they purge the personnel, hoping to be left with loyal skeleton crews—because they aren't yet sure who those crews had better be loyal to. Oh, I saw generals and commissioners scuttling around like toads in a chamberpot, believe me." Now I turned my head to confront his eyes. "And believe me," I added, "we were lucky they happened to include one Decatur man."

Again, under the tranquilization and the stimulation (how keenly I saw the wrinkles around his mouth, heard cleft air brawl, felt the shiver of speed, snuffed stale bodies, registered the prickle of hairs and sweat glands, the tightened belly muscles and self-seizing guts beneath!), fear fluttered in me, and under the fear I was hollow. The man on whom I had turned my back could put a gun muzzle at the base of my skull.

Wagner nodded. "Yes-s-s."

Though it was too early to allow myself relief, I saw I'd passed the first watchdog. The Society might have been keeping such close surveillance that Wagner would know there had in fact been no mysterious travels of assorted missilemen.

This wasn't plausible, Mannix had declared. The Society was limited in what it could do. Watching every nonmember's every movement was ridiculous.

"Have they reached a decision?" Wagner asked.

"Yes." No matter how level I tried to keep it, my voice seemed to shiver the bones in my head. "American personnel will be replaced by foreigners till the crisis is past. I suppose you know West Europe has a good many competent rocketeers. In civilian jobs, of course; still, they could handle a military assignment. And they'd be docile, regardless of who gave orders. The Spanish and French especially, considering how the purges went through those countries. In short, they'd not be players in the game, just parts of the machinery."

My whetted ears heard him let out a breath. "When?"

"Not certain. A move of that kind needs study and planning

beforehand. A couple—three weeks? My word is that we'd better compress our own timetable."

"Indeed, Indeed." Wagner bayoneted me with his stare. "If you are correct."

"You mean if I'm telling the truth," I said on his behalf.

"You understand, Colonel Dowling, you'll have to be quizzed and examined. And we'll meet an ironic obstacle in your conditioning against involuntary betrayal of secrets."

"Eventually you'd better go ahead and trust me . . . after all these years."

"I think that will be decided on the top level."

They took me to a well-equipped room somewhere and put me through the works. They were no more unkind than necessary, but extremely thorough. Never mind details of those ten or fifteen hours. The thoroughness was not quite sufficient. My immunity and my story held up. The physical checks showed nothing suspicious. Mannix had said, "I expect an inhibition too deep for consciousness will prevent the idea from occurring to them." I'd agreed. The reality was what had overrun me.

Afterward I was given a meal and—since I'd freely admitted being full of stim—some hours under a sleep inducer. It didn't prevent dreams which I still shiver to recall. But when I was allowed to wake, I felt rested and ready for action.

Whether I'd get any was an interesting question. Mannix's hope was that I'd be taken to see persons high in the outfit, from whom I might obtain information on plans and membership. But maybe I'd be sent straight home. My yarn declared that, after the bout of talks was over, I'd requested a few days' leave, hinting to my superiors that I had a girlfriend out of town.

My guards, two young men now grown affable, couldn't guess what the outcome would be. We started a poker game, but eventually found ourselves talking. These were full-time undergrounders. I asked what made them abandon their original identities. The first said, "Oh, I got caught strewing pamphlets and had to run. What brought me into the Society to start with was . . . well, one damn thing after another, like when I was a miner and they boosted our quota too high for us to maintain safety structures and a cave-in killed a buddy of mine."

The second, more bookish, said thoughtfully: "I believe in God."

I raised my brows. "Really? Well, you're not forbidden to go to church. You might not get a good job, positively never a clearance, but—"

"That's not the point. I've heard a lot of preachers in a lot of different places. They're all wind-up toys of the state. The Social Gospel, you know—no, I guess you don't."

Wagner arrived soon afterward. His surface calm was like Dacron crackling in a wind. "Word's come, Dowling," he announced. "They want to interview you, ask your opinions, your impressions, you having been our sole man on the spot."

I rose. "They?"

"The main leadership. Sotomayor himself, and his chief administrators. Here." Wagner handed me a wallet. "Your new I.D. card, travel permit, ration tab, the works, including a couple of family snapshots. Learn it. We leave in an hour."

I scarcely heard the latter part. Alfredo Sotomayor! The half-legendary president of the whole Society!

I'd wondered plenty about him. Little was known. His face was a fixture on post-office walls, wanted for a variety of capital crimes, armed and dangerous. The text barely hinted at his political significance. Evidently the government didn't wish to arouse curiosity. The story told me, while I was in the long process of joining, was that he'd been a firebrand in his youth, an icily brilliant organizer in middle life, and in his old age was a scholar and philosopher, at work on a proposal for establishing a "free country," whatever that meant. Interested, I'd asked for some of his writings. They were denied me. Possession was dangerous. Why risk a useful man unnecessarily?

I was to meet rebellious Lucifer.

Whom once I had served. Whom I would be serving yet had not the political police laid hand on me and mine.

Not that those fingers had closed on Bonnie or the kids. They would if I didn't undo my own rebelliousness. Camp La Pasionara. What was Sotomayor to me?

How could I believe a bandit had any real interest in America, except to plunder her? I had *not* been shown those writings.

"You feel well, Jim?" asked the man who believed in God. "You look kind of pale."

"Yeah, I'm okay," I mumbled. "Better sit down, though, and learn my new name."

A fake security car, windows blanked, could bring me to an expendable hidey-hole like this, off in a lonely section of hills.

The method was too showy for a meeting which included brains, heart, and maybe spinal cord of Decatur. Wagner and I would use public transportation.

We walked to the nearest depot, a few kilometers off. I'd have enjoyed the sunlight, woods, peace asparkle with birdsong, if Bonnie had been my companion (and I whole, I whole). As was, neither of us spoke. At the newsstand I bought a magazine and read about official plans for my future while the train was an hour late. It lost another hour, for some unexplained reason, en route. About par for the course. Several times the coach rattled to the sonic booms of military jets. Again, nothing unusual, especially in time of crisis. The People's Republic keeps abundant warcraft.

Our destination was Oakland. We arrived at 2000, when the factories were letting out, and joined the pedestrian swarm. I don't like city dwellers. They smell sour and look grubby. Well, that's not their fault; if soap and hot water are in short supply, people crowded together will not be clean. But their grayness goes deeper than their skins—except in ethnic districts, of course, which hold more life but which you'd better visit in armed groups.

Wagner and I found a restaurant and made the conversation of two petty production managers on a business trip. I flatter myself that I gave a good performance. Concentration on it took my mind off the food and service.

Afterward we saw a movie, an insipidity about boy volunteer on vacation meets girl on collective. When it and the political reel had been endured, meeting time was upon us. We hadn't been stopped to show our papers, and surely any plainclothesman running a random surveillance had lost interest in us. A street car groaned us to a surprisingly swank part of town; and the house to which we walked was a big old mansion in big old grounds full of the night breath of roses.

"Isn't this too conspicuous?" I wondered.

"Ever tried being inconspicuous in a tenement?" Wagner responded. "The poor may hate the civil police, but the prospect of reward money makes them eyes and ears for the P.P."

He hesitated. "Since you could check it out later anyway," he said, "I may as well tell you we're at the home of Lorenzo Berg, commissioner of electric power for Northern California. He's been one of us since his national service days."

I barely maintained my steady pace. This fact alone would buy me back my life.

* * *

A prominent man is a watched man. Berg's task in the Society had been to build, over the years, the image of a competent bureaucrat who had no further ambitions and therefore was no potential menace to anybody, but who amused himself by throwing little parties where screwball intellectuals would gather to discuss the theory of chess or the origin of Australopithecus. Most of these affairs were genuine. For the few that weren't, he had the craft to nullify the bugs in his house and later play tapes for them which had been supplied him. Of course, a mobile tapper could have registered what was actually said—he dared not screen the place—but the P.P. had more to do than make anything but spot checks on a harmless eccentric.

Thus Berg could provide a scene for occasional important Society meetings. He could temporarily shelter fugitives. He could maintain for this area that vastly underrated tool—a reference library; who'd look past the covers of his many books and microreels? Doubtless his services went further, but never into foolish flamboyancies.

I don't recall him except as a blur. He played his role that well, even that night among those men. Or was it his role? You needn't be a burning-eyed visionary to live by a cause.

A couple like that were on hand. They must have been able in their fields. But one spoke of his specialty, massive sabotage, too lovingly for me. My missiles were counter-force weapons, not botulin mists released among women and children. Another, who was a black, dwelt on Russian racism. I'm sure his citations were accurate, of how the composition of the Politburo has never since the beginning reflected the nationalities in the Soviet Union. Yet what had that to do with us and why did his eyes dwell so broodingly on the whites in the room?

The remaining half dozen were entirely businesslike in their various ways, except Sotomayor, who gave me a courteous greeting and then sat quietly and listened. They were ordinary Americans, which is to say a mixed lot; a second black man, a Jew to judge by the nose (it flitted across my mind how our schools keep teaching that the People's Republic has abolished the prejudices of the imperialist era, which are described in detail), a Japanese-descended woman, the rest of them like me . . . except, again, Sotomayor, who I think was almost pure Indio. His features were rather long and lean for that, but he had the cheekbones, the enduringly healthy brown skin, dark eyes altogether alive under straight white hair, flared nostrils, and a sensitive mouth. He dressed elegantly, and sat and stood as erect as a burning candle.

I repeated my story, was asked intelligent questions, and carried everything off well. Maybe I was helped by Bonnie having told me a lot about theater and persuading me to take occasional bit parts. The hours ticked by. Finally, around 0100, Sotomayor stirred and said in his soft but youthful voice: "Gentlemen, I think perhaps we have done enough for the present, and it might arouse curiosity if the living-room lights shone very late on a midweek night. Please think about this matter as carefully as it deserves. You will be notified as to time and place of our next meeting."

All but one being from out of town, they would sleep here. Berg led them off to their cots. Sotomayor said he would guide me. Smiling, as we started up a grand staircase the Socialist Functionalist critics would never allow to be built today, he took my arm and suggested a nightcap.

He rated a suite cleared for his use.

Although a widower, Berg maintained a large household. Four grown sons pleaded the apartment shortage as a reason for living here with their families and so prevented the mansion's conversion to an ordinary tenement. They and the wives the Society had chosen for them had long since been instructed to stay completely passive, except for keeping their kids from overhearing anything, and to know nothing of Society affairs.

Given that population under this roof, plus a habit of inviting visiting colleagues to bunk with him, plus always offering overnight accommodations when parties got wet, Berg found that guests of his drew no undue notice.

All in all, I'd entered quite a nest. And the king hornet was bowing me through his door.

The room around me was softly lit, well furnished, dominated by books and a picture window. The latter overlooked a sweep of city—lanes of street lamps cut through humpbacked darknesses of buildings—and the Bay and a deeper spark-speckled shadow which was San Francisco. A nearly full moon bridged the waters with frailty. I wondered if men would ever get back yonder. The requirements of defense against the revisionists—

Why in the name of madness was I thinking about that?

Sotomayor closed the door and went to a table whereon stood a bottle, a carafe of water, and an ice bucket which must be an heirloom. "Please be seated, Colonel Dowling," he said. "I have only this to offer you, but it is genuinely from Scotland. You need a drink, I'm sure, tense as you are."

"D-does it show that much?" Hearing the idiocy of the question, I hauled myself to full awareness. Tomorrow morning, when the group dispersed, Wagner would conduct me home and I would report to Mannix. My job was to stay alive until then.

"No surprise." He busied himself. "In fact, your conduct has been remarkable throughout. I'm grateful for more than your service, tremendous though that may turn out to be. I'm joyful to know we have a man like you. The kind is rare and precious."

I sat down and told myself over and over that he was my enemy. "You, uh, you overrate me, sir."

"No. I have been in this business too long to cherish illusions. Men are limited creatures at best. This may perhaps make their striving correspondingly more noble, but the limitations remain. When a strong, sharp tool comes to hand, we cherish it."

He handed me my drink, took a chair opposite me, and sipped at his own. I could barely meet those eyes, however gentle they seemed. Mine stung. I took a long gulp and blurted the first words that it occurred to me might stave off silence: "Why, when being in the Society is such a risk, sir, would anybody join who's not, well, unusual?"

"Yes, in certain cases, through force of circumstance. We have taken in criminals—murderers, thieves—when they looked potentially useful."

After a moment of stillness, he added slowly: "In fact, revolutionaries, be they Decaturists or members of other outfits or isolated in their private angers—revolutionaries have always had motivations as various as their humanity. Some are idealists; yet let us admit that some of the ideals are nasty, like racism or religious fanaticism. Some want revenge for harm done them or theirs by officials who may have been sadistic or corrupt, but often were merely incompetent or overzealous in a system which allows the citizen no appeal. Some hope for money or power or fame under a new dispensation. Some are old-fashioned patriots who want us out of the empire. Am I right that you fall in that category, Colonel Dowling?"

"Yes," I said, you were.

Sotomayor's gaze went into me and beyond me, across city and waters, skyward. "One reason I want to know you better," he said, "is that I think you can be educated to a higher ideal."

I discovered, with a sort of happiness, that I was interested enough to take my mind off the fact I was drinking the liquor of a man who believed I was his friend and a man. "To your own purposes, sir?" I asked. "You know, I never have been told what you yourself are after."

"On as motley a collection as our members are, the effect of an official doctrine would be disruptive. Nor is any required. The history of communist movements in the last century gives ample proof. I've dug into history, you realize. The franker material is hard to find, after periodic purges of the libraries. But it's difficult to eliminate a book totally. The printing press is a more powerful weapon than any gun—for us or for our masters." Sotomayor smiled and sighed. "I ramble. Getting old. Still, I have spent these last years of mine trying to understand what we are doing in the hope we can do what is right."

"And what are your conclusions, sir?"

"Let us imagine our takeover plan succeeds," he answered. "We hold the rocket bases. Given those, I assure you there are enough members and sympathizers in the rest of the armed services and in civilian life that, while there will doubtless be some shooting, the government will topple and we will take over the nation."

The drink slopped in my hand. Sweat prickled forth on my skin and ran down my ribs.

Sotomayor nodded. "Yes, we are that far along," he said. "After many years and many human sacrifices, we are finally prepared. The war has given us the opportunity to use what we built."

Surely, I thought wildly, the P.P., military intelligence, high Party officials, surely they knew something of the sort was in the wind. You can't altogether conceal a trend of such magnitude.

Evidently they did not suspect how far along it was.

Or . . . wait . . . You didn't need an enormous number of would-be rebels in the officer corps. You really only needed access to the dossiers and psychographs kept on everybody. Then in-depth studies would give you a good notion of how the different key men would react.

"Let us assume, then, a junta," Sotomayor was saying. "It cannot, must not, be for more than the duration of the emergency. Civilian government must be restored and made firm. But *what* government? That is the problem I have been working on."

"And?" I responded in my daze.

"Have you ever read the original Constitution of the United Stares? The one drawn in Philadelphia in 1787?"

"Why . . . well, no. What for?"

"It may be found in scholarly works. A document so widely

disseminated cannot be gotten rid of in thirty or forty years. Though if the present system endures, I do not give the old Constitution another fifty.'' Sotomayor leaned forward. Beneath his softness, intensity mounted. ''What were you taught about it in school?''

''Oh . . . well, uh, let me think . . . Codification of the law for the bourgeoisie of the cities and the slaveowners of the South . . . Modified as capitalism evolved into imperialism . . .''

''Read it sometime.'' A thin finger pointed at a shelf. ''Take it to bed with you. It's quite brief.''

After a moment: ''Its history is long, though, Colonel Dowling, and complicated, and not always pleasant—especially toward the end, when the original concept had largely been lost sight of. Yet it was the most profoundly revolutionary thing set down on paper since the New Testament.''

''Huh?''

He smiled again. ''Read it, I say, and compare today's version, and look up certain thinkers who are mentioned in footnotes if at all—Hobbes, Locke, Hamilton, Burke, and the rest. Then do your own thinking. That won't be easy. Some of the finest minds which ever existed spent centuries groping toward the idea that law should be a contract the people make among each other, and that every man has absolute rights, which protect him in making his private destiny and may never be taken from him.''

His smile had dissolved. I have seldom heard a bleaker tone: ''Think how radical that is. Too radical, perhaps. The world found it easier to bring back overlords, compulsory belief, and neolithic god-kings.''

''W-would you . . . revive the old government?''

''Not precisely. The country and its people are too changed from what they were. I think, however, we could bring back Jefferson's original idea. We could write a basic law which does not compromise with the state, and hope that in time the people will again understand.''

He had spoken as if at a sacrament. Abruptly he shook himself, laughed a little, and raised his glass. ''Well!'' he said. ''You didn't come here for a lecture. *A vuestra salud.*''

My hand still shook when I drank with him.

''We'd better discuss your personal plans,'' he suggested. ''I know you've had a hatful of business lately, but none of us dare stay longer than overnight here. Where might you like to go?''

"Sir?" I didn't grasp his meaning at once. Drug or no, my brain was turning slowly under its burdens. "Why . . . home. Back to base. Where else?"

"Oh, no. Can't be. I said you have proved you are not a man we want to risk."

"Bu-but . . . if I don't go back, it's a giveaway!"

"No fears. We have experts at this sort of thing. You will be provided unquestionable reasons why your leave should be extended. A nervous collapse, maybe, plausible in view of the recent strains on you, and fakeable to fool any military medic into prescribing a rest cure. Why, your family can probably join you at some pleasant spot." Sotomayor chuckled. "Oh, you'll work hard. We want you in consultation, and between times I want to educate you. We'll try to arrange a suitable replacement at Reed. But one missile base is actually less important than the duties I have in mind for you."

I dropped my glass. The room whirled. Through a blur I saw Sotomayor jump up and bend over me, heard his voice: "What's the matter? Are you sick?"

Yes, I was. From a blow to the . . . the belly.

I rallied, and knew I might argue for being returned home, and knew it would be no use. Fending off his anxious hands, I got to my feet. "Exhaustion, I guess," I slurred. "Be okay in a minute. Which way's, uh, bathroom?"

"Here." He took my arm again.

When the door had closed on him, I stood in tiled sterility and confronted my face. But adrenalin pumped through me; and Mannix's chemicals were still there. Everything Mannix had done was still there.

If I stalled until too late . . . the Lomonosov Institute might or might not survive. If it did, I might or might not be admitted. If it didn't, something equivalent might or might not be built elsewhere in some latter year. I might or might not get the benefit thereof, before I was too old.

Meanwhile Bonnie—and my duty was not, not to anybody's vague dream—and I had barely a minute to decide—and it would take longer than that to change my most recent programming—

Act! yelled the chemicals.

I zipped down my pants, took my gun in my right hand, and opened the door.

Sotomayor had waited outside. At his back I saw the main room, water, moon, stars. Astonishment smashed his dignity.

"Dowling, *¿está Usted loco?* What the flaming hell—?"

Each word I spoke made me more sure, more efficient: "This is a weapon. Stand back."

Instead, he approached. I remembered he had been in single combats and remained vigorous and leathery. I aimed past him and squeezed as I had been taught. The flash of light burned a hole through carpet and floorboards at his feet. Smoke spurted from the pockmark. It smelled harsh.

Sotomayor halted, knees bent, hands cocked. Once, hunting in the piny woods of my boyhood, we'd cornered a bobcat. It had stood the way he did, teeth peeled but body crouched motionless, watching every instant for a chance to break free.

I nodded. "Yeah," I said. "A zap gun. Sorry, I've changed teams."

He didn't stir, didn't speak, until he forced me to add: "Back. To yonder phone I see. I've got a call to make." My lips twitched sideways. "I can't very well do otherwise, can I?"

"Has that thing—" he whispered, "has that thing been substituted for the original?"

"Yes," I said. "Forget your *machismo*. I've got the glands."

"Pugilist," he breathed, almost wonderingly.

Faintly through the blood-filled stiffness of me, I felt surprise. "What?"

"The ancient Romans often did the same to their pugilists," he said in a monotone. "Slaves who boxed in the arenas, iron on their fists. The man kept his physical strength, you see, but his bitterness made him fight without fear or pity . . . Yes. Pavlov and those who used Pavlov's discoveries frequently get good reconditioning results from castration. Such a fundamental shock. This is more efficient. Yes."

Fury leaped in me. "Shut your mouth! They'll grow me back what I've lost. I love my wife."

Sotomayor shook his head. "Love is a convenient instrument for the almighty state, no?"

He had no right to look that scornful, like some aristocrat. History has dismissed them, the damned feudal oppressors; and when the men in this house were seized, and the information in its files, his own castle would crash down.

He made a move. I leveled my weapon. His right hand simply gestured, touching brow, lips, breast, left and right shoulders. "Move!" I ordered.

He did—straight to me, shouting loud enough to wake the dead in Philadelphia.

I fired into his mouth. His head disintegrated. A cooked eyeball rolled out. But he had such speed that his corpse knocked me over.

I tore free of the embrace of those arms, spat out his blood, and leaped to lock the hall door. Knocking began a minute afterward, and the cry, "What's wrong? Let me in!"

"Everything's all right," I told the panel. "Comrade Sotomayor slipped and nearly fell. I caught him."

"Why's he silent? Let us in!"

I'd expected nothing different, and was already dragging furniture in front of the door. Blows and kicks, clamor and curses waxed beyond. I scuttled to the telephone—sure, they provided this headquarters well—and punched the number Mannix had given me. An impulse would go directly to a computer which would trace the line and dispatch an emergency squad here. Five minutes?

They threw themselves at the door, thud, thud, thud. That isn't as easy as the movies pretend. It would go down before long, though. I used bed, chairs, and tables to barricade the bathroom door. I chinked my fortress with books and placed myself behind, leaving a loophole.

When they burst through, I shot and I shot and I shot. I grew hoarse from yelling. The air grew sharp with ozone and thick with cooked meat.

Two dead, several wounded, the attackers retreated. It had dawned on them that I must have summoned help and they'd better get out.

The choppers descended as they reached the street.

My rescuers of the civil police hadn't been told anything, merely given a Condition A order to raid a place. So I must be held with the other survivors to wait for higher authority. Since the matter was obviously important, this house was the jail which would preserve the most discretion.

But they had no reason to doubt my statement that I was a political agent. I'd better be confined respectfully. The captain offered me my pick of rooms, and was surprised when I asked for Sotomayor's if the mess there had been cleaned up.

Among other features, it was the farthest away from everybody else, the farthest above the land.

Also, it had that bottle. I could drink if not sleep. When that didn't lift my post-combat sadness, I started thumbing through books. There was nothing else to do in the night silence.

I read: "We hold these Truths to be self-evident, that all Men are created equal, that they are endowed by their Creator with certain inalienable Rights, that among these are Life, Liberty, and the Pursuit of Happiness—That to secure these Rights, Governments are instituted among Men, deriving their just Powers from the Consent of the Governed, that whenever any Form of Government becomes destructive of those Ends, it is the Right of the People to alter or to abolish it, and to institute a new Government, laying its Foundation on such Principles, and organizing its Powers in such Form, as to them shall seem most likely to effect their Safety and Happiness."

I read: "We the people of the United States . . . secure the blessings of liberty to ourselves and our posterity. . . ."

I read: "Congress shall make no law respecting an establishment of religion, or prohibiting the free exercise thereof; or abridging the freedom of speech, or of the press; or the right of the people peacefully to assemble, and to petition the Government for a redress of grievances."

I read: "The powers not delegated to the United States by the Constitution, nor prohibited by it to the States, are reserved to the States respectively, or to the people."

I read: "I have sworn upon the altar of God eternal hostility toward every form of tyranny over the mind of man."

I read: "In giving freedom to the slave, we assure freedom to the free—honorable alike in what we give and what we preserve."

I read: "But they shall sit every man under his vine and under his fig tree; and none shall make them afraid. . . ."

When Mannix arrived—in person—he blamed my sobbing on sheer weariness. He may have been right.

Oh, yes, he kept his promise. My part in this affair could not be completely shielded from suspicion among what rebels escaped the roundup. A marked man, I had my best chance in transferring to the technical branch of the political police. They reward good service.

So, after our internal crisis was over and the threat of our rockets made the Kunin faction quit, with gratifyingly little damage done the Motherland: I went to Moscow and returned whole.

Only it's no good with Bonnie, I'm no good at all.

Night Piece

He had not gone far from the laboratory when he heard the footsteps. Even then he could sense they were not human, but he stopped and turned about with a fluttering hope that they might be, after all.

It was late on Wednesday night. His assistants had quit at five, leaving him to phone his wife that she had better not wait up, then fry some hash over a Bunsen burner and return to the instrument that was beginning to function. He had often done so, and afterward walked the mile to a bus stop where he could get a ride directly home. His wife worried about him, but he told her this was a peaceful industrial section, himself nearly the last living man after dark, in no danger of robbery or murder. The walk relaxed him, filled his lungs with cool air and cleared his brain of potential dreams.

Tonight, when the symptoms began, sheer habit had made him lock the door and start out afoot. The steps behind made him wonder if he should have called a taxi. Not that wheels could outpace the thing, but there might have been some comfort in the driver's stolid presence. *To be sure,* he thought, *if it is a holdup man—*

The hope died as he looked backward. The sidewalk stretched gray and hard and lifeless, under widely spaced lamps: first a gaunt pole, a globe of glare on top, a dingy yellow puddle of light below; then a thickening murkiness, becoming night itself, until the next globe stood forth, scattering sickly-colored illumination into emptiness. The street ran black of hue, like a river which moved in some secret fashion. Along the other edge of the sidewalk rose brick walls, where an occasional doorway or window made a blocked-off hole. Everything went in straight lines that converged toward an infinity hidden by the dark.

All the pavement was quite bare. A thin breeze sent a scrap of paper tumbling and clicking past his feet. Otherwise he heard nothing, not even the follower.

He tried to slow his heartbeat. *It can't hurt me,* he told himself, knowing he lied. For a while he stood immobile, not so much unwilling to turn his back on the footsteps (for they could be anywhere; more accurately, they were nowhere) as unwilling to hear them again.

"But I can't stay here all night," he said. The whisper made a relieving counterpoint to his pulse. He felt sweat run from his armpits and down his ribs, tickling. "It'll only take a different form. I'd better get home, at least."

He had not known he possessed enough courage to resume walking.

The footsteps picked up. They weren't loud, which was just as well, for they seemed less human each second he listened. There was a slithering quality to them: not wet but dry, a scaly dryness that went sliding over dirty concrete. He didn't even know how many feet there were. More than two, surely. Perhaps so many that they weren't feet at all, but one supple length. And the head rose, weaving about in curves that rippled and rustled—becoming less sinuous as the hood swelled until the sidewise figure eight upon it stood forth plain; a thin little tongue flickered as if frantic, but there was an immortal patience in the eyes, which were lidless.

"Of course this is ridiculous," he told himself. "Giving pictorial form to that which is, by definition, beyond any form whatsoever—" His voice came out small. The rustling stopped. For a moment he heard only the clack of his own shoes and the millrace blood in his body. He hopped crazily through all the gibberish in his head.

Faustus is the name, good sir, not Frankenstein but Faustus in the Faustian sense if you please and means fortunate in the Latin but one may wonder if the Latin was not constructed with a hitherto unsuspected sense of irony, e.g., my wife awaits me, she may not have gone to bed yet and lamplight would fall on her hair but my shoes are too tight and too loud.

That it might have abandoned him. Or rather, the scientific brain cells corrected, that he had somehow slipped back from the state of awareness of these things. *Because,* he thought, *I deny that rationality is dead in the cosmos, and even that my experiments with the ESP amplifier opened hell gate. Rather, they sensitized me to an unsuspected class of phenomena, one for which human evolution has not prepared me because humankind never encountered it before. (Except, perhaps, in the thinnest and swiftest accidental glimpses, revelation, nightmare, and madness.) I am the early student of X-rays, the alchemist heating liquid mercury, the half-ape burned by fire, the mouse strayed onto a battlefield. I shall be destroyed if I cannot escape, but the universe will still live, her and me and them and a certain willow on a hilltop which fills with sunset light each summer evening. I pray that this be true.*

Then the scales uncoiled and went scrabbling toward him, louder now, and he caught a hot cedary odor. But the night breeze was cold in his hair. He cried out, once, and began to run.

The street lamps reached ahead of him, on to an unseen infinity, like stars in space. No, lonelier than that. Each lamp was an island universe, spinning up there a million years from the next neighbor. Surely, in all that darkness, a man might find some hiding place! He was out of condition. Soon he was breathing through a wide-open, dried-out mouth. His lungs were twin fires and he felt his eyeballs bulge from pressure. His shoes grew so heavy that he thought he ran with two planets on his feet.

Through thunder and breakings he heard the rustle, closer still, and his shoes going slap-slap-slap on bare pavement, under the purulent street lamps. Up ahead were two of them, whose globes looked close together from where he was, and the shadows they cast made a dark shaft between that reached straight upward to an infinity from which stars fountained in horrible fire. He had not imagined there could be so grim a sight. He had no breath left, but his brain screamed for him.

Somewhere there must be darkness. A tunnel to hide in, to close off and seal. There must be warmth and the sound of waters. And darkness again. If he was caught, let it at least not happen in the light. But he begged the tunnel would hide him.

The current up which he waded was strong. It slid heavily and sensuously about him, pushing on breast and belly, loins and thighs. He was totally blind now, but that was good, he was far from the world-spewing globes. The water's noise echoed from the tunnel walls, ringing and booming. Now and then a wave splashed against them, a loud clear sound followed by a thin shower of drops, like laughter. His feet slipped, he flailed about with his arms, touched the warm curved odorous wall of the tunnel and shoved himself back upright. He had a sense of wading uphill, and the current strengthened with each step he achieved. A *hyperbola,* he thought in upsurging weariness. *I'll never reach the end. That's at infinity.*

After centuries he heard the pumps that drove the waters, pumps as big as the world, throbbing in the dark. He stopped, afraid to go on, afraid the rotors would seize him and grind him and squirt him from a cylinder.

But when the hooded swimmer struck him and he went under, he must shriek.

Too late now! The waters took him, stopped his voice, cataracted down his throat and churned in his guts. A momentary gulp of air smelled like cedar. The swimmer closed its jaws. He heard his skin tear under the fangs, and the poisons began to tingle down the skein of his nerves. The head marked with a sideways figure eight shook him as a dog shakes a rat. Nevertheless he planted feet on the tunnel floor, gripped the monstrous barrel of a body, and threw his last energies against it. Back and forth they swayed, the tunnel trembled under their violence, they smashed into its walls. The pumps began to skip beats, the walls began to crack and dissolve, the waters rushed forth across the world. But still he was gripped.

He shook off the hand, leaned his face against blessed scratchy brick and tried to vomit. But nothing happened. The policeman took him by the arm again, but more gently. "What's the matter?"

A lamp near the alley mouth dribbled in just enough light to show the large blue shape with the star on the breast. "What's wrong?" insisted the policeman. "I thought you was drunk, but you don't smell like it. Sick?"

"Yes." He controlled himself, suppressed the last belly spasm and turned around to face the policeman. The other voice came faintly to him, with a curious heterodyned whine, a rise and fall like speech heard through high fever. "End of the world, you know."

"Huh?"

For a moment he considered asking the policeman's help. The fellow looked so substantial and blue. His big jowly face was not unkind. But of course the policeman could not help. *He can take me home, if I so request. Or put me in jail, if I act oddly enough. Or call a doctor if I fall boneless at his feet. But what's the use? There is no cure for being in an ocean.*

He glanced at his watch. Only a few minutes had passed since he left the laboratory. At that time he had wanted companionship, a human face to look at if not to take along on his flight. Now he had his wish, and there was no comfort. The policeman was as remote as the lamp. A part of him could talk to the policeman, just as another part could direct heart and lungs and glands in their work. But the essential *I* had departed this world. The I was not even human any longer. No man could help him find his way back.

"I'm sorry," he said. "I get a bit stupid." His reasoning faculties worked very fast. "During these attacks, I mean."

"What attacks?"

"Diabetes. You know, diabetics get fainting spells. I didn't quite pass out this time, but I got rather woozy. I'll be okay, though."

"Oh." The policeman's ignorance of medicine proved as great as hoped. "I see. Want I should call you a cab?"

"No thanks, officer. Not necessary. I'm on my way to the bus stop. Honest, I'll be fine."

"Well, I better come along with you," said the policeman.

They walked side by side, unspeaking. Presently they emerged on an avenue that had restaurants and theaters as well as darkened shops. Light glittered, blinked, quivered in red and yellow and cold blue, cars went slithering past, men and somewhat fewer women drifted along the sidewalks. The air was full of noise, feet, tires, think it'll rain tomorrow close the deal for paper, mister? A neon sign across from the bus stop made *Idle Hour* Bar & Grill, blink, *Idle Hour* blink *Idle Hour* blink *Idle Hour* blink.

"Here you are," said the policeman. "You sure you'll be okay?"

"Quite sure. Thank you, officer." To please the policeman and make him go away, he sat down on the bench.

"Well, good luck to you." The big blue man walked off and was lost in the drift.

A woman sat at the other end of the bench. In a tired and middle-aged fashion she looked a little bit like his sister. He noticed her casting glances in his direction and wondered why. Probably curious to know the reason he came here escorted, but afraid to ask lest he think she was trying to get picked up. It didn't matter. She was hollow anyway. They all were, himself included. They were infinitesimal skins of distorted space enclosing nothing whatever, not even space. The lights were hollow and the noise was hollow. All fullness was ocean.

He felt much at peace. Now that he was no longer pursued . . . well, why should he be? It had happened to completion. And then after the tunnel broke, the waters had covered everything. They reached vast and gray, warm and still, with a faint taste of salt like tears. In the translucent greenish gray where he lay, easily rocking, there was no place for pursuit, for anything except everything.

Time flowed in the ocean, but a slow soft kind of time. First the light strengthened, sourceless, eventually revealing the eternal overcast, which was cool nacre. Sometimes a lower stratum would form, mare's tails whipped on a sharp wind or blue-black masses rearing up with lightning in their heads. But when that happened, he could sink undersurface, where the water was forever still and greenish. . . . Finally the light faded. The nights were altogether dark. He liked them best, for then he could lie and feel the tides pass through him. A tide was more than a rolling of his body; it was a deep secret thrill, somehow each atom of him was touched by the force as it passed and a tingle scarcely sensed would go down all molecular lengths. By day he enjoyed the tides too, but not so much, for then other life forms were about. He had only the dimmest awareness of these, but they did pass by, sometimes brushing him or considering him with patient lidless eyes.

"Excuse me, sir, do you know if this bus goes to Seventh Street?"

It startled him a little that his body should start. Surely there was no sense to the chilly prickles of sweat that burst out all over him. "No," he said. His voice came out so harsh that the woman edged even further away. Somehow that was an additional flick across his soft skin. He twisted, trying to escape; he grew plates of bone so that they must leave him in peace.

"No," he said, "I don't believe it does. I get off before then myself—I've never ridden as far as Seventh Street—so I'm not sure. But I don't believe it does."

His logical faculty grew furious with him for talking so idiotically. "Oh," she said. "Thank you." He said, "You can ask the driver." She said, "Yes, I suppose I can. Thank you." He said, "You're welcome." She obviously wanted to break off the misbegotten conversation and didn't quite see how. For his part, he couldn't take any more. The noises and skins were hollow, no doubt, but they kept striking at him. He jumped up and crossed the street. Her eyes pursued him. He hadn't seen her blink.

The *Idle Hour* was dim. A couple sat in a booth along one wall; a discouraged man hunched at the bar opposite; a juke box made garish embers but remained mercifully unfed. The bartender was a thin man in the usual white shirt and black bow tie. He was washing some glasses and said without enthusiasm, "Be closing time pretty soon, mister."

"That's all right. Scotch and soda." Speech was automatic, like breath. When he had the glass, he retired to a booth of his own. He leaned back on faded plastic cushioning, set the glass before him and stared at the ice cubes. He didn't want to drink.

Who would want to drink in the ocean? he thought with a touch of wryness.

But this is wrong!

He didn't want to make jokes, he wanted the tides and the plankton swirling into his mouth, the thin warm saltiness, the good sound of rainstorms lashing the surface when he was snugly down among seaweeds. *They* were cool and silken, they caressed. He changed the awkward bony plates that protected him from the others for scales, which were not quite as strong but left him slippery and flexible and alive to the stroking, streaming green weed. Now he could slip through their most secret grottos, nose about on the oozy bottom and look with incurious lidless eyes at the fossils he uncovered.

"Let's examine the superman thesis," he said to his wife. "I don't mean the Nietzschean Uebermensch. I mean Superior, the nonhuman animal with nonhuman powers making him as much stronger than us as we are stronger than the apes. Traditionally, he's supposed to be born of man and woman. In hard biological fact, we know this isn't possible. Even if the simultaneous alteration of millions of genes could take place, the resulting embryo would be so alien in blood type, enzyme system, the very proteins, that it would hardly be created before the outraged uterus destroyed it."

"Perhaps in a million years, man could evolve into superman," she answered.

"Perhaps," he said skeptically. "I'm inclined to doubt it, though. The great apes, even the monkeys, aren't likely to evolve into men. They branched off from our common ancestor too long ago; they've followed their special path too far. Likewise, men may improve their reasoning, visualizing, imagining ability—what we're pleased to call their conscious intelligence—their own characteristic as a species—they may improve that through a megayear or so of slow evolution. But they'd still be men, wouldn't they? A later model, but still men.

"Now the truly superior being . . ." He held his wine glass up to the light. "Let's speculate aloud. What is superiority anyhow, in a biological sense? Isn't it an ability—a mode of behavior, I'll say—that enables the species to cope more effectively with environment?

"Okay. So let's inquire what modes of behavior there are. The simplest, practiced by unicellular organisms as well as higher ones like sunflowers, is tropism. A mere chemical response to a fixed set of stimuli. More complicated and adaptable are sets of reflexes. That's the characteristic insectal mode. Then you get true instincts: inherited behavior patterns, but generalized, flexible and modifiable. Finally, in the higher mammals, you get a degree of conscious intelligence. Man, of course, has made this his particular strength. He also has quite a bit of instinct, some reflexes, and maybe a few tropisms. His ability to reason, though, is what's gotten him as far as he's come on this planet.

"To surpass us, should Superior try to outhuman humanity? Shouldn't he rather possess only a modicum of reasoning ability by our standards, very weak instincts, a few reflexes, and no tropisms? But his specialty, his characteristic mode, would be something we can't imagine. We may have a bare touch of it, as the apes and dogs have a touch of logical reasoning power. But we can no more imagine its full development than a dog could follow Einstein's equations."

"What might this ability be?" his wife wondered.

He shrugged. "Who knows? Conceivably in the ESP field— Now I'm letting my hobby horse run away with me again. (Damn it, though, I *am* starting to get reproducible results!) Whatever it is, it's something much more powerful than logic or imagination. And as futile for us to speculate about as for the dog to ponder Einstein."

"Do you really believe there are such superbeings?" She had come to expect almost any hypothesis of him.

"Oh, no," he laughed. "I'm just playing a game with ideas. Like your kitten with a ball of string. But assuming Superior does exist . . . hm. Do mice know that men exist? All a mouse knows is that the world contains good things like houses and cheese, bad things like weatherstripping and traps, without any orderly pattern that his instincts could adapt him to. He sees men, sure, but how can he know they're a different order of life, responsible for all the strangeness in his world? In the same way, we may have coexisted with Superior for a million years, and never known it. The part of him we can detect may be an accepted feature of our universe, like the earth's magnetic field; or an unexplained feature like occasional lights in the sky; or he may be quite undetectable. His activities would never impinge on ours, except once in a while by sheerest accident—and then another 'miracle' is recorded that science never does find an explanation for."

She smiled, enjoying his own pleasure. "Where do these beings come from? Another planet?"

"I doubt that. They probably evolved here right along with us. All life on earth has an equally ancient lineage. I've no idea what the common ancestor of man and Superior could have been. Perhaps as recent as some half ape in the Pliocene, perhaps as far back as some amphibian in the Carboniferous. We took one path, they took another, and never the twain shall meet."

"I hope not. We'd have no more chance than the mice, would we?"

"I don't know. But we'd certainly best cultivate our own garden."

Which, however, he had not done. He wasn't sure how he had blundered onto the Superior plane of existence: or, rather, how his mind or his rudimentary ESP or whatever-it-was had suddenly begun reacting to the behavior-mode of that race. He only knew, with the flat sureness of immediate experience, that it had happened.

His logical mind, unaffected as yet, searched in a distant and dreamy fashion for a rationale. The amplifier alone could hardly be responsible. But maybe the remembrance of his speculative fable had provided the additional impetus necessary? If that were so, then his fate was a most improbable accident. Other men could still go ahead and study ESP phenomena as much as they cared to, learn a lot, use their knowledge, all in perfect safety, with never a hint that on a higher level of those phenomena Superior carried out huge purposes.

Himself, though, was sunk in a gray ocean on a gray world. Let him so remain. Never had he imagined such peace, or the tides or the kissing seaweeds; and as for the lightning storms, he could hide when they flashed. Down he went then, into a green well of silence whose roof coruscated with light shards; further down, the well darkened, the light shrank to a spot overhead (if that meant anything here where there was no weight, no heaviness, no force or current or pursuit) and then the dark enfolded him. On the bottom it was always night.

He lay in the ooze, which was cool though the water stayed warm, he wrapped the dear darkness around him like another skin, closed the lids he had grown to keep daylight off, he could taste salt and feel the tides go through his molecules. High above rolled the clouds, thunder banged from horizon to horizon, the sky was all one blaze of great lightnings; wind yammered, driving spindrift flat off the crests of the waves, which foamed and snarled and shivered the bones of the world. Even down in the depths—

No! What a storm that must be! Fear tinged him. He didn't want to remember lightnings, which worked their length across heaven and sizzled like hastening scales. He burrowed into the mud until he touched bedrock and, and, and felt it quiver.

Even the storm could not be as dreadful as that deep earthquake vibration. He wailed voicelessly and fled back upward. The others swarmed around him, driven from their grottos by the growing violence. Teeth snapped at him, lidless eyes glowed like twinned globes. Some had been torn apart; he tasted blood in the waters.

Another crash and another went through him, as deeply as ever the tides had done, but bruising and ripping. He burst the surface.

Rain and scud whipped him. Wallowing on the wrinkled back of a wave, he looked straight up at the lightning. Thunder filled his skull.

A deeper noise responded. Across many wild miles he saw the mountain rise from the waters. Black and enormous it was lifted; water cascaded off its flanks, fire and sulfur boiled from its throat. Shock followed shock, flinging him to and fro, over and under. He felt, rather than saw, the whole sea bottom lifting beneath him.

He gibbered in the foam and fled, seeking depths, seeking a place where he could not see the mountain. Its pinnacle had already gone through the clouds. In that wounded sky the stars blazed gruesomely.

Somewhere through the explosions, he thought he must be able to get free. Surely all the ocean was not convulsed. But a basalt peak smote him from beneath. The water squirted from his gills; he went sick and dizzy. Raised into naked air, he felt the delicate gill membranes shrivel and drew a breath that burned him down throat and lungs to his inmost cell. The black reef continued rising. Soon it would be part of the mountainside. He made one sprawling flop, all his strength expended: slid off the rock, back down into the sea. But a wave grabbed him in its white teeth and shook him.

He pushed the hand from his shoulder. "All right, all right, all right," he mumbled. "Let me alone."

"Closing time, I told you," said the bartender. "You deaf or something? I gotta close this place."

"Let me alone." He covered his ears against the screaming.

"Don't make me call a cop. Go on home, mister. You look like you could stand a night's rest." The bartender was thin but expert. He applied leverage in the right places, got his customer to his feet and shambling across the floor. "You just go on home now. Good night. Closing time, you know."

The door swung shut, as if to deny the bartender's existence. Other hollow people were on the street, some going for coffee, some entering the bus that waited on the opposite curb.

My bus, he thought. *The one that may or may not go as far as Seventh Street.* The thought was unreal. All thought was. Reality consisted in a black mountain, rising and rising, himself trapped in a pool on the slope where the surf had cast him, gasping raw air, scourged by rain, deafened by wind and thunder, and lifted toward the terrible stars.

He crouched in his wretchedness, implored the ocean to come back, but at the same time he hissed to the fire and the wind and the sulfurous reek, *If you won't let me go, I'll destroy you. See if I don't!*

Habit had taken him over the street to the bus. He stopped in front of the doors. What was he doing here? The thing was an iron box. No, he must not enter the box. The hollow people sat there in rows, waiting for him. He must tear down the mountain instead.

What mountain?

He knew in the thinking part of himself that somewhere in space and time was an existence not all harm and hatred. The night was too loud now, beneath winter stars, for him to return thither. He must pull down the mountain, so he could regain the ocean. . . . But his logical faculties spun free, down and down a hyperbolic path. They considered the abstract unreal proposition that he would not be hollow if he could become human again. And then he would be happy, though at present he didn't want to be human, he wanted to rip the mountain and re-enter the sea. But as a logical exercise, to pass the time for the unused part of his brain, *why* had he suffered and fought and been hunted, since that moment when he was first sensitized to . . . to Superior's mode of behavior?

He could no more understand the situation with reason than a dog could use instinct to puzzle out the machinery of this bus and the why of its existence. (No, he would not enter that box. He didn't know why, except that the box was hollow and waited for him. But he was sure it went to Seventh Street.) Nonetheless, reason was not absolutely useless. The activities of Superior were always and forever incomprehensible to him, but he could describe their general tendency. Violence, cruelty, destruction. Which didn't make sense! No species could survive that used its powers only for such ends.

Therefore, Superior did not. Most of the time, he/she/it/? was just being Superior, and as such was completely beyond human perception. Occasionally, though, there was conflict. By analogy, mankind—all animals—behaved constructively on the whole, but sometimes engaged in strife. Superior? Well, of course Superior didn't have wars in the human sense of the word. No use speculating what they did have. Conflicts of some kind, anyhow, where an issue was decided not by reason or compromise but by force. And the force employed was (to give it a name) of an ESP nature.

A mouse could not understand human art or science. In a way, he couldn't even see them. But a mouse could be affected by the crudest, most animal-like manifestation of human behavior: physical combat. A mathematical theorem did not exist for the mouse; a bullet did.

By analogy again, he, the human, was a mouse that had wandered onto a battlefield. By some accident, he had been sensitized to the lowest mode of Superior behavior and was thereby being affected; he was caught in the opposing tides of a death struggle.

Not that he was directly experiencing what Superior actually performed. Everything that had happened was merely the way the forces, the currents, felt to him. Frantically seeking a balance, his mind interpreted those unnatural stimuli in the nearest available human terms.

He thought his sensations must dimly reflect the course of the battle. One side or entity or . . . Aleph . . . had gotten the upper hand and in some sense pursued the other till it found a momentary shelter. Zayin had then had a breathing space until Aleph found it again, pursued it again. Cornered, Zayin fought back so fiercely that Aleph must in turn retreat. Now, having recovered during the lull that followed, Zayin was renewing the battle. . . . But none of this made any difference. The doings of Superior were, in themselves, irrelevant to Sapiens. He was the mouse on the battlefield, nothing else.

With luck, a mouse could escape from bursting shells and burning tracers before they smashed him. A man could escape from this other conflict before it burned out his mind: by desensitizing himself, by ceasing to perceive the transcendent energies around him, much as one could get relief from too brilliant a light by closing one's eyes. But what was the method of desensitization?

Clouds broke further, and he saw the moon flying pocked among the stars. Its light was as cold as the wind. His flesh quivered in the pain of cold and earthquake shocks. But the ocean tumbled not far off, white under the moon. He felt that impact reverberate in the mountain. He began to crawl from his dwindling pool.

How can I get away?

"Hey, mister, you gonna board this bus or not?"

The currents carried me first in one direction, then in another. Down to the sea depths, up to the stars. Whether I go forward or backward, seaward or skyward, I am still within the currents.

"I said, you comin' aboard? Don't just stand there blocking the door."

Lightning burned his eyes. He felt the thunder in his bones. But louder, now, was the hate in him: for the mountain which had ruined his sea and for the sea which had cast him onto the mountain. *I will destroy them all.*

And then fear smote him, for through the noise and the gigantic white flashes he heard himself asking: "Do you go to Seventh Street?"

The driver said across lightyears, "Yeah, that's the end of my run. Come on, hop in. I got a schedule to keep."

"No—" he whimpered, stumbling backward toward the ocean. His teeth clattered with cold. The waves retreated from him. *I am not going in a box to Seventh Street!*

"Where do you wanna go, then?" asked the driver, elaborately sarcastic.

"Go?" he repeated in a numb voice. "Why . . . home."

Please, he called to the surf. But still the tide withdrew, a monstrous hollow rumble. He turned about, hissing at the mountain where it flamed overhead. *All right, then,* said his hatred. He started to crawl up the wet black rocks. *All right, if you won't tell me the way home, I'll climb up over your peak.*

But you do know the way home, said his human logical faculty.

What? He stopped. The wind hooted and whipped him. If he didn't keep moving he would freeze.

Of course. Consider the pattern. Forward or backward, you are still moving within the currents. But if you remain still—

No! he screamed, and in his fear he reared up and clawed at the stars for support.

It won't take long.

Oh, God, no, I'm too afraid. No man should have to do this twice.

The cold and lightning and earthquake struck at him. He cowered on the beach, under the mountain, too frightened to hate. *No, I must climb. I can't stay here.*

The bus driver snorted and closed the door in his face.

Where the courage came from, he never knew. For an instant he was able to remember his wife's eyes, and that she was waiting for him. He raised his hand and rapped on the door. The driver groaned.

If he goes off and leaves me—if he delays half a minute letting me in—I'll never go aboard. I won't be able to.

The door folded back.

He gathered the last rags of himself around himself, climbed up the step and over the threshold.

Something snatched at him. The wind drove in between his ribs, lightning hit him, he had never conceived such pain. He opened his mouth to yell.

No! That's part of the pattern. Don't do it.

Somehow he maintained silence, clung to the stanchion as the bus got under way and felt the galaxies sundered. The earth-shaken rocks on the mountainside rolled beneath him, thrusting him upward. He planted his feet on the ground and said: "To Seventh Street."

The world drained out of him.

As blackness faded again, he found hismelf sprawled on one of the longitudinal seats up front. "Now look, buster," said the driver, "drunk or not, you pay the fare, see? I don't want no trouble. Just gimme the fare."

He drew a breath deep into starved lungs. The bus was noisy, with a stench from the motor; tired people sagged down its length, under improbably bright-colored advertisements. On either side he could see the lighted windows of houses.

How still the night was!

"What is the fare?" he asked. *Ridiculous,* his logical mind scolded him, wearily but not very angrily. After all, the rest of him had shown up well too, when the crisis came. *I've ridden this line a hundred times. But I can't quite remember the cost. It feels so new to be human.*

"Two bits."

"Oh, is that all? I'd have paid more." His knees were weak, but he managed to stand up and fish out a quarter. It clinked in the coin box with a noise whose metal clarity he savored.

Perhaps a little sympathetic, or perhaps from a sense of duty, the driver asked him, "D'you say you was going to Seventh Street?"

"No." He sat down again. "Not tonight, after all. My home isn't quite that far."

The Voortrekkers

—And he shall see old planets change and alien stars arise—

So swift is resurrection that the words go on which had been in me when last I died. Only after pulsebeats does the strangeness raining through my senses reach my awareness, to make me know that four more decades, and almost nine light-years, have flowed between me and the poet.

Light-years. Light. Everywhere light. Once, a boy, I spent a night camped on a winter mountaintop. Then it entered my bones—and how can anyone who has done likewise ever believe otherwise?—that space is not dark. Maybe this was when the need was born in me, to go up and out into the sky.

I am in the sky now, and of it. Around me stars and stars and stars are crowding, until there is no room for blackness to be more than a crystal which holds them. They are all the colors of reality, from lightning through gold to the duskiest rose, but each one singingly keen. Nebulae are flung among them like veils and clouds, where great suns have died or new worlds are whirling to birth. The Milky Way is a cool torrent, here cloven by the thunderstorm masses of galactic center, there open a-glint toward endlessness. I magnify my vision and trace the spiral of our sister maelstrom, a million and a half light-years hence in Andromeda.

Sol is a small glow on the edge of Hercules. Brightest is Sirius, whose blue-white luminance casts shadows of fittings and housings across my hull. I seek and find its companion.

This is not done by optics. The dwarf is barely coming around the giant, lost in glare. What I see, through different sensors, is the X-radiation; what I snuff is a sharp breath of neutrinos mingled with the gale that streams from the other; I swim in an intricate interplay of force-fields, balancing, thrusting, while they caress me; I listen to the skirls and drones, the murmurs and melodies of a universe.

At first I do not hear Korene. If I was a little slow to leave Kipling for these heavens, so I am to leave them for her. Maybe it's more excusable. I must make certain at once, as much as possible, that we are not in danger. Probably we aren't, or the automatons would have restored us to existence before the scheduled moment. But automatons can only judge what they were designed and programmed to judge, by people nine light-years away from yonder mystery, people most likely dust, even as Korene and Joel are surely dust.

Joel, Joel! Korene calls from within me. *Are you there?*

I open my interior scanners. Her principal body, the one which houses her principal brain, is in motion, carefully testing every part after forty-three years of death. For the thousandth time, the beauty of this seat of her consciousness strikes me. Its darkly sheening shape is only humanlike in the way that an abstract sculpture might be on far, far Earth—those several arms, for instance, or the dragonfly head which is not really a head at all—and only this for functional reasons. But something about the slimness and grace of movement recalls Korene who is dust.

She has not yet made contact with any of the specialized auxiliary bodies around her. Instead she has joined a communication circuit to one of mine.

Hi, I flash, rather shakily, for in spite of studies and experiments and simulations, years of them, it is still too tremendous to comprehend, that we are actually approaching Sirius. *How are you?*

Fine. Everything okay?

Near's I can tell. Why didn't you use voice?

I did. No answer. I yelled. No answer. So I plugged in.

My joy gets tinged with embarrassment. *Sorry. I, uh, I guess I was too excited.*

She breaks the connection, since it is not ideally convenient, and says, "Quite something out there?"

"You wouldn't believe," I respond by my own speaker. "Take a look."

I activate the viewscreens for her. "O-o-o-ohh; O God," she breathes. Yes, breathes. Our artificial voices copy those which once were in our throats. Korene's is husky and musical; it was a pleasure to hear her sing at parties. Her friends often urged her to get into amateur theatricals, but she said she had neither the time nor the talent.

Maybe she was right, though Lord knows she was good at plenty of other things, her astronautical engineering, painting, cookery, sewing fancy clothes, throwing feasts, playing tennis and poker, ranging over hills, being a wife and mother, in her first life. (Well, we've both changed a lot since then.) On the other hand, that utterance of hers, when she sees the star before her, says everything for which I can only fumble.

From the beginning, when the first rockets roared into orbit, some people have called astronauts a prosaic lot, if they weren't calling us worse; and no doubt in some cases this was true. But I think mainly it's just that we grow tongue-tied in the presence of the Absolute.

"I wish—" I say, and energize an auxiliary of my own, a control-module maintainer, to lay an awkward touch upon her—"I wish you could sense it the way I do, Korene. Plug back in—full psychoneural—when I've finished my checkouts, and I'll try to convey a little."

"Thanks, my friend." She speaks with tenderness. "I knew you would. But don't worry about my missing something because of not being wired up like a ship. I'll be having a lot of experiences you can't, and wishing I could share them with you." She chuckles. "*Vive la différence.*"

Nonetheless I hear the flutter in her tone and, knowing her, am unsurprised when she asks anxiously, "Are there . . . by any chance . . . planets?"

"No trace. We're a long ways off yet, of course. I might be missing the indications. So far, though, it looks as if the astronomers were right" who declared minor bodies cannot condense around a star like Sirius. "Never mind, we'll both find enough to keep us out of mischief in the next several years. Already at this range, I'm noticing all kinds of phenomena which theory did not predict."

"Then you don't think we'll need organics?"

"No, 'fraid not. In fact, the radiation—"

"Sure. Understood. But damn, next trip I'm going to insist on a destination that'll probably call for them."

She told me once, back in the Solar System, after we had first practiced the creation of ourselves in flesh: "It's like making love again."

They had not been lovers in their original lives. He an American, she a European, they served the space agencies of their respective confederations and never chanced to be in the same cooperative venture. Thus they met only occasionally and casually, at professional conventions or celebrations. They were still young when the interstellar exploration project was founded. It was a joint undertaking of all countries—no one bloc could have gotten its taxpayers to bear the cost—but research and development must run for a generation before hardware would become available to the first true expeditions. Meanwhile there was nothing but a few unmanned probes, and the interplanetary studies wherein Joel and Korene took part.

She retired from these, to desk and laboratory, at an earlier age than he did, having married Olaf and wishing children. Olaf himself continued on the Lunar shuttle for a while. But that wasn't the same as standing on the peaks of Rhea beneath the rings of Saturn or pacing the million kilometers of a comet, as afire as the scientists themselves with what they were discovering. Presently he quit, and joined Korene on one of the engineering teams of the interstellar group. Together they made important contributions, until she accepted a managerial position. This interested her less in its own right; but she handled it ferociously well, because she saw it as a means to an end—authority, influence. Olaf stayed with the work he liked best. Their home life continued happy.

In that respect, Joel at first differed. Pilots on the major expeditions (and he got more berths than his share) could seldom hope to be family men. He tried, early in the game; but after he realized what a very lonely kind of pain drove a girl he had loved to divorce him, he settled for a succession of mistresses. He was always careful to explain to them that nothing and nobody could make him stop faring before he must.

This turned out to be not quite true. Reaching mandatory age for "the shelf," he might have finagled a few extra years skyside. But by then, cuts in funding for space were marrow-deep. Those who still felt that man had business beyond Earth agreed that what resources were left had better go mostly toward the stars. Like Korene, Joel saw that the same was true of him. He enrolled in the American part of the effort. Experience and natural talent equipped him uniquely to work on control and navigation.

In the course of this, he met Mary. He had known a good many female astronauts, and generally liked them as persons—often as bodies too, but long voyages and inevitable promiscuity were as discouraging to stable relationships for them as for him. Mary used her reflexes and spirit to test-pilot experimental vehicles near home.

This didn't mean that she failed to share the dream. Joel fell thoroughly in love with her. Their marriage likewise proved happy.

He was forty-eight, Korene sixty, when the word became official: The basic machinery for reaching the stars now existed. It needed merely several years' worth of refinement and a pair of qualified volunteers.

It *is* like making love again.

How my heart soared when first we saw that the second planet has air a human can breathe! Nothing can create that except life. Those months after Joel went into orbit around it and we observed, photographed, spectroanalyzed, measured, sampled, calculated, mainly reading what instruments recorded but sometimes linking ourselves directly to them and feeling the input as once we felt wind in our hair or surf around our skins—

Why do I think of hair, skin, heart, love, I who am embodied in metal and synthetics and ghostly electron-dance? Why do I remember Olaf with this knife sharpness?

I suppose he died well before Korene. Men usually do. (What does death have against women, anyway?) Then was her aftertime until she could follow him down; and in spite of faxes and diaries and every other crutch humankind has invented, I think he slowly became a blur, never altogether to be summoned forth except perhaps in sleep. At least, with this cryogenic recall of mine which is not programmed to lie, I remember how aging Korene one day realized, shocked, that she had nothing left except aging Olaf, that she could no longer see or feel young Olaf except as words.

Oh, she loved him-now, doubtless in a deeper fashion than she-then had been able to love him-then, after all their shared joy, grief, terror, toil, hope, merry little sillinesses which stayed more clear across the years than many of the big events—yes, their shared furies and frustrations with each other, their few and fleeting intense involvements with outsiders, which somehow also were always involvements between him and her—she loved her old husband, but she had lost her young one.

Whereas I have been given him back, in my flawless new memory. And given Joel as well, or instead, or—Why am I thinking this nonsense? Olaf is dust.

Tau Ceti is flame.

It's not the same kind of fire as Sol. It's cooler, yellower, something autumnal about it, even though it will outlive man's home star. I don't suppose the unlikenesses will appear so great to human eyes. I know the entire spectrum. (How much more does Joel sense! To me, every sun is a once-in-the-universe individual; to him, every sunspot is.) The organic body/mind is both more general and more specific than this . . . like me *vis-à-vis* Joel. (I remember, I remember: striding the Delphi road, muscle-play, boot-scrunch, spilling sunlight and baking warmth, bees at hum through wild thyme and rosemary, on my upper lip a taste of sweat, and that tremendous plunge down to the valley where Oedipus met his father. . . . Machine, I would not experience it in quite those terms. There would be too many other radiations, forces, shifts and subtleties which Oedipus never felt. But would it be less beautiful? Is a deaf man, suddenly cured, less alive because afterward his mind gives less time to his eyes?)

Well, we'll soon know how living flesh experiences the living planet of Tau Ceti.

It isn't the infinite blue and white of Earth. It has a greenish tinge, equally clear and marvelous, and two moons for the lovers whom I, sentimental old crone, keep imagining. The aliennesses may yet prove lethal. But Joel said, in his dear dry style:

"The latest readouts convince me. The tropics are a shirt-sleeve environment." His mind grinned, I am sure, as formerly his face did. "Or a bare-ass environment. That remains to be seen. I'm certain, however, organic bodies can manage better down there than any of yours or mine."

Was I the one who continued to hesitate because I had been the one more eager for this? A kind of fear chilled me. "We already know they can't find everything they need to eat, in that biochemistry—"

"By the same token," the ship reminded, not from intellectual but emotional necessity, "nothing local, like germs, can make a lunch off them. The survival odds are excellent," given the concentrated dietary supplements, tools, and the rest of what we have for them. "Good Lord, Korene, you could get smashed in a rock storm, prospecting some wretched asteroid, or I could run into too much radiation for the screens and have my brain burned out. Or whatever. Do we mind?"

"No," I whispered. "Not unendurably."

"So *they* won't."

"True. I shouldn't let my conscience make a coward of me. Let's go right ahead."

After all, when I brought children into the world, long ago, I knew they might be given straight over to horror; or it might take them later on; or at best, they would be born to trouble as the sparks fly upward, and in an astonishingly few decades be dust. Yet I never took from them, while they lay innocent in my womb, their chance at life.

Thus Joel and I are bringing forth the children who will be ourselves.

He wheels like another moon around the world, and his sensors drink of it and his mind reasons about it. I, within him, send forth my auxiliary bodies to explore its air and waters and lands; through the laser channels, mine are their labors, triumphs, and—twice—deaths. But such things have become just a part of our existence, like the jobs from which we hurried home every day. (Though here job and home go on concurrently.) The rest of us, the most of us, is linked in those circuits that guide our children into being.

We share, we are a smile-pattern down the waves and wires, remembering how chaste the agency spokesman made it sound, in that first famous interview. Joel and I had scarcely met then, and followed it separately on television. He told me afterward that, having heard the spiels a thousand times before, both pro and con, he'd rather have gone fishing.

(Neither was especially likable, the commentator small and waspish, the spokesman large and Sincere. The latter directed his fleshy countenance at the camera and said:

"Let me summarize, please. I know it's familiar to you in the audience, but I want to spell out our problem.

"In the state of the art, we can send small spacecraft to the nearer stars, and back, at an average speed of about one-fifth light's. That means twenty-odd years to reach Alpha Centauri, the closest; and then there's the return trip; and, naturally, a manned expedition would make no sense unless it was prepared to spend a comparable time on the spot, learning those countless things which unmanned probes cannot. The trouble is, when I say small spacecraft, I mean small. Huge propulsion units but minimal hull and payload. No room or mass to spare for the protection and life support that even a single human would require: not to mention the fact that confinement and monotony would soon drive a crew insane."

"What about suspended animation?" asked the commentator.

The spokesman shook his head. "No, sir. Aside from the bulkiness of the equipment, radiation leakage would destroy too many cells en route. We can barely provide shielding for those essential items which are vulnerable." He beamed. "So we've got a choice. Either we stay with our inadequate probes, or we go over to the system being proposed."

"Or we abandon the whole boondoggle and spend the money on something useful," the commentator said.

The spokesman gave him a trained look of pained patience and replied: "The desirability of space exploration is a separate question, that I'll be glad to take up with you later. If you please, for the time being let's stick to the mechanics of it."

"'Mechanics' may be a very good word, sir," the commentator insinuated. "Turning human beings into robots. Not exactly like Columbus, is it? Though I grant you, thinkers always did point out how machine-like the astronauts were . . . and are."

"If you please," the spokesman repeated, "value judgments aside, who's talking about making robots out of humans? Brains transplanted into machinery? Come! If a body couldn't survive the trip, why imagine that a brain in a tank might? No, we'll simply employ ultra-sophisticated computer-sensor-effector systems."

"With human minds."

"With human psychoneural patterns mapped in, sir. That is all." Smugly: "True, that's a mighty big 'all.' The pattern of an individual is complex beyond imagination, and dynamic rather than static; our math boys call it n-dimensional. We will have to develop methods for scanning it without harm to the subject, recording it, and transferring it to a different matrix, whether that matrix be photonic-electronic or molecular-organic." Drawing breath, then portentously: "Consider the benefits, right here on Earth, of having such a capability."

"I don't know about that," said the commentator. "Maybe you could plant a copy of my personality somewhere else; but *I'd* go on in this same old body, wouldn't I?"

"It would hardly be your exact personality anyhow," admitted the spokesman. "The particular matrix would . . . um . . . determine so much of the functioning. The important thing, from the viewpoint of extrasolar exploration, is that this will give us machines which are not mere robots, but which have such human qualities as motivation and self-programming.

"At the same time, they'll have the advantages of robots. For example, they can be switched off in transit; they won't experience those empty years between stars; they'll arrive sane."

"Some of us wonder if they'll have departed sane. But look," the commentator challenged, "if your machines that you imagine you can program to be people, if they're that good, then why have them manufacture artificial flesh-and-blood people at the end of a trip?"

"Only where circumstances justify it," said the spokesman. "Under some conditions, organic bodies will be preferable. Testing the habitability of a planet is just the most obvious possibility. Consider how your body heals its own wounds. In numerous respects it's actually stronger, more durable, than metal or plastic."

"Why give them the same minds—if I may speak of minds in this connection—the same as the machines?"

"A matter of saving mass." The spokesman smirked at his own wit. "We know the psychoneural scanner will be far too large and fragile to carry along. The apparatus which impresses a pattern on the androids will have to use pre-existent data banks. It can be made much lighter than would otherwise be necessary, if those are the same banks already in use."

He lifted a finger. "Besides, our psychologists think this will have a reinforcing effect. I'd hardly dare call the relationship, ha, ha, parental—"

"Nor I," said the commentator. "I'd call it something like obscene or ghastly.")

When Joel and I, together, month after month guide these chemistries to completion, and when—O climax outcrying the seven thunders!—we send ourselves into the sleeping bodies—maybe, for us at least, it is more than making love ever was.

Joel and Mary were on their honeymoon when he told her of his wish.

Astronauts and ranking engineers could afford to go where air and water were clean, trees grew instead of walls, bird-song resounded instead of traffic, and one's fellow man was sufficiently remote that one could feel benign toward him. Doubtless that was among the reasons why politicians got re-elected by gnawing at the space program.

This evening the west was a fountain of gold above a sea which far out shimmered purple, then broke upon the sands in white thunder. Behind, palms made traces on a blue where Venus had kindled. The air was mild, astir with odors of salt and jasmine.

They stood, arms around each other's waists, her head leaned against him, and watched the sun leave. But when he told her, she stepped from him and he saw terror.

"Hey, what's wrong, darling?" He seized her hands.

"No," she said. "You mustn't."

"What? Why ever not? You're working for it too!"

The sky-glow caught tears. "For somebody else to go, that's fine. It, it'd be like winning a war—a just war, a triumph—when somebody else's man got to do the dying. Not you," she pleaded.

"But . . . good Lord," he tried to laugh, "it won't be me, worse luck. My satisfaction will be strictly vicarious. Supposing I'm accepted, what do I sacrifice? Some time under a scanner; a few calls for chromosome templates. Why in the cosmos should you care?"

"I don't know. It'd be . . . oh, I never thought about it before, never realized the thing might strike home like this—" She swallowed. "I guess it's . . . I'd think, there's a Joel, locked for the rest of his existence inside a machine . . . and there's a Joel in the flesh, dying some gruesome death, or marooned forever."

Silence passed before he replied, slowly: "Why not think, instead, there's a Joel who's glad to pay the price and take the risk—" he let her go and swept a gesture around heaven— "for the sake of getting out yonder?"

She bit her lip. "He'd even abandon his wife."

"I hoped you'd apply also."

"No. I couldn't face it. I'm too much a, an Earthling. This is all too dear to me."

"Do you suppose I don't care for it? Or for you?" He drew her to him.

They were quite alone. On grass above the strand, they won to joy again.

"After all," he said later, "the question won't get serious for years and years."

I don't come back fast. They can't just ram a lifetime into a new body. That's the first real thought I have, as I drift from a cave where voices echoed on and on, and then slowly lights appeared, images, whole scenes, my touch on a control board, Dad lifting me to his shoulder which is way up in the sky, leaves above a brown secret pool, Mary's hair tickling my nose, a boy who stands on his head in the schoolyard, a rocket blastoff that shakes my bones with its sound and light, Mother giving me a fresh-baked ginger cookie, Mother laid out dead and the awful strangeness of her and Mary holding my hand very tight, Mary, Mary, Mary.

No, that's not her voice, it's another woman's, whose, yes, Korene's, and I'm being stroked and cuddled more gently than I ever knew could be. I blink to full consciousness, free-fall afloat in the arms of a robot.

"Joel," she murmurs. "Welcome."

It crashes in on me. No matter the slow awakening: suddenly this. I've taken the anesthetic before they wheel me to the scanner, I'm drowsing dizzily off, then *now* I have no weight, metal and machinery cram everywhere in around me, those are not eyes I look into but glowing optical sensors, "Oh, my God," I say, "it happened to me."

This me. Only I'm Joel! Exactly Joel, nobody else.

I stare down the nude length of my body and know that's not true. The scars, the paunch, the white hairs here and there on the chest are gone. I'm smooth, twenty years in age, though with half a century inside me. I snap after breath.

"Be calm," says Korene.

And the ship speaks with my voice: "Hi, there. Take it easy, pal. You've got a lot of treatment and exercise ahead, you know, before you're ready for action."

"Where are we?" breaks from me.

"Sigma Draconis," Korene says. "In orbit around the most marvelous planet—intelligent life, friendly, and their art is beyond describing, 'beautiful' is such a weak little word—"

"How are things at home?" I interrupt. "I mean, how were they when you . . . we . . . left?"

"You and Mary were still going strong, you at age seventy," she assures me. "Likewise the children and grandchildren." *Ninety years ago.*

I went under, in the laboratory, knowing a single one of me would rouse on Earth and return to her. I am not the one.

I didn't know how hard that would lash.

Korene holds me close. It's typical of her not to be in any hurry to pass on the last news she had of her own self. I suppose, through the hollowness and the trying to cry in her machine arms, I suppose that's why my body was programmed first. Hers can take this better.

"It's not too late yet," she begged him. "I can still swing the decision your way."

Olaf's grizzled head wove back and forth. "No. How many times must I tell you?"

"No more," she sighed. "The choices will be made within a month."

He rose from his armchair, went to her where she sat, and ran a big ropy-veined hand across her cheek. "I am sorry," he said. "You are sweet to want me along. I hate to hurt you." She could imagine the forced smile above her. "But truly, why would you want a possible millennium of my grouchiness?"

"Because you are Olaf," Korene answered.

She got up likewise, stepped to a window, and stood looking out. It was a winter night. Snow lay hoar on roofs across the old city, spires pierced an uneasy glow, a few stars glimmered. Frost put shrillness into the rumble of traffic and machines. The room, its warmth and small treasures, felt besieged.

She broke her word by saying, "Can't you see, a personality inside a cybernet isn't a castrated cripple? In a way, we're the ones caged, in these ape bodies and senses. There's a whole new universe to become part of. Including a universe of new closenesses to me."

He joined her. "Call me a reactionary," he growled, "or a professional ape. I've often explained that I like being what I am, too much to start over as something else."

She turned to him and said low: "You'd also start over as what you were. We both would. Over and over."

"No. We'd have these aged minds."

She laughed forlornly. "'If youth knew, if age could.'"

"We'd be sterile."

"Of necessity. No way to raise children on any likely planet. Otherwise—Olaf, if you refuse, I'm going regardless. With another man. I'll always wish he were you."

He lifted a fist. "All right, God damn it!" he shouted. "All right! I'll tell you the real reason why I won't go under your bloody scanner! I'd die too envious!"

It is fair here beyond foretelling: beyond understanding, until slowly we grow into our planet.

For it isn't Earth. Earth we have forever laid behind us, Joel and I. The sun is molten amber, large in a violet heaven. At this season its companion has risen about noon, a gold-bright star which will drench night with witchery under the constellations and three swift moons. Now, toward the end of day, the hues around us—intensely green hills, tall blue-plumed trees, rainbows in wings which jubilate overhead—are become so rich that they fill the air; the whole world glows. Off across the valley, a herd of beasts catches the shiningness on their horns.

We took off our boots when we came back to camp. The turf, not grass nor moss, is springy underfoot, cool between the toes. The nearby forest breathes out fragrances; one of them recalls rosemary. Closer is smoke from the fire Korene built while we were exploring. It speaks to my nostrils and the most ancient parts of my brain: of autumn leaves burning, of blazes after dark in what few high solitudes remained on Earth, of hearths where I sat at Christmas time with the children.

"Hello, dears," says my voice out of the machine. (It isn't the slim fleet body she uses aboard ship; it's built for sturdiness, is the only awkward sight in all the landscape.) "You seem to have had a pleasant day."

"Oh, my, oh, my!" Arms uplifted, I dance. "We *must* find a name for this planet. Thirty-six Ophiuchi B Two is ridiculous."

"We will," says Joel in my ear. His palm falls on my flank. It feels like a torch.

"I'm on the channel too," says the speaker with his voice. "Uh, look, kids, fun's fun, but we've got to get busy. I want you properly housed and supplied long before winter. And while we ferry the stuff, do the carpenteering, et cetera, I want more samples for us to analyze. So far you've just found some fruits and such that're safe to eat. You need meat as well."

"I hate to think of killing," I say, when I am altogether happy.

"Oh, I reckon I've got enough hunter instinct for both of us," says Joel, my Joel. Breath gusts from him, across me. "Christ! I never guessed how good elbow room and freedom would feel."

"Plus a large job," Korene reminds: the study of a world, that she and her Joel may signal our discoveries back to a Sol we can no longer see with our eyes alone; that in the end, they may carry back what we have gathered, to an Earth that perhaps will no longer want it.

"Sure. I expect to love every minute." His clasp on me tightens. Waves shudder outward, through me. "Speaking of love—"

The machine grows still. A shadow has lengthened across its metal, where firelight weaves reflected. The flames talk merrily. A flying creature cries like a trumpet.

"So you have come to that," says Korene at last, a benediction.

"Today," I declare from our glory.

There is another quietness.

"Well, congratulations," says Korene's Joel. "We, uh, we were planning a little wedding present for you, but you've caught us by surprise." Mechanical tendrils reach out. Joel releases me to take them in his fingers. "All the best, both of you. Couldn't happen to two nicer people, even if I am one of them myself, sort of. Uh, well, we'll break contact now, Korene and I. See you in the morning?"

"Oh, no, oh, no," I stammer, between weeping and laughter, and cast myself on my knees to embrace this body whose two spirits brought us to life and will someday bury us. "Stay. We want you here, Joel and I. You, you are us." *And more than us and pitifully less than us*. "We want to share with you."

The priest mounted to his pulpit. Tall in white robes, he waited there against the shadows of the sanctuary; candles picked him out and made a halo around his hood. When silence was total in the temple, he leaned forward. His words tolled forth to the faces and the cameras:

"Thou shalt have none other gods but me, said the Lord unto the children of Israel. Thou shalt love thy neighbor as thyself, said Christ unto the world. And sages and seers of every age and every faith warned against *hubris,* that overweening pride which brings down upon us immortal anger.

"The Tower of Babel and the Flood of Noah may be myths. But in myth lies a wisdom of the race which goes infinitely beyond the peerings and posturings of science. Behold our sins today and tremble.

"Idolatry: man's worship of what he alone has made. Uncharity: man's neglect, yes, forsaking of his brother in that brother's need, to whore after mere adventure. *Hubris:* man's declaration that he can better the work of God.

"You know what I mean. While the wretched of Earth groan in their billions for succor, treasure is spewed into the barrenness of outer space. Little do the lords of lunacy care for their fellow mortals. Nothing do they care for God.

"'To follow knowledge like a sinking star, Beyond the utmost bound of human thought' is a pair of lines much quoted these days. Ulysses, the eternal seeker. May I remind you, those lines do not refer to Homer's wanderer, but to Dante's, who was in hell for breaking every constraint which divine Providence had ordained.

"And yet how small, how warm and understandable was his sin! His was not that icy arrogance which today the faceless engineers of the interstellar project urge upon us. Theirs is the final contempt for God and for man. In order that we may violate the harmony of the stars, we are to create, in metal and chemicals, dirty caricatures of a holy work; we are actually to believe that by our electronic trickery we can breathe into them souls."

Nat the rhesus monkey runs free. The laboratory half of the cabin is barred to him; the living quarters, simply and sturdily equipped, don't hold much he can harm. He isn't terribly mischievous anyway. Outdoors are unlimited space and trees where he can be joyful. So, when at home with Korene and Joel, he almost always observes the restrictions they have taught him.

His wish to please may stem from memory of loneliness. It was a weary while he was caged on the surface, after he had been grown in the tank. (His body has, in fact, existed longer than the two human ones.) He had no company save rats, guinea pigs, tissue cultures, and the like—and, of course, the machine which tended and tested him. That that robot often spoke, petted and played games, was what saved his monkey sanity. When at last living flesh hugged his own, what hollow within him was suddenly filled?

What hollow in the others? He skips before their feet, he rides on their shoulders, at night he shares their bed.

But today is the third of cold autumn rains. Though Korene has given to this planet of Eighty-two Eridani the name Gloria, it has its seasons, and now spins toward a darker time. The couple have stayed inside, and Nat gets restless. No doubt, as well, the change in his friends arouses an unease.

There ought to be cheer. The cabin is amply large for two persons. It is more than snug, it is lovely, in the flowing grain of its timbers and the crystal-glittering stones of its fireplace. Flames dance on the hearth; they laugh; a bit of their smoke escapes to scent the air like cinnamon; through the brightness of fluorescent panels, their light shimmers off furnishings and earthenware which Joel and Korene made together in the summer which is past—off the racked reels of an audiovisual library and a few beloved pictures—off twilit panes where rain sluices downward. Beyond a closed door, wind goes *broo-oom*.

Joel sits hunched at his desk. He hasn't bathed or shaved lately, his hair is unkempt, his coverall begrimed and sour. Korene has maintained herself better; it is dust in the corners and unwashed dishes in a basin which bespeak what she has neglected while he was trying to hunt. She sprawls on the bed and listens to music, though the ringing in her ears makes that hard.

Both have grown gaunt. Their eyes are sunken, their mouths and tongues are sore. Upon the dried skin of hands and faces, a rash has appeared.

Joel casts down his calculator. "Damn, I can't think!" he nearly shouts. "Screw those analyses! What good are they?"

Korene's reply is sharp. "They just might show what's gone

wrong with us and how to fix it."

"Judas! When I can't even sleep right—" He twists about on his chair to confront the inactive robot. "You! You damned smug machines, where are you? What're you doing?"

A tic goes ugly along Korene's lip. "They're busy, yonder in orbit," she says. "I suggest you follow their example."

"Yah! Same as you?"

"Quite—anytime you'll help me keep our household running, Sir Self-Appointed Biochemist." She starts to lift herself but abandons the effort. Tears of self-pity trickle forth. "Olaf wouldn't have turned hysterical like you."

"And Mary wouldn't lie flopped-out useless," he says. However, the sting she has given sends him back to his labor. Interpreting the results of gas chromatography on unknown compounds is difficult at best. When he has begun to hallucinate—when the graphs he has drawn slide around and intertwine as if they were worms—

A crash resounds from the pantry. Korene exclaims. Joel jerks erect. Flour and the shards of a crock go in a tide across the floor. After them bounds Nat. He stops amidst the wreckage and gives his people a look of amazed innocence. Dear me, he all but says, how did this happen?

"You lousy little sneak!" Joel screams. "You know you're not allowed on the shelves!" He storms over to stand above the creature. "How often—" Stooping, he snatches Nat up by the scruff of the neck. A thin tone of pain and terror slips between his fingers.

Korene rises. "Let him be," she says.

"So he can finish the . . . the havoc?" Joel hurls the monkey against the wall. The impact is audible. Nat lies twisted and wailing.

Silence brims the room, inside the wind. Korene gazes at Joel, and he at his hands, as if they confronted these things for the first time. When at last she speaks, it is altogether without tone. "Get out. Devil. Go."

"But," he stammers. "But. I didn't mean."

Still she stares. He retreats into new anger. "That pest's been driving me out of my skull! You know he has! We may be dead because of him, and yet you gush over him till I could puke!"

"Right. Blame him for staying healthy when we didn't. I find depths in you I never suspected before."

"And I in you," he jeers. "He's your baby, isn't he? The baby you've been tailored never to bear yourself. Your spoiled brat."

She brushes past him and kneels beside the animal.

Joel utters a raw kind of bark. He lurches to the door, hauls it open, disappears as if the dusk has eaten him. Rain and chill blow in.

Korene doesn't notice. She examines Nat, who pants, whimpers, watches her with eyes that are both wild and dimming. Blood mats his fur. It becomes clear that his back is broken.

"My pretty, my sweet, my bouncy-boy, please don't hurt. Please," she sobs as she lifts the small form. She carries him into the laboratory, prepares an injection, cradles him and sings a lullaby while it does its work.

Afterward she brings the body back to the living room, lies down holding it, and cries herself into a half-sleep full of nightmares.

—Her voice rouses her, out of the metal which has rested in a corner. She never truly remembers, later, what next goes on between her selves. Words, yes; touch; a potion for her to drink; then the blessing of nothingness. When she awakens, it is day and the remnant of Nat is gone from her.

So is the robot. It returns while she is leaving the bed. She would weep some more if she had the strength; but at least, through a headache she can think.

The door swings wide. Rain has ended. The world gleams. Here too are fall colors, beneath a lucent sky where wandersongs drift from wings beating southward. The carpet of the land has turned to sallow gold, the forest to bronze and red and a purple which bears tiny flecks like mica. Coolness streams around her.

Joel enters, half leaning on the machine, half upheld by it. Released, he crumples at her feet. From the throat which is not a throat, his voice begs:

"Be kind to him, will you? He spent the night stumbling around the woods till he caved in. Might've died, if a chemosensor of ours hadn't gotten the spoor."

"I wanted to," mumbles the man on the floor. "After what I did."

"Not his fault," says the ship anxiously, as if his identity were also involved and must clear itself of guilt. "He wasn't in his right mind."

The female sound continues: "An environmental factor, you see. We have finally identified it. You weren't rational either, girl. But never blame yourself, or him." Hesitation. "You'll be all right when we've taken you away from here."

Korene doesn't observe how unsteady the talking was, nor think about its implications. Instead, she sinks down to embrace Joel.

"How could I do it?" he gasps upon her breast.

"It wasn't you that did," says Korene in the robot, while Korene in the woman holds him close and murmurs.

—They are back aboard ship, harnessed weightless. Thus far they haven't asked for explanations. It was enough that their spirits were again together, that the sadness and the demons were leaving them, that they slept unhaunted and woke to serenity. But now the soothing drugs have worn off and healing bodies have, afresh, generated good minds.

They look at each other, whisper, and clasp hands. Joel says aloud, into the metal which encloses them: "Hey. You two."

His fellow self does not answer. Does it not dare? Part of a minute goes by before the older Korene speaks. "How are you, my dears?"

"Not bad," he states. "Physically."

How quiet it grows.

Until the second Korene gives challenge. "Hard news for us. Isn't that so?"

"Yes," her voice sighs back.

They stiffen. "Go on," she demands.

The answer is hasty. "You were suffering from pellagra. That was something we'd never encountered before; not too simple to diagnose, either, especially in its early stages. We had to ransack our whole medical data bank before we got a clue as to what to look for in the cell and blood samples we took. It's a deficiency disease, caused by lack of niacin, a B vitamin."

Protest breaks from Joel. "But hell, we knew the Glorian biochemistry doesn't include B complex! We took our pills."

"Yes, of course. That was one of the things which misled us, along with the fact that the animals throve on the same diet as yours. But we've found a substance in the native food—all native food; it's as integral to life as ATP is on Earth—a material that seemed harmless when we made the original analyses—" pain shrills forth—"when we decided we could create you—"

"It acts with a strictly human-type gene," the ship adds roughly. "We've determined which one, and don't see how to block the process. The upshot is release of an enzyme which destroys niacin in the bloodstream. Your pills disguised the situation at first, because the concentration of antagonist built up slowly. But equilibrium has been reached at last, and you'd get no measurable help from swallowing extra doses; they'd break down before you could metabolize them."

"Mental disturbances are one symptom," Korene says from the speaker. "The physical effects in advanced cases are equally horrible. Don't worry. You'll get well and stay well. Your systems have eliminated the chemical, and here is a lifetime supply of niacin."

She does not need to tell them that here is very little which those systems can use as fuel, nor any means of refining the meats and fruits on which they counted.

The ship gropes for words. "Uh, you know, this is the kind of basic discovery, I think, the kind of discovery we had to go into space to make. A piece of genetic information we'd never have guessed in a million years, staying home. Who knows what it'll be a clue to? Immortality?"

"Hush," warns his companion. To the pair in the cabin she says low, "We'll withdraw, leave you alone. Come out in the passageway when you want us. . . . Peace." A machine cannot cry, can it?

For a long while, the man and the woman are mute. Finally, flatly, he declares, "What rations we've got should keep us, oh, I'd guess a month."

"We can be thankful for that." When she nods, the tresses float around her brow and cheekbones.

"Thankful! Under a death sentence?"

"We knew . . . our selves on Earth knew, some of us would die young. I went to the scanner prepared for it. Surely you did likewise."

"Yes. In a way. Except it's happening to me." He snaps after air: "And you, which is worse. This you, the only Korene that this I will ever have. Why *us?*"

She gazes before her, then astonishes him with a smile. "The question which nobody escapes. We've been granted a month."

He catches her to him and pleads, "Help me. Give me the guts to be glad."

—The sun called Eighty-two Eridani rises in white-gold radiance over the great blue rim of the planet. That is a blue as deep as the ocean of its winds and weather, the ocean of its tides and waves, surging aloft into flame and roses. The ship orbits on toward day. Clouds come aglow with morning light. Later they swirl in purity above summer lands and winter lands, storm and calm, forest, prairie, valley, height, river, sea, the flocks upon flocks which are nourished by this world their mother.

Korene and Joel watch it through an hour, side by side and hand in hand before a screen, afloat in the crowdedness of machinery. The robot and the ship have kept silence. A blower whirrs its breeze across their bare skins, mingling for them their scents of woman and man. Often their free hands caress, or they kiss, but they have made their love and are now making their peace.

The ship swings back into night. Opposite, stars bloom uncountable and splendid. She stirs. "Let us," she says.

"Yes," he replies.

"You could wait," says the ship. His voice need not be so harsh; but he does not think to control it. "Days longer."

"No," the man tells him. "That'd be no good," seeing Korene starve to death; for the last food is gone. "Damn near as bad as staying down there," and watching her mind rot while her flesh corrupts and withers.

"You're right," the ship agrees humbly. "Oh, Christ, if we'd thought!"

"You couldn't have, darling," says the robot with measureless gentleness. "No one could have."

The woman strokes a bulkhead, tenderly as if it were her man, and touches her lips to the metal.

He shakes himself. "Please, no more things we've talked out a million times," he says. "Just goodbye."

The robot enfolds him in her clasp. The woman joins them. The ship knows what they want, it being his wish too, and "*Sheep May Safely Graze*" brightens the air.

The humans float together. "I want to say," his words stumble, "I never stopped loving Mary, and missing her, but I love you as much, Korene, and, and thanks for being what you've been.

"I wish I could say it better," he finishes.

"You don't need to," she answers, and signals the robot.

They hardly feel the needle. As they float embraced, toward darkness, he calls drowsily, "Don't grieve too long, you there

Don't ever be afraid o' making more lives. The universe'll always surprise us."

"Yes." She laughes a little through the sleep which is gathering her in. "Wasn't that good of God?"

We fare across the light-years and the centuries, life after life, death after death. Space is our single home. Earth has become more strange to us than the outermost comet of the farthest star.

For to Earth we have given:

Minds opened upon endlessness, which therefore hold their own world, and the beings upon it, very precious.

A knowledge of natural law whereby men may cross the abyss in the bodies their mothers gave them, short years from sun to sun, and planets unpeopled for their taking, so that their kind will endure as long as the cosmos.

A knowledge of natural law whereby they have stopped nature's casual torturing of them through sickness, madness, and age.

The arts, histories, philosophies and faiths and things once undreamable, of a hundred sentient races; and out of these, an ongoing renaissance which does not look as if it will ever die.

From our gifts have sprung material wealth at each man's fingertips, beyond the grasp of any whole Earth-bound nation; withal, a growing calm and wisdom, learned from the manyfoldedness of reality. Each time we return, strife seems less and fewer seem to hate their brothers or themselves.

But does our pride on behalf of them beguile us? They have become shining enigmas who greet us graciously, neither thrust us forth again nor seek to hold us against our wills. Though finally each of us never comes back, they make no others. Do they need our gifts any longer? Is it we the wanderers who can change and grow no more?

Well, we have served; and one service will remain to the end. Two in the deeps, two and two on the worlds, we alone remember those who lived, and those who died, and Olaf and Mary.

Afterword

Let's put rhetoric aside for a moment and look at a few facts.

Though the space program has had its human share of inefficiencies and absurdities, it has never been a losing proposition. Rather, it has *already* repaid the modest investment, and returned a huge profit as well.

Modest? Of course. The budget of the National Aeronautics and Space Administration—for all of its varied activities—peaked at about the time of Apollo 11. Yet in those palmy days it got less than eight cents for every dollar the federal government spent on health, education, and welfare: a figure which takes no account of state and local undertakings or of private philanthropies. We would be unkind if we compared the actual accomplishments. But at least we can deny that NASA has ever taken bread out of the mouths of the poor.

Profit? Certainly. The revolution in meteorology alone, brought about by weather satellites, proves that claim. The lives and treasure saved because hurricanes can be accurately predicted offer a spectacular example. However, precise forecasts as a routine matter, year after year, are the open-ended payoff, especially for agriculture and transportation and thus for mankind. Or think of communications. Never mind if many television programs strike you as inane—never mind, even, educational uses in primitive areas—the core truth is that transmission over great distances was bound to come, and that relaying through space is cheaper than across the surface. Cash economies are mere shorthand for labor set free and natural resources conserved.

We are on the verge of reaping rich harvest from terrestrial resources satellites. Not much further off is a real comprehension of geophysics and geochemistry, by way of examining the cosmic environment of our planet and comparing it with its neighbors. The practical, humane applications should be obvious. Likewise, astrophysics is a key to the full description and control of matter and energy; and the place for that research is above an atmosphere. Meanwhile we can hope for deeper insights into how life works. Early biological experiments out there have indicated how little we know today, how badly we need to carry on studies under conditions found nowhere but in space. A golden age of medicine ought to result.

Well and good, some say; but can't we do this with unmanned probes, vehicles, robots, devices? Why go to the enormous cost of sending men?

Having patiently explained once more that the cost isn't enormous, and added that further development can make it small, I respond: Machines are invaluable aids. Still, do you seriously believe they could have replaced the direct experiences of a Cook, Stanley, Lyell, Darwin, Boas—in our own day, a Cousteau, Leakey, or Goodall? Man, or woman, is the only computer which continuously reprograms itself, the only sensor system which records data it is not planned to detect, the only thing which gives a damn.

Six fleeting visits to a single barren globe scarcely constitute exploration. If we stop now, it will be as if European mariners had stopped when Columbus reported his failure to reach India. What he did find was enough to bring legions overseas. What the astronauts have found in the tiny times granted them is astonishingly much: not material wealth, but the stuff of knowledge, whence all else arises. Shall we end the enterprise at its very beginning?

Discussing such pragmatic questions with ordinary folk like myself, including dwellers in poverty areas, I have never had any difficulty in getting the point across, the value to them and their children. It seems to be the cocktail party intellectuals whom dynamite won't blast loose from preconceptions. Perhaps I have met the wrong ones and do their class an injustice.

Or perhaps, pitiably, they have not eyes to see.

There are human creations as glorious as the rising of a spaceship witnessed close at hand. There are realities here on Earth as mysterious and miraculous as any in the astronomical deeps. But there are none which are more so. And yonder is where the endlessness lies—not simply of adventure and learning but of the spirit, which must have revelations from the greater than human if it is to grow, even as a flower must have sunlight.

Why not build a machine to climb Everest?

Or a machine to make love?

Or a machine to exist?

Because we are what we are. First come the wish and the vision, then the understanding. However cruel this world, it is less cutthroat than it might be, thanks to the prophets of the high faiths; but what they sought was not civilization but salvation. Maybe the reason that some persons cannot imagine what we have to gain beyond Earth is that heaven has not touched them with wonder.

Go out, the next clear night. Look up.

Gibraltar Falls

The Time Patrol base would only remain for the hundred-odd years of inflow. During that while, few people other than scientists and maintenance crew would stay there for long at a stretch. Thus it was small, a lodge and a couple of service buildings, nearly lost in the land.

Five and a half million years before he was born, Tom Nomura found that southern end of Iberia still more steep than he remembered it. Hills climbed sharply northward until they became low mountains walling the sky, riven by canyons where shadows lay blue. It was dry country, rained on violently but briefly in winter, its streams shrunken to runnels or nothing as its grass burnt yellow in summer. Trees and shrubs grew far apart, thorn, mimosa, acacia, pine, aloe; around the waterholes palm, fern, orchid.

Withal, it was rich in life. Hawks and vultures were always

at hover in cloudless heaven. Grazing herds mingled their millions together; among their scores of kinds of zebra-striped ponies, primitive rhinoceros, okapi-like ancestors of the giraffe, sometimes mastodon—thinly red-haired, hugely tusked—or peculiar elephants. Among the predators and scavengers were sabertooths, early forms of the big cats, hyenas, and scuttering ground apes which occasionally walked on their hind legs. Ant-heaps lifted six feet into the air. Marmots whistled.

It smelled of hay, scorch, baked dung, and warm flesh. When wind awoke, it boomed, pushed, threw dust and heat into the face. Often the earth resounded to hoofbeats, birds clamored or beasts trumpeted. At night a sudden chill struck down, and the stars were so many that one didn't much notice the alienness of their constellations.

Thus had things been until lately. And as yet there was no great change. But now had begun a hundred years of thunder. When that was done, nothing would ever be the same again.

Manse Everard regarded Tom Nomura and Feliz a Rach for a squinting moment before he smiled and said, "No, thanks, I'll just poke around here today. You go have fun."

Did an eyelid of the big, bent-nosed, slightly grizzled man droop a little in Nomura's direction? The latter couldn't be sure. They were from the same milieu, indeed the same country. That Everard had been recruited in New York, 1954 A.D., and Nomura in San Francisco, 1972, ought to make scant difference. The upheavals of that generation were bubble pops against what had happened before and what would happen after. However, Nomura was fresh out of the Academy, a bare twenty-five years of lifespan behind him. Everard hadn't told how much time his own farings through the world's duration added up to; and given the longevity treatment the Patrol offered its people, it was impossible to guess. Nomura suspected the Unattached agent had seen enough existence to have become more foreign to him than Feliz—who was born two millenniums past either of them.

"Very well, let's start," she said. Curt though it was, Nomura thought her voice made music of the Temporal language.

They stepped from the veranda and walked across the yard. A couple of other corpsmen hailed them, with a pleasure directed at her. Nomura agreed. She was young and tall, the curve-nosed strength of her features softened by large green eyes, large mobile mouth, hair that shone auburn in spite of being hacked off at the ears. The usual gray coverall and stout boots could not hide her figure or the suppleness of her stride. Nomura knew he himself wasn't bad-looking—a stocky but limber frame, high-cheeked regular features, tawny skin—but she made him feel drab.

Also inside, he thought. *How does a new-minted Patrolman—not even slated for police duty, a mere naturalist—how does he tell an aristocrat of the First Matriarchy that he's fallen in love with her?*

The rumbling which always filled the air, these miles from the cataracts, sounded to him like a chorus. Was it imagination, or did he really sense an endless shudder through the ground, up into his bones?

Feliz opened a shed. Several hoppers stood inside, vaguely resembling wheelless two-seater motorcycles, propelled by anti-gravity and capable of leaping across several thousand years. (They and their present riders had been transported hither in heavy-duty shuttles.) Hers was loaded with recording gear. He had failed to convince her it was overburdened and knew she'd never forgive him if he finked on her. His invitation to Everard—the ranking officer on hand, though here-now simply on vacation—to join them today had been made in a vague hope that the latter would see that load and order her to let her assistant carry part of it.

She sprang to the saddle. "Come on!" she said. "The morning's getting old."

He mounted his vehicle and touched controls. Both glided outside and aloft. At eagle height, they leveled off and bore south, where the River Ocean poured into the Middle of the World.

Banks of upflung mist always edged that horizon, argent smoking off into azure. As one drew near afoot, they loomed topplingly overhead. Further on, the universe swirled gray, shaken by the roar, bitter on human lips, while water flowed off rock and gouged through mud. So thick was the cold salt fog that it was unsafe to breathe for more than a few minutes.

From well above, the sight was yet more awesome. There one could see the end of a geological epoch. For a million and a half years the Mediterranean basin had lain a desert. Now the Gates of Hercules stood open and the Atlantic was coming through.

The wind of his passage around him, Nomura peered west across unrestful, many-hued and intricately foam-streaked immensity. He could see the currents run, sucked toward the new-made gap between Europe and Africa. There they clashed together and recoiled, a white and green chaos whose violence toned from earth to heaven and back, crumbled cliffs, overwhelmed valleys, blanketed the shore in spume for miles inland. From them came a stream, snow-colored in its fury, with flashes of livid emerald, to stand in an eight-mile wall between the continents and bellow. Spray roiled aloft, dimming the torrent after torrent, wherein the sea crashed onward.

Rainbows wheeled through the clouds it made. This far aloft, the noise was no more than a monstrous millstone grinding. Nomura could clearly hear Feliz's voice out of his receiver, as she stopped her vehicle and lifted an arm. "Hold. I want a few more takes before we go on."

"Haven't you enough?" he asked.

Her words softened. "How can we get enough of a miracle?"

His heart jumped. *She's not a she-soldier, born to lord it over a ruck of underlings. In spite of her early life and ways, she isn't. She feels the dread, the beauty, yes, the sense of God at work—*

A wry grin at himself: *She'd better!*

After all, her task was to make a full-sensory record of the whole thing, from its beginning until that day when, a hundred years hence, the basin was full and the sea lapped calm where Odysseus would sail. It would take months of her lifespan. *(And mine, please, mine.)* Everybody in the corps wanted to experience this stupendousness; the hope of adventure was practically required for recruitment. But it wasn't feasible for many to come so far downstairs, crowding into so narrow a time-slot. Most would have to do it vicariously. Their chiefs would not have picked someone who was not a considerable artist, to live it on their behalf and pass it on to them.

Nomura remembered his astonishment when he was assigned to assist her. Short-handed as it was, could the Patrol afford artists?

Well, after he answered a cryptic advertisement and took several puzzling tests and learned about intertemporal traffic, he had wondered if police and rescue work were possible and been told that, usually, they were. He could see the need for administrative and clerical personnel, resident agents, historiographers, anthropologists, and, yes, natural scientists like himself. In the weeks they had been working together, Feliz convinced him that a few artists were at least as vital. Man does not live by bread alone, nor guns, paperwork, theses, naked practicalities.

She re-stowed her apparatus. "Come," she ordered. As she flashed eastward ahead of him, her hair caught a sunbeam and shone as if molten. He trudged mute in her wake.

The Mediterranean floor lay ten thousand feet below sea level. The inflow took most of that drop within a fifty-mile strait. Its volume amounted to ten thousand cubic miles a year, a hundred Victoria Falls or a thousand Niagaras.

Thus the statistics. The reality was a roar of white water, spray-shrouded, earth-sundering, mountain-shaking. Men could see, hear, feel, smell, taste the thing; they could not imagine it.

When the channel widened, the flow grew smoother, until it ran green and black. Then mists diminished and islands appeared, like ships which cast up huge bow waves; and life could again grow or go clear to the shore. Yet most of those islands would be eroded away before the century was out, and much of that life would perish in weather turned strange. For this event would move the planet from its Miocene to its Pliocene epoch.

And as he flitted onward, Nomura did not hear less noise, but more. Though the stream itself was quieter here, it moved toward a bass clamor which grew and grew till heaven was one brazen bell. He recognized a headland whose worn-down remnant would someday bear the name Gibraltar. Not far beyond, a cataract twenty miles wide made almost half the total plunge.

With terrifying ease, the waters slipped over that brink. They were glass-green against the darkling cliffs and umber grass of the continents. Light flamed off their heights. At their bottom another cloud bank rolled white in never-ending winds. Beyond reached a blue sheet, a lake whence rivers hewed canyons, out and out across the alkaline sparkle, dust devils and mirage shimmers of the furnace land which they would make into a sea.

It boomed, it brawled, it querned.

Again Feliz poised her flyer. Nomura drew alongside. They were high; the air whittered chilly around them.

"Today," she told him, "I want to try for an impression of the sheer size. I'll move in close to the top, recording as I go, and then down."

"Not too close," he warned.

She bridled. "I'll judge that."

"Uh, I . . . I'm not trying to boss you or anything." *I'd better not. I, a plebe and a male.* "As a favor, please—" Nomura flinched at his own clumsy speech. "—be careful, will you? I mean, you're important to me."

Her smile burst upon him. She leaned hard against her safety harness to catch his hand. "Thank you, Tom." After a moment, turned grave: "Men like you make me understand what is wrong in the age I come from."

She had often spoken kindly to him: most times, in fact. Had she been a strident militant, no amount of comeliness would have kept him awake nights. He wondered if perhaps he had begun loving her when first he noticed how conscientiously she strove to regard him as her equal. It was not easy for her, she being almost as new in the Patrol as he—no easier than it was for men from other areas to believe, down inside where it counted, that she had the same capabilities they did and that it was right she use herself to the full.

She couldn't stay solemn. "Come on!" she shouted. "Hurry! That straight dropoff won't last another twenty years!"

Her machine darted. He slapped down the face screen of his helmet and plunged after, bearing the tapes and power cells and other auxiliary items. *Be careful,* he pleaded, *oh, be careful, my darling.*

She had gotten well ahead. He saw her like a comet, a dragonfly, everything vivid and swift, limned athwart yonder mile-high precipice of sea. The noise grew in him till there was nothing else, his skull was full of its doomsday.

Yards from the waters, she rode her hopper chasmward. Her head was buried in a dial-studded box, her hands at work on its settings, she steered with her knees. Salt spray began to fog Nomura's screen. He activated the self-cleaner. Turbulence clawed at him; his carrier lurched. His eardrums, guarded against sound but not changing pressure, stabbed with pain.

He had come quite near Feliz when her vehicle went crazy. He saw it spin, saw it strike the green immensity, saw it and her engulfed. He could not hear himself scream through the thunder.

He rammed the speed switch, swooped after her. Was it blind instinct which sent him whirling away again, inches before the torrent grabbed him too? She was gone from sight. There was only the water wall, clouds below and unpitying blue calm above, the noise that took him in its jaws to shake him apart, the cold, the damp, the salt on his mouth that tasted like tears.

He fled for help.

* * *

Noonday glowered outside. The land looked bleached, lay moveless and lifeless except for a carrion bird. The distant falls alone had voice.

A knock on the door of his room brought Nomura off the bed, onto his feet. Through an immediately rackety pulse he croaked, "Come in. Do."

Everard entered. In spite of air conditioning, sweat spotted his garments. He gnawed a fireless pipe and his shoulders slumped.

"What's the word?" Nomura begged of him.

"As I feared. Nothing. She never returned home."

Nomura sank into a chair and stared before him. "You're certain?"

Everard sat down on the bed, which creaked beneath his weight. "Yeah. The message capsule just arrived. In answer to my inquiry, et cetera, Agent Feliz a Rach has not reported back to her home milieu base from the Gibraltar assignment, and they have no further record of her."

"Not in *any* era?"

"The way agents move around in time and space, nobody keeps dossiers, except maybe the Danellians."

"Ask them!"

"Do you imagine they'd reply?" Everard snapped—they, the supermen of the remote future who were the founders and ultimate masters of the Patrol. One big fist clenched on his knee. "And don't tell me we ordinary mortals could keep closer tabs if we wanted to. Have you checked your personal future, son? We don't want to, and that's that."

The roughness left him. He shifted the pipe about in his grip and said most gently. "If we live long enough, we outlive those we've cared for. The common fate of man; nothing unique to our corps. But I'm sorry you had to strike it so young."

"Never mind me!" Nomura exclaimed. "What of her?"

"Yes . . . I've been thinking about your account. My guess is, the airflow patterns are worse than tricky around that fall. What should've been expected, no doubt. Overloaded, her hopper was less controllable than usual. An air pocket, a flaw, whatever it was, something like that grabbed her without warning and tossed her into the stream."

Nomura's fingers writhed against each other. "And I was supposed to look after her."

Everard shook his head. "Don't punish yourself worse. You were simply her assistant. She should have been more careful."

"But—God damn it, we can rescue her still, and you won't allow us to?" Nomura half screamed.

"Stop," Everard warned. "Stop right there."

Never say it: that several Patrolmen could ride backward in time, lay hold on her with tractor beams and haul her free of the abyss. Or that I could tell her and my earlier self to beware. It did not happen, therefore it will not happen.

It must *not happen.*

For the past becomes in fact mutable, as soon as we on our machines have transformed it into our present. And if ever a mortal takes himself that power, where can the changing end? We start by saving a glad girl; we go on to save Lincoln, but somebody else tries to save the Confederate States—No, none less than God can be trusted with time. The Patrol exists to guard what is real. Its men may no more violate that faith than they may violate their own mothers.

"I'm sorry," Nomura mumbled.

"It's okay, Tom."

"No, I . . . I thought . . . when I saw her vanish, my first thought was that we could make up a party, ride back to that very instant and snatch her clear—"

"A natural thought in a new man. Old habits of the mind die hard. The fact is, we did not. It'd scarcely have been authorized anyway. Too dangerous. We can ill afford to lose more. Certainly we can't when the record shows that our rescue attempt would be foredoomed if we made it."

"Is there no way to get around that?"

Everard sighed. "I can't think of any. Make your peace with fate, Tom." He hesitated. "Can I . . . can we do anything for you?"

"No." It came harsh out of Nomura's throat. "Except leave me be for a while."

"Sure." Everard rose. "You weren't the only person who thought a lot of her," he reminded, and left.

When the door had closed behind him, the sound of the falls seemed to wax, grinding, grinding. Nomura stared at emptiness. The sun passed its apex and began to slide very slowly toward night.

I should have gone after her myself, at once.

And risked my life.

Why not follow her into death, then?

No. That's senseless. Two deaths do not make a life. I couldn't have saved her, I didn't have the equipment or—The sane thing was to fetch help.

Only the help was denied—whether by man or by fate hardly matters, does it?—and so she went down. The stream hurled her into the gulf, she had a moment's terror before it smashed the awareness out of her, then at the bottom it crushed her, plucked her apart, strewed the pieces of her bones across the floor of a sea that I, a youngster, will sail upon one holiday, unknowing that there is a Time Patrol or ever was a Feliz. Oh, God, I want my dust down with hers, five and a half million years from this hour!

A remote cannonade went through the air, a tremor through earth and floor. An undercut bank must have crumbled into the torrent. It was the kind of scene she would have loved to capture.

"Would have?" Nomura yelled and surged from the chair. The ground still vibrated beneath him. "She will!"

He ought to have consulted Everard, but feared—perhaps mistakenly, in his grief and his inexperience—that he would be refused permission and sent upstairs at once.

He ought to have rested for several days, but feared that his manner would betray him. A stimulant pill must serve in place of nature.

He ought to have checked out a tractor unit, not smuggled it into the locker on his vehicle.

When he took the hopper forth, a Patrolman who saw asked where he was bound. "For a ride," Nomura answered. The other nodded sympathetically. He might not suspect that a love had been lost, but the loss of a comrade was bad enough. Nomura was careful to get well over the northern horizon before he swung toward the seafall.

Right and left, it reached further than he could see. Here, more than halfway down that cliff of green glass, the very curve of the planet hid its ends from him. Then as he entered the spume clouds, whiteness enfolded him, roiling and stinging.

His face shield stayed clear, but vision was ragged, upward along immensity. The helmet warded his hearing but could not stave off the storm which rattled his teeth and heart and skeleton. Winds whirled and smote, the carrier staggered, he must fight for every inch of control.

And to find the exact second—

Back and forth he leaped across time, reset the verniers, reflicked the main switch, glimpsed himself vague in the mists, and peered through them toward heaven: over and over, until abruptly he was *then*.

Twin gleams far above . . . He saw the one strike and go under, go down, while the other darted around until soon it ran away. Its rider had not seen him, where he lurked in the chill salt mists. His presence was not on any damned record.

He darted forward. Yet patience was upon him. He could cruise for a long piece of lifespan if need be, seeking the trice which would be his. The fear of death, even the knowing that she might be dead when he found her, were like half-remembered dreams. The elemental powers had taken him. He was a will that flew.

He hovered within a yard of the water. Gusts tried to cast him into its grip, as they had done to her. He was ready for them, danced free, returned to peer—returned through time as well as space, so that a score of him searched along the fall in that span of seconds when Feliz might be alive.

He paid his other selves no heed. They were merely stages he had gone through or must still go through.

THERE!

The dim dark shape tumbled past him, beneath the flood, on its way to destruction. He spun a control. A tractor beam locked onto the other machine. His reeled and went after it, unable to pull such a mass free of such a might.

The tide nearly had him when help came. Two vehicles, three, four, all straining together, they hauled Feliz's loose. She sagged horribly limp in her saddle harness. He didn't go to her at once. First he went back those few blinks in time, and back, and back, to be her rescuer and his own.

When finally they were alone among fogs and furies, she freed and in his arms, he would have burnt a hole through the sky to get ashore where he could care for her. But she stirred, her eyes blinked open, after a minute she smiled at him. Then he wept.

Beside them, the ocean roared onward.

The sunset to which Nomura had leaped ahead was not on anybody's record either. It turned the land golden. The falls must be afire with it. Their song resounded beneath the evening star.

Feliz propped pillows against headboard, sat straighter in the bed where she was resting, and told Everard: "If you lay charges against him, that he broke regulations or whatever male stupidity you are thinking of, I'll also quit your bloody Patrol."

"Oh, no." The big man lifted a palm as if to fend off attack. "Please. You misunderstand. I only meant to say, we're in a slightly awkward position."

"How?" Nomura demanded, from the chair in which he sat and held Feliz' hand. "I wasn't under any orders not to attempt this, was I? All right, agents are supposed to safeguard their own lives if possible, as being valuable to the corps. Well, doesn't it follow that the salvaging of a life is worthwhile too?"

"Yes. Sure." Everard paced the floor. It thudded beneath his boots, above the drumbeat of the flood. "Nobody quarrels with success, even in a much tighter organization than ours. In fact, Tom, the initiative you showed today makes your future prospects look good, believe me." A grin went lopsided around his pipe-stem. "As for an old soldier like myself, it'll be forgiven that I was too ready to give up." A flick of somberness: "I've seen so many lost beyond hope."

He stopped in his treading, confronted them both, and stated: "But we cannot have loose ends. The fact is, her unit does not list Feliz a Rach as returning, ever."

Their clasps tightened on each other.

Everard gave him and her a smile—haunted, nevertheless a smile—before he continued: "Don't get scared, though. Tom, earlier you wondered why we, we ordinary humans at least, don't keep closer track of our people. Now do you see the reason?

"Feliz a Rach never checked back into her original base. She may have visited her former home, of course, but we don't ask officially what agents do on their furloughs." He drew breath. "As for the rest of her career, if she should want to transfer to a different headquarters and adopt a different name, why, any officer of sufficient rank could approve that. Me, for example.

"We operate loose in the Patrol. We dare not do otherwise."

Nomura understood, and shivered.

Feliz recalled him to the ordinary world. "But who might I become?" she wondered.

He pounced on the cue. "Well," he said, half in laughter and half in thunder, "how about Mrs. Thomas Nomura?"

Windmill

—and though it was night, when land would surely be colder than sea, we had not looked for such a wind as sought to thrust us away from Calforni. Our craft shuddered and lurched. Wickerwork creaked in the gondola, rigging thrummed, the gasbag boomed, propeller noise mounted to a buzz saw whine. From my seat I glimpsed, by panel lights whose dimness was soon lost in shadows, how taut were the faces of Taupo and Wairoa where they battled to keep control, how sweat ran down their necks and bare chests and must be drenching their sarongs even in this chill.

Yet we moved on. Through the port beside me I saw ocean glimmer yield to gray and black, beneath high stars. A deeper dark, blotted far inland, must be the ruins of Losanglis. The few fires which twinkled there gave no comfort, for the squatters are known to be robbers and said to be cannibals. No Merican lord has ever tried to pacify that concrete wilderness; all who have claimed the territory have been content to cordon its dwellers off in their misery. I wonder if we Sea People should—

But I drift, do I not, Elena Kalakaua? Perhaps I write that which you have long been aware of. Forgive me. The world is so big and mysterious, civilization so thin a web across it, bound together by a few radio links and otherwise travel which is so slow, it's hard to be sure what any one person knows of it, even a best-beloved girl whose father is in Parliament. Let me drift, then. You have never been outside the happy islands of the Maurai Federation. I want to give you something of the feel, the reality, of this my last mission.

I was glad when meganecropolis fell aft out of sight and we neared the clean Muahvay. But then Captain Bowenu came to me. His hair glowed white in the gloom, yet he balanced himself with an ease learned during a youth spent in the topmasts of ships. "I'm afraid we must let you off sooner than planned," he told me. "This head wind's making the motors gulp power, and the closest recharging station is in S'Anton."

Actually it was northward, at Sannacruce. But we couldn't risk letting the Overboss there know of our presence—when that which I sought lay in country he said was his. The Meycan realm was safely distant and its Dons friendly.

One dare not let the accumulators of an aircraft get too low. For a mutinous moment I wished we could have come in a jet. But no, I understand well, such machines are too few, too precious, above all too prodigal of metal and energy; they must be reserved for the Air Force. I only tell you this passing mood of mine because it may help give you sympathy for my victims. Yes, my victims.

"Indeed, Rewi Bowenu," I said. "May I see the map?"

"Of course, Toma Nakamuha." Sitting down beside me, he spread a chart across our laps and pinpointed our location. "If you bear east-northeast, you should reach Hope before noon. Of course, your navigation can't be too accurate, with neither compass nor timepiece. But the terrain shouldn't throw you so far off course that you can't spy the windmills when they come over your horizon."

He left unspoken what would follow if he was wrong or I blundered. Buzzards, not gulls, would clean my bones, and they would whiten very far from our sea.

But the thought of those windmills and what they could mean nerved me with anger. Also, you know how Wiliamu Hamilitonu was my comrade from boyhood. Together we climbed after coconuts, prowled gillmasked among soft-colored corals and fanciful fish, scrambled up Mauna Loa to peer down its throat, shipped on a trimaran trader whose sails bore us around this whole glorious globe till we came back to Awaii and drank rum and made love to you and Lili beneath an Island moon. Wiliamu had gone before me, seeking to learn on behalf of us all what laired in the settlement that called itself Hope. He had not returned, and now I did not think he ever would.

That is why I volunteered, yes, pulled ropes for the task. The Service had other men available, some better qualified, maybe. But we are always so short of hands that I did not need to wrangle long. When will they see in Wellantoa how undermanned we are, in this work which matters more than any other?

I unbuckled, collected my gear, and went to hang on a strap by an exit hatch. The craft slanted sharply downward. Crosscurrents tore at us like an orca pack at a right whale. I hardly noticed, being busy in a last-minute review of myself.

Imagine me: tall for the Meycan I would claim to be, but not impossibly so, and you yourself have remarked on the accidents of genetics which have blent parts of my ancestry in a jutting Inio-like nose and coppery skin. Language and manners: In sailor days I was often in Meycan ports, and since joining the Service have had occasion to visit the hinterlands in company with natives. Besides, the deserts are a barrier between them and Calforni which is seldom crossed. My Spanyol and behavior ought to pass. Dress: shirt, trousers, uniform jacket, serape, sombrero, boots, all worn and dirty. Equipment: bedroll, canteen, thin pack of dried-out rations, knife, *spada* slung across back for possible machete work or self-defense. I hoped greatly I would not need it for that last. We learn the use of weapons, as well as advanced judo and karate arts, in training; nonetheless, the thought of opening up human flesh made a knot in my guts.

But what had been done to Wiliamu?

Maybe nothing. Maybe Hope was altogether innocent. We could not call in the armed forces unless we were certain. Even under the Law of Life, even under our covenant with the Overboss of Sannacruce, not even the mighty Maurai Federation can invade foreign territory like that without provoking a crisis. Not to speak of the hurt and slain, the resources and energy. We *must* be sure it was worth the cost— Now I do go astray, telling this to a politician's daughter who's spent as much time in N'Zealann as Awaii. I am too deeply back in my thoughts, as I clung there waiting.

"Level off!" Taupo sang from his seat forward. The ship struggled to a somewhat even keel. Evidently the altimeter said we were in rope's length of the ground.

Rewi, who had been beside me, squeezed my shoulder. "Tanaroa be with you, Toma," he murmured underneath the racket. He traced a cross. "Lesu Haristi deliver you from evil."

Wairoa laughed and called: "No need for deliverance from shark-toothed Nan! You'd never catch him in those dunes!" He must always have his joke. Yet his look at me was like a handclasp.

We opened the hatch and cast out a weighted line. When its windlass had stopped spinning. I threw a final glance around the cabin. I wouldn't see this gaiety of tapa and batik soon again, if ever. Supposing Hope proved harmless, I'd still have to make my own way, with mule train after mule train from trading post to trading post, to Sandago and our agents there. It would not do to reveal myself as a Maurai spy and ask to use Hope's transmitter to call for an airlift. That could make other people, elsewhere around the world, too suspicious of later strangers in their midst. (You realize, Elena, this letter is for none save you.)

"Farewell, shipmate," the men said together; and as I went out and down the rope, I heard them begin the Luck-Wishing Song.

The wind tore it from me. That was a tricky passage down, when the cord threshed like an eel and I didn't want to burn the hide off my palms. But at last I felt earth underfoot. I shook a signal wave up the rope, stepped back, and watched.

For a minute the long shape hung over me, a storm cloud full of propeller thunder. Then the line was gathered in and the craft rose. It vanished astonishingly fast.

I looked around. Deserts had never much appealed to me. But this one was different: natural, not man-made. Life had not died because water was gone, topsoil exhausted, poisons soaked into the ground. Here it had had all the geological time it needed to grow into a spare environment.

The night was as clear as I've ever seen, fantastic with stars, more stars than there was crystal blackness in between them, and the Milky Way a torrent. The land reached pale under heavenglow, speckled by silver-gray of scattered sagebrush and black weird outlines of joshua trees; I could see across its rises and arroyos to hills on the horizon, which stood blue. The wind was cold, flowing under my thin fluttering garments and around my flesh, but down here it did not shout, it murmured, and pungencies were borne upon it. From afar I heard coyotes yip. When I moved, the sandy soil crunched and gave a little beneath my feet, as alive in its own way as water.

I picked my guiding constellations out of the swarm overhead and started to walk.

Dawn was infinitely shadowed, in that vast wrinkled land. I saw a herd of wild sheep and rejoiced in the grandeur of their horns. The buzzard which took station high up in sapphire was no more terrible than my gulls, and no less beautiful. An intense green darkness against rockslopes red and tawny meant stands of piñon or juniper.

And it was April. My travels around western Meyco had taught me to know some of the wildflowers I came upon wherever shade and moisture were: bold ocotillo, honey-hued nolina plume, orchids clustered around a tiny spring. Most, shy beneath the sage and greasewood and creosote bush, I did not recognize by name. I've heard them called bellyflowers, because you have to get down on your belly to really see and love them. It amazed me how many they were, and how many kinds.

Lesser animals scuttered from me, lizards, snakes, mantises; dragonflies hovered over that mini-oasis on wings more splendid than an eagle's; I surprised a jackrabbit, which went lolloping off with a special sort of gracefulness. But a couple of antelope surprised me in turn, because I was watching a dogfight between a hawk and a raven while I strode. Suddenly I rounded a clump of chaparral and we found each other. The first antelope I'd ever met, they were delightful as dolphins and almost as fearless: because I was not wolf or grizzly or cougar; their kind had forgotten mine, which had not come slaughtering since the War of Judgment. At least, not until lately—

I discovered that I cared for the desert, not as a thing which the books said was integral to the whole regional ecology, but as a miracle.

Oh, it isn't our territory, Elena. We'll never want to live there.

Risen, the sun hammered on my temples and speared my eyeballs, the air seethed me till my mouth was gummed, sand crept into my boots to chew my feet and the jumping cholla lived up to its name, fang-sharp burrs coming at me from nowhere. Give me Mother Ocean and her islands. But I think one day I'll return for a long visit. And . . . if Wiliamu had lost his way or perished in a sandstorm or otherwise come to natural grief in these reaches, as the Hope folk said he must have done . . . was that a worse death than on the reefs or down into the deeps?

—Rewi Bowenu had been optimistic. The time was midafternoon and the land become a furnace before I glimpsed the windmills. Their tall iron skeletons wavered through heat-shimmer. Nonetheless I felt a chill. Seven of them were much too many.

Hope was a thousand or so adults and their children. It was white-washed, red-tiled adobes centered on a flagged plaza where a fountain played: no extravagance in this dominion of dryness, for vision has its own thirst, which that bright leaping slaked. (Flower beds as well as vegetable gardens surrounded most houses, too.) It was irrigation ditches fanning outward to turn several square kilometers vivid with crops and orchards.

And it was the windmills.

They stood on a long hill behind the town, to catch every shift of air. Huge they were. I could but guess at the man-years of toil which had gone into shaping them, probably from ancient railway tracks or bridge girders hauled across burning emptiness, reforged by the muscles of men who themselves could not be bent. Ugly they were, and in full swing they filled my ears with harsh creakings and groanings. But beauty and quietness would come, I was told. This community had been founded a decade and a half ago. The first several years had gone for barebones survival. Only of late could people begin to take a little ease, think beyond time's immediate horizon.

Behind the hill, invisible from the town, stood a large shedlike building. From it, handmade ceramic pipes, obviously joined to the mill system, led over the ridge to a great brick tank, just below the top on this side. From that tank in turn, sluices fed the canals, the dwellings and workshops, and—via a penstock—a small structure at the foot of the hill which Danil Smit said contained a hydroelectric generator. (Some days afterward, I was shown that machine. It was pre-Judgment. The labor of dragging it here from its ancient site and reconstructing it must have broken hearts.)

He simply explained at our first encounter: "The mills raise water from the spring, you see, it bein' too low for proper irrigation. On the way down again, the flow powers that dynamo, which charges portable accumulators people bring there. This way we get a steady supply of electricity, not big, but enough for lights an' such." (Those modern Everlast fluorescents were almost shockingly conspicuous in homes where almost everything else was as primitive as any woods-runner's property.)

"Why do you not use solar screens?" I asked. "Your power supply would be limited only by the number of square meters you could cover with them."

My pronunciation of their dialect of Ingliss passed quite easily for a Spanyol accent. As for vocabulary, well, from the start I hadn't pretended to be an ordinary wandering worker. I was Miwel Arruba y Gonsals, of a *rico* family in Tamico, fallen on ill days when our estates were plundered during the Watemalan War. Trying to mend my fortunes, I enlisted with a mercenary company. We soldiered back and forth across the troubled lands, Tekkas, Zona, Vada, Ba-Calforni, till the disaster at Montrey, of which the *señores* had doubtless heard, from which I counted myself lucky to escape alive. . . .

Teeth gleamed in Smit's beard. "Ha! Usin' what for money to buy 'em? Remember, we had to start here with no more'n we could bring in oxcarts. Everything you see around you was dug, forged, sawed an' dovetailed together, fire-baked, planted, plowed, cultivated, harvested, threshed, with these."

He held out his hands, and they were like the piñon boles, strong, hard, but unmercifully gnarled. I watched his eyes more, though. In that shaggy, craggy face they smoldered with a prophet's vision.

Yet the mayor of Hope was no backwoods fanatic. Indeed, he professed indifference to rite and creed. "Oktai an' his fellow gods are a bunch of Asians, an' Calforni threw out the Mong long ago," he remarked once to me. "As for Tanaroa, Lesu Haristi, an' that lot, well, the sophisticated thing nowadays in Sannacruce is to go to their church, seein' as how the Sea People do. No disrespect to anybody's faith, understand. I know you Meycans also worship—uh—Esu Carito, is that what you call him? But me, my trust is in physics, chemistry, genetics, an' a well-trained militia." For he had been a prosperous engineer in the capital, before he led the migration hither.

I would have liked to discuss philosophy with him and, still more, applied science. It's so hard to learn how much knowledge of what kind has survived, even in the upper classes of a realm with which we have as regular intercourse as we do with Sannacruce.

Do you fully realize that? Many don't. I didn't, till the Service academy and Service experience had educated me. You can't help my sorrow unless you know its source. Let me therefore spell out what we both were taught as children, in order then to point out how oversimplified it is.

The War of Judgment wiped out a number of cities, true; but most simply died on the vine, in the famines, plagues, and worldwide political collapse which followed; and the reason for the chaos was less direct destruction than it was the inability of a resources-impoverished planet to support a gross overpopulation when the industrial machinery faltered for just a few years. (The more I see and ponder, the more I believe those thinkers are right who say that crowding, sensory deprivation, loss of all touch with a living world in which mankind evolved as one animal among millions—that that very unnaturalness brought on the mass lunacy which led to thermonuclear war. If this be true, my work is sacred. Help me never to believe, Elena, that any of the holiness has entered my own self.)

Well, most of the books, records, even technical apparatus remained, being too abundant for utter destruction. Thus, during the dark centuries, barbarians might burn whole libraries to keep alive through a winter; but elsewhere, men preserved copies of the same works, and the knowledge of how to read them. When a measure of stability returned, in a few of the least hard-hit regions, it was not ignorance which kept people from rebuilding the old high-energy culture.

It was lack of resources. The ancestors used up the rich deposits of fuel and minerals. Then they had the means to go on to exploit leaner substances. But once their industrial plant had stopped long enough to fall into decay, it was impossible to reconstruct. This was the more true because nearly all human effort must go into merely keeping half-alive, in a world whose soil, water, forests and wildlife had been squandered.

If anything, we are more scientific nowadays, we are more ingenious engineers, than ever men were before—we islands of civilization in the barbarian swamp which slowly, slowly we try to reclaim—but we must make do with what we have, which is mostly what the sun and living things can give us. The amount of that is measured by the degree to which we have nursed Earth's entire biosphere back toward health.

Thus the text we offer children. And it is true, of course. It's just not the whole truth.

You see—this is the point I strive to make, Elena, this is why I started by repeating the tricky obvious—our machinations are only one small force in a typhoon of forces. Traveling, formerly as a sailor, now as an agent of the Ecological Service, I have had borne in upon me how immense the world is, how various and mysterious. We look through Maurai eyes. How well do those see into the soul of the Calfornian, Meycan, Orgonian, Stralian . . . of folk they often meet . . . and what have they glimpsed of the depths of Sudamerca, Africa, Eurasia? We may be the only great power; but we are, perhaps, ten million among, perhaps, twenty times our number; and the rest are strangers to us, they were blown on different winds during the dark centuries, today they begin to set their own courses and these are not ours.

Maurai crewmen may carouse along the waterfront of Sannacruce. Maurai captains may be invited to dine at the homes of merchants, Maurai admirals with the Overboss himself. But what do we know of what goes on behind the inner walls, or behind the faces we confront?

Why, a bare three years ago we heard a rumor that an emigrant colony was flourishing in the Muahvay fringe. Only one year ago did we get around to verifying this from the air, and seeing too many windmills, and sending Wiliamu Hamilitonu to investigate and die.

Well. I would, as I said, have liked to talk at length with this intelligent and enigmatic man, Mayor Danil Smit. But my role as a *cab'llero* forbade. Let my tale go on.

They had received me with kindness in the settlement. Eager curiosity was there too, of course. Their communal radio could pick up broadcasts from Sannacruce city; but they had turned their backs on Sannacruce, and anyhow, it's not what we would call a thriving cultural center. Periodic trips to trading posts maintained by the Sandagoan Mercanteers, albeit the caravans brought books and journals back among the supplies, gave no real satisfaction to their news-hunger. Besides, having little to barter with and many shortages of necessities, they could not afford much printed matter.

Yet they seemed, on the whole, a happy folk.

Briun Smit, son of Danil, and his wife Jeana gave me lodging. I shared the room of their five living children, but that was all right, those were good, bright youngsters; it was only that I was hard put to invent enough adventures of Lieutenant Arruba for them, when we lay together on rustling cornshuck pallets and they whispered and giggled in the dark before sleep or the dawn before work.

Briun was taller, leaner and blonder than his father, and seemingly less fervent. He cultivated hardly any land, preferring to serve the community as a ranger. This was many things: to ride patrol across the desert against possible bandits, to guard the caravans likewise when they traveled, to prospect for minerals, to hunt bighorn, antelope and mustang for meat. Besides crossbow and blowgun, he was deadly expert with ax, recurved hornbow, sling, lasso and bolas. The sun had leathered him still more deeply than his neighbors and carved crow's-feet around his eyes. His clothes were the general dull color—scant dyestuff was being made thus far—but flamboyant in cut and drape and in the cockade he bore on his curve-brimmed hat.

"Sure, Don Miwel, you just stay with me long's you've a mind to," he said out of the crowd which gathered when I made my dusty way into town.

"I fear I lack the skill to help you at farming, sir," I answered quite truthfully. "But perhaps I have some at carpentry, ropework and the like," which every sailor must and a landed aristocrat might.

Jeana was soon as delighted by what I could do as by what I could tell. It pleased me to please her—for instance, by making a bamboo-tube sprinkler grid for her garden, or a Hilsch arrangement out of sheet metal not immediately needed elsewhere, that really cooled the house whenever the frequent winds blew, or by telling her that Maurai scientists had developed insects and germs to prey on specific plant pests and how to order these through the Mercanteers. She was a small woman, but beautifully shaped beneath the drab gown, of elfin features and vivid manner and a fair complexion not yet bleached by the badlands.

"You have a lovely wife, *señor,* if I may so," I remarked to Briun, the second evening at his home. We sat on the verandah, taking our ease after the day's jobs. Our feet were on the rail, we had pipes in our right hands and mugs of cider in our left, which she had fetched us. Before us stood only a couple of other houses, this one being on the edge of town; beyond gleamed the canals, palm trees swaying along their banks, the first shoots of grain an infinitely delicate green, until far, far out, on the edge of sight, began the umber of untouched desert. Long light-beams cast shadows from the west and turned purple the eastern hills. It was blowing, coolness borne out of lands already nighted, and I heard the iron song .he unseen windmills.

"Thanks," the ranger said to me. He grinned. "I think the same." He took a drink and a puff before adding, slowly now and soberly: "She's a reason we're here."

"Really?" I leaned forward.

"You'd learn the story regardless. Might as well tell you right off, myself." Briun scowled. "Her father was a forester o' rank in Sannacruce. But that didn't help much when the Overboss' eye lit on her, an' she fourteen. He liked—likes 'em young, the swine. When she refused presents, he started pressurin' her parents. They held out, but everybody knew it couldn't be for long. If nothin' else, some night a gang o' bully boys would break in an' carry her off. Next mornin', done bein' done, her parents might as well accept his bribes, hopin' when he was tired of her he'd find a poor man who'd take another gift to marry her. We'd seen cases."

"Terrible," I said. And it is. Among them, it's more than an angering, perhaps frightening episode of coercion; they set such store by virginity that the victim is apt to be soul-scarred for life. My question which followed was less honest, since I already knew the answer: "Why do the citizens tolerate that kind of ruler?"

"He has the men-at-arms," Briun sighed. "An', o' course, he don't directly offend a very big percentage. Most people like bein' secure from pirates or invaders, which the bastard does give 'em. Finally, he's hand in glove with the Sea People. Long's they support him, or at least don't oppose an' boycott him, he's got the metal to hire those soldiers." He shook his head. "I can't see why they do. I really can't. The Maurai claim to be decent folk."

"I have heard," I said cautiously, "he follows their advice about things like reforestation, soil care, bio-control, wildlife management, fisheries."

"But not about human bein's!"

"Perhaps not, Mister Briun. I do not know. I do know this,

however. The ancestors stripped the planet nearly to its bones. Unless and until we put flesh back, no human beings anywhere will be safe from ruin. In truth, my friend, we cannot maintain what technology we have except on a biological basis. For example, when almost everything has to be made from wood, we must keep the forests in equilibrium with the lumberers. Or, since the oil is gone, or nearly gone, we depend greatly on microbial fuel cells . . . and the fuels they consume are by-products of life, so we require abundant life. If the oil did come back—if we made some huge strike again, by some miracle—we would still not dare burn much. The ancestors found what happens when you poison the environment."

He gave me a sharp look. I realized I had stepped out of character. In haste, I laughed and said: "I have had more than one Maurai agent lecture me, in old days on our estate, you see. Now tell me, what happened in Sannacruce?"

"Well—" He relaxed, I hoped. "The discontent had been growin' for quite a while anyway, you understand. Not just Overboss Charl; the whole basic policy, which won't change while the Sea People keep their influence. We're becomin' too many to live well, when not enough fallow land or fishin' ground is bein' opened for use."

I refrained from remarks about birth control, having learned that what seems only natural to a folk who spend their lives on shipboard and on islands, comes slowly indeed to those who imagine they have a continent at their free disposal. Until they learn, they will die back again and again; we can but try to keep them from ravaging too much nature in the meantime. Thus the doctrine. But, Elena, can you picture how hard it is to apply that doctrine to living individuals, to Briun and Jeana, eager hobbledehoy Rodj and little, trusting Dorthy?

"There'd been some explorin'," he continued after another sip and another pungent blue smoke-plume trailed forth into the evening. "The good country's all taken where it isn't reserved. But old books told how desert had been made to bloom, in places like Zona. Maybe a possibility closer to home? Well, turned out true. Here, in the Muahvay, a natural wellspring, ample water if it was channeled. Dunno how the ancestors missed it. My father thinks it didn't exist back then; an earthquake split the strata, sometime durin' the dark centuries, an' opened a passage to a bigger water table than had been suspected before.

"Anyhow, Jeana's case was sort of a last straw. Her dad an' mine led a few pioneers off, on a pretext. They did the basic work of enclosin' the spring, diggin' the first short canal, erectin' the first windmill an' makin' an' layin' the first pipelines. They hired nomad Inios to help, but nevertheless I don't see how they did it, an' in fact several died o' strain.

"When the rest came back, families quietly sold out, swappin' for wagons, tools, gene-tailored seed an' such. The Overboss was took by surprise. If he'd tried to forbid the migration, he'd've had a civil war on his hands. He still claims us, but we don't pay him any tax or any mind. If ever we link up to anybody else, I reckon it'll be Sandago. But we'd rather stay independent, an' I think we can. This territory will support a big population once it's developed."

"A heroic undertaking," I said low.

"Well, a lot died in the second group, too, and a lot are half crippled from overwork in those early days, but we made it." His knuckles stood forth around the handle of his mug, as if it were a weapon. "We're self-supportin' now, an' our surplus to trade grows larger every year. We're free!"

"I admire what you have done, also as a piece of engineering," I said. "Perhaps you have ideas here we could use when at last I go home again. Or perhaps I could suggest something to you?"

"Um." He sucked on his pipe and frowned, abruptly uncomfortable.

"I would like to see your whole hydraulic system," I said; and my heart knocked within me. "Tomorrow can you introduce me to the man in charge, and I go look at the water source and the windmills?"

"No!" He sprang from his chair. For a moment he loomed over me, and I wondered if he'd drop his pipe and snatch the knife at his belt. Shadows were thickening and I couldn't make out his face too well, but eyes and teeth stood aglisten.

After a long few seconds he eased. His laugh was shaky as he sat down. "Sorry, Don Miwel." He was not a skilled liar. "But we've had that kind o' trouble before, which is why I, uh, overreacted." He sought solace in tobacco. "I'm afraid Windmill Ridge is off limits to everybody except the staff an' the mayor; likewise the springhouse. You see, uh, we've got just the one source, big though it is, an' we're afraid o' pollution or damage or—All right, in these lands water's worth more than blood. We can't risk any spy for a possible invader seein' how our defenses are arranged. No insult meant. You understand, don't you, guest-friend?''

Sick with sorrow, I did.

Still, the Service would require absolute proof. It seemed wise to bide my time, quietly study the layout for a few weeks, observe routines, gather bits and pieces of information, while the dwellers in Hope came fully to accept Miwel Arruba.

The trouble was, I in my turn came to accept them.

When Briun's boy Rodj told me about their winter visitor, his excitement glowed. "Clear from Awaii, he was, Miwel! A geologist, studyin' this country; an' the stories he could tell!" Quickly: ''Not full of action like yours. But he's been clear around the world.''

Wiliamu hadn't expected he would need a very thick cover.

Not wanting to prompt Briun's suspicion, I asked further of Jeana, one day when he was out and the children napping or at school. It bespoke a certain innocence that, despite the restrictive sexual customs, none looked askance at my hostess and me for the many hours we spent alone together. I confess it was hard for me to keep restraint—not only this long celibacy, but herself, sweet, spirited and bright, as kindled by my newness as her own children.

I'd finished the sprinkler layout and hooked it to the cistern on the flat roof. ''See,'' I said proudly, and turned the wooden spigot. Water danced over the furrows she hoed alone. ''No more lugging a heavy can around.''

''Oh, Miwel!'' She clapped small work-bitten hands. ''I don't know how to— This calls for a celebration. We'll throw a party come Saddiday. But right now—'' She caught my arm. ''Come inside. I'm bakin'.'' The rich odors had already told me that. ''You get the heels off the first loaf out o' the oven.''

There was tea as well, rare and costly when it must be hauled from Sina, or around the Horn from Florda. We sat on opposite sides of a plank table, in the kitchen dimness and warmth, and smiled at each other. Sweat made tiny beads on her brow; the thin dress clung. ''I wish I could offer you lemonade,'' she said. ''This is lemonade weather. My mother used to make it, back home. She died in Sandstorm Year an' never—Well.'' A forlorn cheerfulness: ''Lemonade demands ice, which we haven't yet.''

"You will?"

"Father Danil says prob'ly nex' year we—Hope'll have means to buy a couple o' fridges, an' the power plant'll be expanded enough so we can afford to run them."

"Will you build more windmills for that?" A tingle went through me. I struggled to be casual. "Seems you already have plenty for more than your fluorolights."

Her glance was wholly frank and calm. "We have to pump a lot o' water. It don't gush from a mountainside, remember, it bubbles from low ground."

I hated to risk spoiling her happiness, but duty made me press in: "A Maurai geologist visited here not long before, I have heard. Could he not have given you good advice?"

"I . . . I don't know. That's man talk. Anyway, you heard how we can't let most of ourselves in there—I've never been—let alone strangers, even nice ones like you."

"He would have been curious, though. Where did he go on to? Maybe I can find him later."

"I don't know. He left sudden-like, him an' his two Inic guides. One mornin' they were gone, nary a word o' good-by except, naturally, to the mayor. I reckon he got impatient."

Half of me wanted to shout at her: *When our "Geological Institute" radioed inquiries about its man, your precious village elders gave us the same answer, that he'd departed, that if he failed to arrive elsewhere he must have met with some misfortune on the way. But that wouldn't happen! Would it? An experienced traveler, two good natives at his side, well supplied, no rumor of bandits in this region for years past. . . . Have you thought about that, Jeana? Have you dared think about it?*

But the rest of me held my body still. "More tea?" she asked.

I am not a detective. Folk less guileless would have frozen at my questions. I did avoid putting them in the presence of fierce old Danil Smit, and others who had spent adult years in the competition and intrigues of Sannacruce city. As for the rest, however . . . they invited me to dinner, we drank and yarned, we shared songs beneath that unutterably starry sky, several times we rode forth to see a spectacular canyon or simply for the joy of riding. . . . It was no trick to niggle information out of them.

For example, I wondered aloud if they might be over-hunting the range. Under the Law of Life, it could be required that a qualified game warden be established among them, directly responsible to the International Conservation Tribunal. Briun bristled a moment, then pointed out correctly that man always upsets nature's balance when he enters a land, and that what counts is to strike a new balance. Hope was willing to keep a trained wildlife manager around; but let him be a local person, albeit educated abroad, somebody who knew local conditions. (And would keep local secrets.)

In like manner, affable men assigned to duty on Windmill Ridge told me their schedules, one by one, as I inquired when they would be free for sociability. My work for the younger Smit household had excited a great deal of enthusiasm; in explaining it, I could slip in questions about their own admirable hydraulic system. Mere details about rate of flow, equipment ordered or built, equipment hoped for—mere jigsaw fragments.

Presently I had all but the final confirmation. My eyewitness account would be needed to call in the troops. What I had gained hitherto justified the hazard in entering the forbidden place.

A caravan was being organized for Barstu trading post. I could accompany it, and thence make my way to Sandago. And that, I trusted, I feared, would be my last sight of these unbreakable people whom I had come to love.

The important thing was that no sentry was posted after dark. The likelihood of trouble was small, the need of sleep and of strength for next day's labor was large.

I slipped from among the children. Once I stepped on a pallet in the dark, the coarseness crackled beneath my bare foot, Dorthy whimpered in her blindness and I stiffened. But she quieted. The night was altogether deserted as I padded through the memorized house, out beneath stars and a bitter-bright gibbous moon. It was cold and breezy; I heard the windmills. Afar yelped coyotes. (There were no dogs. They hadn't yet any real need for them. But soon would come the cattle and sheep, not just a few kept at home but entire herds. Then farewell, proud bighorn and soaring antelope.) The streets were gritty. I kept out of the gray-white light, stayed in the shadows of gray-white houses. Beyond the village, rocks barked my toes, sagebrush snatched at my ankles, while I trotted around to the other side of the Ridge.

There stood the low, wide adobe structure which, I was told, covered the upwelling water, to minimize loss by evaporation and downfall of alkaline dust into it. From there, I was told, it was lifted by the mills into the brick basin, from which it went to its work. Beyond the springhouse the land rolled upward, dim and empty of man. But I could make out much else, sage, joshua trees, an owl ghosting by.

My knife had electromagnetic devices built into its handle. I scarcely needed it to get in, save for not wanting to leave signs of breakage. The padlock on the door was as flimsy as the walls proved to be thin. Pioneers in a stern domain had had nothing to spare for more than the most pathetic of frauds.

I entered, closed the door behind me, flashed light from that gem-pommel on my knife, which was actually a lens. The air was cold in here, too. I saw moisture condensed on pipes which plunged into the clay floor and up through the roof, and somehow smelled it. Otherwise, in an enormous gloom, I barely glimpsed workbenches, toolracks, primitive machinery. I could not now hear the turning sails of the windmills which drove the pumps; but the noise of pistons in crudely fashioned tallow-lubricated cylinders was like bones sliding across each other.

There was no spring. I hadn't expected any.

A beam stabbed at me. I doused my own, reversed it to make a weapon, recoiled into murk. From behind the glare which sought about, a deep remembered voice said, more weary than victorious: "Never mind, Miwel or whoever you are, I know you haven't got a gun. I do. The town's firearm. Buckshot loaded."

Crouched among bulky things and my pulsebeats, I called back: "It will do you less than good to kill me, Danil Smit"—and shifted my position fast. The knife was keen in my hand, my thumb braced easily against the guard. I was young, in top shape, trained; I could probably take him in the dark. I didn't want to. Lesu Haristi knows how I didn't want to, and knows it was not merely for fear of having to flee ill prepared into the desert.

He sighed, like the night wind beyond these walls. "You're a Maurai spy, aren't you?"

"An agent of the Ecological Service," I answered, keeping moving. "We've treaty arrangements with the Overboss. I agree he's a rat in some ways, but he co-operates in saving his land for his great-grandchildren . . . and yours."

"We weren't sure, me an' my partners," Danit Smit said. "We figured we'd take turns watchin' here till you left. You might've been honest."

"Unlike you—you murderers." But somehow I could not put anger into that word, not even for Wiliamu my shipmate and his two nameless guides.

"I s'pose you've got backup?" he called.

"Yes, of course," I said. "Losing our first man was plenty to make us suspicious. Losing the second . . . imagine." Leap, leap went my crouch-bent legs. I prayed the noise of the pumping masked my foot-thuds from him. "It's clear what your aim is, to grow in obscurity till you're so large and strong you can defy everybody—the Federation itself—from behind your barrier of desert distances. But don't you see," I panted, "my superiors have already guessed this? And they don't propose to let the menace get that big!"

You know I exaggerated. Manpower and equipment is spread so thin, close to the breaking point. It might well be decided that there are more urgent matters than one rebellious little community. Wiliamu and I might be written off. Sweat stood chill upon me. So many seas unsailed, lands unwalked, girls unloved, risings of Orion and the Cross unseen!

"You haven't realized how determined we are," I told him. "The Law of Life isn't rhetoric, Danil Smit. It's survival."

"What about our survival?" he groaned.

"Listen," I said, "if I come out into view, can we talk before Tanaroa?"

"Huh? . . . Oh." He stood a while, and in that moment I knew what it is to be of a race who were once great and are no longer. Well, in their day *they* were the everywhere-thrusting aliens; and if they devoured the resources which were the very basis of their power, what could they expect but that Earth's new masters would come from the poor and forgotten who had had less chance to do likewise? Nevertheless, that was long ago, it was dead. Reality was Danil Smit, humbled into saying, "Yes," there in the dark of the shed, he who had seen no other way than murder to preserve his people's freedom.

I switched my own flash back on and set it down by his on a bench, to let light reflect off half-seen shapes and pick his beard and hands and pleading eyes out of the rattling, gurgling murk. I said to him, fast, because I did not like saying it:

"We suspected you weren't using a natural outflow. After centuries, the overnight discovery of such a thing would have been strange. No, what you found was a water table, and you're pumping it dry, in this land of little rain, and that breaks the Law of Life."

He stood before me, in the last rags of his patriarchy, and cried: "But why? All right, all right, eventually we'll've exhausted it. But that could be two-three hundred years from now! Don't you see, we could use that time for livin'?"

"And afterward?" I challenged, since I must keep reminding myself that my cause is right, and must make him believe that my government is truly fanatical on this subject. (He would not have met enough of our easy-going islanders to realize crusades are impossible to us—that, at most, a tiny minority of devotees strive to head off disaster at the outset, before the momentum of it has become too huge.) My life might hang upon it. The shotgun dangled yet in his grasp. He had a good chance of blasting me before I could do more than wound him.

I went on: "Afterward! Think. Instead of what life we have today, to enlarge human knowledge and, yes, the human spirit . . . instead of that, first a sameness of crops and cattle, then a swarm of two-legged ants, then barrenness. We must resist this wherever it appears. Otherwise, in the end—if we can't, as a whole species, redeem ourselves—will be an Earth given back to the algae, or an Earth as bare as the moon."

"Meanwhile, though," he said desperately, "we'd build aqueducts . . . desalinization plants . . . fusion power—"

I did not speak of rumors I have heard that controlled fusion has in fact been achieved, and been suppressed. Besides its being an Admiralty secret, if true, I had no heart to explain to the crumbling old man that Earth cannot live through a second age of energy outpouring and waste. One remote day, folk may come to know in their blood that the universe was not made for them alone; then they can safely be given the power to go to the stars. But not in our lifetimes.

Not in the lifetime that Wiliamu my comrade might have had.

I closed my teeth on the words: "The fact is, Danil Smit, this community was founded on the exhaustion of ground water vital to an entire ecology. That was a flat violation of the Law and of international convenants. To maintain it, you and your co-conspirators resorted to murder. I'll presume most of the dwellers in Hope are innocent—most believe there is a natural spring here—but where are the bodies of our men? Did you at least have the decency to give them back to the earth?"

The soul went out of him. Hope's founding father crept into my arms and wept.

I stroked his hair and whispered, "It could be worse, it could be worse, I'll work for you, don't give up," while my tears and his ran together.

After all, I will remind my admirals, we have islands to reclaim, stoninesses in the middle of a living ocean.

Give the pioneers topsoil and seeds, give them rainwater cisterns and solar stills, teach them palm and breadfruit culture and the proper ranching of the sea. Man does not have to be always the deathmaker. I know my proposal is a radical break with tradition. But it would be well—it would be a most hopeful precedent—if these, who are not of our kind, could be made into some of our strongest lifebringers. Remember, we have an entire worldful of people, unimaginably diverse, to educate thus, if we can. We must begin somewhere.

I swore I would strive to the utmost to have this accepted. I actually dared say I thought our government could be persuaded to pardon Danil Smit and his few associates in the plot. But if an example must be made, they are ready to hang, begging only that those they have loved be granted exile instead of a return to the tyrant.

Elena, speak to your father. Speak to your friends in Parliament. Get them to help us.

But do not tell them this one last thing that happened. Only think upon it at night, as I do, until I come home again.

We trod forth when dawn was whitening the east, Danil Smit and I. Stars held out in a westward darkness, above the dunes and eldritch trees. But those were remote, driven away by fields and canals carved from the tender desert. And a mordant wind made the mills on the ridge overhead creak and clang and roar as they sucked at the planet.

He raised a hand toward them. His smile was weary and terrible. "You've won this round, Nakamuha, you an' your damned nature worshipers," he said. "My children an' children's children 'ull fit into your schemes, because you're powerful. But you won't be forever. What then, Nakamuha? What then?"

I looked up to the whirling skeletons, and suddenly the cold struck deep into me.

Call Me
Joe

The wind came whooping out of eastern darkness, driving a lash of ammonia dust before it. In minutes, Edward Anglesey was blinded.

He clawed all four feet into the broken shards which were soil, hunched down and groped for his little smelter. The wind was an idiot bassoon in his skull. Something whipped across his back, drawing blood, a tree yanked up by the roots and spat a hundred miles. Lightning cracked, immensely far overhead where clouds boiled with night.

As if to reply, thunder toned in the ice mountains and a red gout of flame jumped and a hillside came booming down, spilling itself across the valley. The earth shivered.

Sodium explosion, thought Anglesey in the drumbeat noise. The fire and the lightning gave him enough illumination to find his apparatus. He picked up tools in muscular hands, his tail gripped the trough, and he battered his way to the tunnel and thus to his dugout.

It had walls and roof of water, frozen by sun-remoteness and compressed by tons of atmosphere jammed onto every square inch. Ventilated by a tiny smoke hole, a lamp of tree oil burning in hydrogen made a dull light for the single room.

Anglesey sprawled his slate-blue form on the floor, panting. It was no use to swear at the storm. These ammonia gales often came at sunset, and there was nothing to do but wait them out. He was tired, anyway.

It would be morning in five hours or so. He had hoped to cast an axhead, his first, this evening, but maybe it was better to do the job by daylight.

He pulled a dekapod body off a shelf and ate the meat raw, pausing for long gulps of liquid methane from a jug. Things would improve once he had proper tools; so far, everything had been painfully grubbed and hacked to shape with teeth, claws, chance icicles, and what detestably weak and crumbling fragments remained of the spaceship. Give him a few years and he'd be living as a man should.

He sighed, stretched, and lay down to sleep.

Somewhat more than one hundred and twelve thousand miles away, Edward Anglesey took off his helmet.

He looked around, blinking. After the Jovian surface, it was always a little unreal to find himself here again, in the clean, quiet orderliness of the control room.

His muscles ached. They shouldn't. He had not really been fighting a gale of several hundred miles an hour, under three gravities and a temperature of 140 absolute. He had been here, in the almost nonexistent pull of Jupiter V, breathing oxynitrogen. It was Joe who lived down there and filled his lungs with hydrogen and helium at a pressure which could still only be estimated, because it broke aneroids and deranged piezoelectrics.

Nevertheless, his body felt worn and beaten. Tension, no doubt—psychosomatics. After all, for a good many hours now he had, in a sense, been Joe, and Joe had been working hard.

With the helmet off, Anglesey held only a thread of identification. The esprojector was still tuned to Joe's brain but no longer focused on his own. Somewhere in the back of his mind, he knew an indescribable feeling of sleep. Now and then, vague forms or colors drifted in the soft black—dreams? Not impossible that Joe's brain should dream a little when Anglesey's mind wasn't using it.

A light flickered red on the esprojector panel, and a bell whined electronic fear. Anglesey cursed. Thin fingers danced over the controls of his chair, he slewed around and shot across to the bank of dials. Yes, there—K tube oscillating again! The circuit blew out. He wrenched the face plate off with one hand and fumbled in a drawer with the other.

Inside his mind, he could feel the contact with Joe fading. If he once lost it entirely, he wasn't sure he could regain it. And Joe was an investment of several million dollars and quite a few highly skilled man-years.

Anglesey pulled the offending K tube from its socket and threw it on the floor. Glass exploded. It eased his temper a bit, just enough so he could find a replacement, plug it in, switch on the current again. As the machine warmed up, once again amplifying, the Joeness in the back alleys of his brain strengthened.

Slowly, then, the man in the electric wheel chair rolled out of the room, into the hall. Let somebody else sweep up the broken tube. To hell with it. To hell with everybody.

Jan Cornelius had never been farther from Earth than some comfortable Lunar resort. He felt much put upon that the Psionics Corporation should tap him for a thirteen-month exile. The fact that he knew as much about esprojectors and their cranky innards as any other man alive was no excuse. Why send anyone at all? Who cared?

Obviously the Federation Science Authority did. It had seemingly given those bearded hermits a blank check on the taxpayer's account.

Thus did Cornelius grumble to himself, all the long hyperbolic path to Jupiter. Then the shifting accelerations of approach to its tiny inner satellite left him too wretched for further complaint. And when he finally, just prior to disembarkation, went up to the greenhouse for a look at Jupiter, he said not a word. Nobody does, the first time.

Arne Viken waited patiently while Cornelius stared. *It still gets me too,* he remembered. *By the throat. Sometimes I'm afraid to look.*

At length Cornelius turned around. He had a faintly Jovian appearance himself, being a large man with an imposing girth. "I had no idea," he whispered. "I never thought . . . I had seen pictures, but . . ."

Viken nodded. "Sure, Dr. Cornelius. Pictures don't convey it."

Where they stood, they could see the dark broken rock of the satellite, jumbled for a short way beyond the landing slip and then chopped off sheer. This moon was scarcely even a platform, it seemed, and cold constellations went streaming past it, around it. Jupiter lay across a fifth of that sky, softly ambrous, banded with colors, spotted with the shadows of planet-sized moons and with whirlwinds as broad as Earth. If there had been any gravity to speak of, Cornelius would have thought, instinctively, that the great planet was falling on him. As it was, he felt as if sucked upward, his hands were still sore where he had grabbed a rail to hold on.

"You live here . . . all alone . . . with this?" He spoke feebly.

"Oh, well, there are some fifty of us all told, pretty congenial," said Viken. "It's not so bad. You sign up for four-cycle hitches—four ship arrivals—and believe it or not, Dr. Cornelius, this is my third enlistment."

The newcomer forbore to inquire more deeply. There was something not quite understandable about the men on Jupiter V. They were mostly bearded, though otherwise careful to remain neat; their low-gravity movements were somehow dreamlike to watch; they hoarded their conversation, as if to stretch it through the year and a month between ships. Their monkish existence had changed them—or did they take what amounted to vows of poverty, chastity, and obedience because they had never felt quite at home on green Earth?

Thirteen months! Cornelius shuddered. It was going to be a long, cold wait, and the pay and bonuses accumulating for him were scant comfort now, four hundred and eighty million miles from the sun.

"Wonderful place to do research," continued Viken. "All the facilities, hand-picked colleagues, no distractions—and, of course . . ." He jerked his thumb at the planet and turned to leave.

Cornelius followed, wallowing awkwardly. "It is very interesting, no doubt," he puffed. "Fascinating. But really, Dr. Viken, to drag me way out here and make me spend a year-plus waiting for the next ship—to do a job which may take me a few weeks . . .'

"Are you sure it's that simple?" asked Viken gently. His face swiveled around, and there was something in his eyes that silenced Cornelius. "After all my time here, I've yet to see any problem however complicated, which when you looked at it the right way didn't become still more complicated."

They went through the ship's air lock and the tube joining it to the station entrance. Nearly everything was underground. Rooms, laboratories, even halls, had a degree of luxuriousness—why, there was a fireplace with a real fire in the common room. God alone knew what *that* cost! Thinking of the huge chill emptiness where the king planet laired, and of his own year's sentence, Cornelius decided that such luxuries were, in truth, biological necessities.

Viken showed him to a pleasantly furnished chamber which would be his own. "We'll fetch your luggage soon, and unload your psionic stuff. Right now, everybody's either talking to the ship's crew or reading his mail."

Cornelius nodded absently and sat down. The chair, like all low-gee furniture, was a mere spidery skeleton, but it held his bulk comfortably enough. He felt in his tunic, hoping to bribe the other man into keeping him company for a while. "Cigar? I brought some from Amsterdam."

"Thanks." Viken accepted with disappointing casualness, crossed long, thin legs and blew grayish clouds.

"Ah . . . are you in charge here?"

"Not exactly. No one is. We do have one administrator, the cook, to handle what little work of that type may come up. Don't forget, this is a research station, first, last, and always."

"What is your field, then?"

Viken frowned. "Don't question anyone else so bluntly, Dr. Cornelius," he warned. "They'd rather spin the gossip out as long as possible with each newcomer. It's a rare treat to have someone whose every last conceivable reaction hasn't been—no, no apologies to me. 'S all right. I'm a physicist, specializing in the solid state at ultra-high pressures." He nodded at the wall. "Plenty of it to be oberved—there!"

"I see." Cornelius smoked quietly for a while. Then: "I'm supposed to be the psionics expert, but, frankly, at present I've no idea why your machine should misbehave as reported."

"You mean those, uh, K tubes have a stable output on Earth?"

"And on Luna, Mars, Venus—everywhere, apparently, but here." Cornelius shrugged. "Of course, psibeams are always persnickety, and sometimes you get an unwanted feedback when—no. I'll get the facts before I theorize. Who are your psimen?"

"Just Anglesey, who's not a formally trained esman at all. But he took it up after he was crippled, and showed such a natural aptitude that he was shipped out here when he volunteered. It's so hard to get anyone for Jupiter V that we aren't fussy about degrees. At that, Ed seems to be operating Joe as well as a Ps. D. could."

"Ah, yes. Your pseudojovian. I'll have to examine that angle pretty carefully, too," said Cornelius. In spite of himself, he was getting interested. "Maybe the trouble comes from something in Joe's biochemistry. Who knows? I'll let you into a carefully guarded little secret, Dr. Viken: psionics is not an exact science."

"Neither is physics," grinned the other man. After a moment, he added more soberly: "Not my brand of physics, anyway. I hope to make it exact. That's why I'm here, you know. It's the reason we're all here."

Edward Anglesey was a bit of a shock the first time. He was a head, a pair of arms, and a disconcertingly intense blue stare. The rest of him was mere detail, enclosed in a wheeled machine.

"Biophysicist originally," Viken had told Cornelius. "Studying atmospheric spores at Earth Station when he was still a young man—accident, crushed him up, nothing below his chest will ever work again. Snappish type, you have to go slow with him."

Seated on a wisp of stool in the esprojector control room, Cornelius realized that Viken had been soft-pedaling the truth.

Anglesey ate as he talked, gracelessly, letting the chair's tentacles wipe up after him. "Got to," he explained. "This stupid place is officially on Earth time, GMT. Jupiter isn't. I've got to be here whenever Joe wakes, ready to take him over."

"Couldn't you have someone spell you?" asked Cornelius.

"Bah!" Anglesey stabbed a piece of prot and waggled it at the other man. Since it was native to him, he could spit out English, the common language of the station, with unmeasured ferocity. "Look here. You ever done therapeutic esping? Not just listening in, or even communication, but actual pedagogic control?"

"No, not I. It requires a certain natural talent, like yours." Cornelius smiled. His ingratiating little phrase was swallowe without being noticed by the scored face opposite him. "I tak it you mean cases like, oh, re-educating the nervous system of palsied child?"

"Yes, yes. Good enough example. Has anyone ever tried t suppress the child's personality, take him over in the most litera sense?"

"Good God, no!"

"Even as a scientific experiment?" Anglesey grinned. "Ha any esprojector operative ever poured on the juice and swampe the child's brain with his own thoughts? Come on, Cornelius, won't snitch on you."

"Well . . . it's out of my line, you understand." The psionicis looked carefully away, found a bland meter face and screwed hi eyes to that. "I have, uh, heard something about . . . Well, yes there were attempts made in some pathological cases to, uh, bu through . . . break down the patient's delusions by sheer force—"

"And it didn't work," said Anglesey. He laughed. "It *can'* work, not even on a child, let alone an adult with a fully develope personality. Why, it took a decade of refinement, didn't it, befor the machine was debugged to the point where a psychiatrist coul even 'listen in' without the normal variation between his patter of thought and the patient's—without that variation setting up a interference scrambling the very thing he wanted to study. Th machine has to make automatic compensations for the difference between individuals. We still can't bridge the differences betwee species.

"If someone else is willing to cooperate, you can very gentl guide his thinking. And that's all. If you try to seize control o another brain, a brain with its own background of experience, it own ego, you risk your very sanity. The other brain will figh back instinctively. A fully developed, matured, hardened huma personality is just too complex for outside control. It has too man resources, too much hell the subconscious can call to its defens if its integrity is threatened. Blazes, man, we can't even maste our own minds, let alone anyone else's!"

Anglesey's cracked-voice tirade broke off. He sat brooding a the instrument panel, tapping the console of his mechanica mother.

"Well?" said Cornelius after a while.

He should not, perhaps, have spoken. But he found it hard to remain mute. There was too much silence—half a billion miles of it, from here to the sun. If you closed your mouth five minutes at a time, the silence began creeping in like fog.

"Well," gibed Anglesey. "So our pseudojovian, Joe, has a physically adult brain. The only reason I can control him is that his brain has never been given a chance to develop its own ego. I *am* Joe. From the moment he was 'born' into consciousness, I have been there. The psibeam sends me all his sense data and sends him back my motor-nerve impulses. Nevertheless, he has that excellent brain, and its cells are recording every trace of experience, even as yours and mine; his synapses have assumed the topography which is my 'personality pattern.'

"Anyone else, taking him over from me, would find it was like an attempt to oust me myself from my own brain. It couldn't be done. To be sure, he doubtless has only a rudimentary set of Anglesey-memories—I do not, for instance, repeat trigonometric theorems while controlling him—but he has enough to be, potentially, a distinct personality.

"As a matter of fact, whenever he wakes up from sleep—there's usually a lag of a few minutes, while I sense the change through my normal psi faculties and get the amplifying helmet adjusted—I have a bit of a struggle. I feel almost a . . . a resistance until I've brought his mental currents completely into phase with mine. Merely dreaming has been enough of a different experience to . . ." Anglesey didn't bother to finish sentence.

"I see," murmured Cornelius. "Yes, it's clear enough. In fact, it's astonishing that you can have such total contact with a being of such alien metabolism."

"I won't for much longer," said the esman sarcastically, "unless you can correct whatever is burning out those K tubes. I don't have an unlimited supply of spares."

"I have some working hypotheses," said Cornelius, "but there's so little known about psibeam transmission—is the velocity infinite or merely very great, is the beam strength actually independent of distance? How about the possible effects of transmission—oh, through the degenerate matter in the Jovian core? Good Lord, a planet where water is a heavy mineral and hydrogen is a metal! What do we know?"

"We're supposed to find out," snapped Anglesey. "That' what this whole project is for. Knowledge. Bull!" Almost, h spat on the floor. "Apparently what little we have learned doesn even get through to people. Hydrogen is still a gas where Jo lives. He'd have to dig down a few miles to reach the solid phase And I'm expected to make a scientific analysis of Jovian cond tions!"

Cornelius waited it out, letting Anglesey storm on while h himself turned over the problem of K-tube oscillation.

"They don't understand back on Earth. Even here they don' Sometimes I think they refuse to understand. Joe's down ther without much more than his bare hands. He, I, we started wit no more knowledge than that he could probably eat the local lif He has to spend nearly all his time hunting for food. It's a mirac he's come as far as he has in these few weeks—made a shelte grown familiar with the immediate region, begun on metallurgy hydrurgy, whatever you want to call it. What more do they wa me to do, for crying in the beer?"

"Yes, yes," mumbled Cornelius. "Yes, I . . ."

Anglesey raised his white bony face. Something filmed ov in his eyes.

"What—" began Cornelius.

"Shut up!" Anglesey whipped the chair around, groped f the helmet, slapped it down over his skull. "Joe's waking. G out of here."

"But if you'll let me work only while he sleeps, how can I—

Anglesey snarled and threw a wrench at him. It was a feeb toss, even in low gee. Cornelius backed toward the door. Anglese was tuning in the esprojector. Suddenly he jerked.

"Cornelius!"

"Whatisit?" The psionicist tried to run back, overdid it, ar skidded in a heap to end up against the panel.

"K tube again." Anglesey yanked off the helmet. It must hav hurt like blazes, having a mental squeal build up uncontrolled ar amplified in your own brain, but he said merely: "Change it f me. Fast. And then get out and leave me alone. Joe didn't wak up of himself. Something crawled into the dugout with me—I' in trouble down there!"

It had been a hard day's work, and Joe slept heavily. He d not wake until the hands closed on his throat.

For a moment then he knew only a crazy smothering wave of panic. He thought he was back on Earth Station, floating in null gee at the end of a cable while a thousand frosty stars haloed the planet before him. He thought the great I beam had broken from its moorings and started toward him, slowly, but with all the inertia of its cold tons, spinning and shimmering in the Earthlight, and the only sound himself screaming and screaming in his helmet trying to break from the cable the beam nudged him ever so gently but it kept on moving he moved with it he was crushed against the station wall nuzzled into it his mangled suit frothed as it tried to seal its wounded self there was blood mingled with the foam his blood *Joe roared.*

His convulsive reaction tore the hands off his neck and sent a black shape spinning across the dugout. It struck the wall, thunderously, and the lamp fell to the floor and went out.

Joe stood in darkness, breathing hard, aware in a vague fashion that the wind had died from a shriek to a low snarling while he slept.

The thing he had tossed away mumbled in pain and crawled along the wall. Joe felt through lightlessness after his club.

Something else scrabbled. The tunnel! They were coming through the tunnel! Joe groped blind to meet them. His heart drummed thickly and his nose drank an alien stench.

The thing that emerged, as Joe's hands closed on it, was only about half his size, but it had six monstrously taloned feet and a pair of three-fingered hands that reached after his eyes. Joe cursed, lifted it while it writhed, and dashed it to the floor. It screamed, and he heard bones splinter.

"Come on, then!" Joe arched his back and spat at them, like a tiger menaced by giant caterpillars.

They flowed through his tunnel and into the room, a dozen of them entered while he wrestled one that had curled itself around his shoulders and anchored its sinuous body with claws. They pulled at his legs, trying to crawl up on his back. He struck out with claws of his own, with his tail, rolled over and went down beneath a heap of them and stood up with the heap still clinging to him.

They swayed in darkness. The legged seething of them struck the dugout wall. It shivered, a rafter cracked, the roof came down. Anglesey stood in a pit, among broken ice plates, under the wan light of a sinking Ganymede.

He could see now that the monsters were black in color and that they had heads big enough to accommodate some brain, less than human but probably more than apes. There were a score of them or so, they struggled from beneath the wreckage and flowed at him with the same shrieking malice.

Why?

Baboon reaction, thought Anglesey somewhere in the back of himself. See the stranger, fear the stranger, hate the stranger, kill the stranger. His chest heaved, pumping air through a raw throat. He yanked a whole rafter to him, snapped it in half, and twirled the iron-hard wood.

The nearest creature got its head bashed in. The next had its back broken. The third was hurled with shattered ribs into a fourth, they went down together. Joe began to laugh. It was getting to be fun.

"Yee-ow! Ti-i-i-iger!" He ran across the icy ground, toward the pack. They scattered, howling. He hunted them until the last one had vanished into the forest.

Panting, Joe looked at the dead. He himself was bleeding, he ached, he was cold and hungry and his shelter had been wrecked—but he'd whipped them! He had a sudden impulse to beat his chest and howl. For a moment he hesitated. Why not? Anglesey threw back his head and bayed victory at the dim shield of Ganymede.

Thereafter he went to work. First build a fire, in the lee of the spaceship—which was little more by now than a hill of corrosion. The monster pack cried in darkness and the broken ground, they had not given up on him, they would return.

He tore a haunch off one of the slain and took a bite. Pretty good. Better yet if properly cooked. Heh! They'd made a big mistake in calling his attention to their existence! He finished breakfast while Ganymede slipped under the western ice mountains. It would be morning soon. The air was almost still, and a flock of pancake-shaped sky-skimmers, as Anglesey called them, went overhead, burnished copper color in the first pale dawn streaks.

Joe rummaged in the ruins of his hut until he had recovered the water-smelting equipment. It wasn't harmed. That was the first order of business, melt some ice and cast it in the molds of ax, knife, saw, hammer he had painfully prepared. Under Jovian conditions, methane was a liquid that you drank and water was a dense hard mineral. It would make good tools. Later on he would try alloying it with other materials.

Next—yes. To hell with the dugout, he could sleep in the open again for a while. Make a bow, set traps, be ready to massacre the black caterpillars when they attacked him again. There was a chasm not far from here, going down a long way toward the bitter cold of the metallic-hydrogen strata: a natural icebox, a place to store the several weeks' worth of meat his enemies would supply. This would give him leisure to—Oh, a hell of a lot!

Joe laughed exultantly and lay down to watch the sunrise.

It struck him afresh how lovely a place this was. See how the small brilliant spark of the sun swam up out of eastern fog banks colored dusky purple and veined with rose and gold; see how the light strengthened until the great hollow arch of the sky became one shout of radiance; see how the light spilled warm and living over a broad fair land, the million square miles of rustling low forests and wave-blinking lakes and feather-plumed hydrogen geysers; and see, see, see how the ice mountains of the west flashed like blued steel!

Anglesey drew the wild morning wind deep into his lungs and shouted with a boy's joy.

"I'm not a biologist myself," said Viken carefully. "But maybe for that reason I can better give you the general picture. Then Lopez or Matsumoto can answer any questions of detail."

"Excellent." Cornelius nodded. "Why don't you assume I am totally ignorant of this project? I very nearly am, you know."

"If you wish," laughed Viken.

They stood in an outer office of the xenobiology section. No one else was around, for the station's clocks said 1730 GMT and there was only one shift. No point in having more, until Anglesey's half of the enterprise had actually begun gathering quantitative data.

The physicist bent over and took a paperweight off a desk. "One of the boys made this for fun," he said, "but it's a pretty good model of Joe. He stands about five feet tall at the head."

Cornelius turned the plastic image over in his hands. If you could imagine such a thing as a feline centaur with a thick prehensile tail . . . The torso was squat, long-armed, immensely muscular; the hairless head was round, wide-nosed, with big deep-set eyes and heavy jaws, but it was really quite a human face. The over-all color was bluish gray.

"Male, I see," he remarked.

"Of course. Perhaps you don't understand. Joe is the complet pseudojovian—as far as we can tell, the final model, with all th bugs worked out. He's the answer to a research question that too fifty years to ask." Viken looked sidewise at Cornelius. "So yo realize the importance of your job, don't you?"

"I'll do my best," said the psionicist. "But if . . . well, let' say that tube failure or something causes you to lose Joe befor I've solved the oscillation problem. You do have other pseudo in reserve, don't you?"

"Oh, yes," said Viken moodily. "But the cost . . . We're no on an unlimited budget. We do go through a lot of money, becaus it's expensive to stand up and sneeze this far from Earth. But fo that same reason our margin is slim."

He jammed hands in pockets and slouched toward the inne door, the laboratories, head down and talking in a low, hurrie voice. "Perhaps you don't realize what a nightmare planet Jupite is. Not just the surface gravity—a shade under three gees, what' that?—but the gravitational potential, ten times Earth's. The tem perature. The pressure. Above all, the atmosphere, and the storms and the darkness!

"When a spaceship goes down to the Jovian surface, it's radio-controlled job; it leaks like a sieve, to equalize pressure, bu otherwise it's the sturdiest, most utterly powerful model ever de signed; it's loaded with every instrument, every servomechanism every safety device the human mind has yet thought up to protec a billion-dollar hunk of precision equipment. And what happens Half the ships never reach the surface at all. A storm snatche them and throws them away, or they collide with a floating chun of Ice Seven—small version of the Red Spot—or, so help me what passes for a flock of *birds* rams one and stoves it in! As fo the fifty per cent which do land, it's a one-way trip. We don' even try to bring them back. If the stresses coming down haven' sprung something, the corrosion has doomed them anyway. Hy drogen at Jovian pressure does funny things to metals.

"It cost a total of about five million dollars to set Joe, on pseudo, down there. Each pseudo to follow will cost, if we'r lucky, a couple of million more."

Viken kicked open the door and led the way through. Beyon was a big room, low-ceilinged, coldly lit and murmurous wit ventilators. It reminded Cornelius of a nucleonics lab; for a mo ment he wasn't sure why, then he recognized the intricacies of remote control, remote observation, walls enclosing forces which could destroy the entire moon.

"These are required by the pressure, of course," said Viken, pointing to a row of shields. "And the cold. And the hydrogen itself, as a minor hazard. We have units here duplicating conditions in the Jovian, uh, stratosphere. This is where the whole project really began."

"I've heard something about that. Didn't you scoop up airborne spores?"

"Not I." Viken chuckled. "Totti's crew did, about fifty years ago. Proved there was life on Jupiter. A life using liquid methane as its basic solvent, solid ammonia as a starting point for nitrate synthesis: the plants use solar energy to build unsaturated carbon compounds, releasing hydrogen; the animals eat the plants and reduce those compounds again to the saturated form. There is even an equivalent of combustion. The reactions involve complex enzymes and—well, it's out of my line."

"Jovian biochemistry is pretty well understood, then."

"Oh, yes. Even in Totti's day they had a highly developed biotic technology: Earth bacteria had already been synthesized and most gene structures pretty well mapped. The only reason it took so long to diagram Jovian life processes was the technical difficulty, high pressure and so on."

"When did you actually get a look at Jupiter's surface?"

"Gray managed that, about thirty years ago. Set a televisor ship down, a ship that lasted long enough to flash him quite a series of pictures. Since then, the technique has improved. We know that Jupiter is crawling with its own weird kind of life, probably more fertile than Earth. Extrapolating from the airborne micro-organisms, our team made trial syntheses of metazoans and—"

Viken sighed. "Damn it, if only there were intelligent native life! Think what they could tell us, Cornelius, the data, the—just think back how far we've gone since Lavoisier, with the low-pressure chemistry of Earth. Here's a chance to learn a high-pressure chemistry and physics at least as rich with possibilities!"

After a moment, Cornelius murmured slyly, "Are you certain there *aren't* any Jovians?"

"Oh, sure, there could be several billion of them." Viken shrugged. "Cities, empires, anything you like. Jupiter has the surface area of a hundred Earths, and we've only seen maybe a dozen small regions. But we do know there aren't any Jovians using radio. Considering their atmosphere, it's unlikely they ever would invent it for themselves—imagine how thick a vacuum tube has to be, how strong a pump you need! So it was finally decided we'd better make our own Jovians."

Cornelius followed him through the lab into another room. This was less cluttered, it had a more finished appearance; the experimenter's haywire rig had yielded to the assured precision of an engineer.

Viken went over to one of the panels which lined the walls and looked at its gauges. "Beyond this lies another pseudo," he said. "Female, in this instance. She's at a pressure of two hundred atmospheres and a temperature of 194 absolute. There's a . . . an umbilical arrangement, I guess you'd call it, to keep her alive. She was grown to adulthood in this, uh, fetal stage—we patterned our Jovians after the terrestrial mammal. She's never been conscious, she won't ever be till she's 'born.' We have a total of twenty males and sixty females waiting here. We can count on about half reaching the surface. More can be created as required. It isn't the pseudos that are so expensive, it's their transportation. So Joe is down there alone till we're sure that his kind *can* survive."

"I take it you experimented with lower forms first," said Cornelius.

"Of course. It took twenty years, even with forced-catalysis techniques, to work from an artificial airborne spore to Joe. We've used the psibeam to control everything from pseudo-insects on up. Interspecies control is possible, you know, if your puppet's nervous system is deliberately designed for it and isn't given a chance to grow into a pattern different from the esman's."

"And Joe is the first specimen who's given trouble?"

"Yes."

"Scratch one hypothesis." Cornelius sat down on a workbench, dangling thick legs and running a hand through thin sandy hair. "I thought maybe some physical effect of Jupiter was responsible. Now it looks as if the difficulty is with Joe himself."

"We've all suspected that much," said Viken. He struck a cigarette and sucked in his cheeks around the smoke. His eyes were gloomy. "Hard to see how. The biotics engineers tell me *Pseudocentaurus sapiens* has been more carefully designed than any product of natural evolution."

"Even the brain?"

"Yes. It's patterned directly on the human, to make psibeam control possible, but there are improvements—greater stability."

"There are still the psychological aspects, though," said Cornelius. "In spite of all our amplifiers and other fancy gadgets, psi is essentially a branch of psychology, even today—or maybe it's the other way around. Let's consider traumatic experiences. I take it the . . . the adult Jovian fetus has a rough trip going down?"

"The ship does," said Viken. "Not the pseudo itself, which is wrapped up in fluid just like you were before birth."

"Nevertheless," said Cornelius, "the two-hundred-atmospheres pressure here is not the same as whatever unthinkable pressure exists down on Jupiter. Could the change be injurious?"

Viken gave him a look of respect. "Not likely," he answered. "I told you the J ships are designed leaky. External pressure is transmitted to the, uh, uterine mechanism through a series of diaphragms, in a gradual fashion. It takes hours to make the descent, you realize."

"Well, what happens next?" went on Cornelius. "The ship lands, the uterine mechanism opens, the umbilical connection disengages, and Joe is, shall we say, born. But he has an adult brain. He is not protected by the only half-developed infant brain from the shock of sudden awareness."

"We thought of that," said Viken. "Anglesey was on the psibeam, in phase with Joe, when the ship left this moon. So it wasn't really Joe who emerged, who perceived. Joe has never been much more than a biological waldo. He can only suffer mental shock to the extent that Ed does, because it *is* Ed down there!"

"As you will," said Cornelius. "Still, you didn't plan for a race of puppets, did you?"

"Oh, heavens, no," said Viken. "Out of the question. Once we know Joe is well established, we'll import a few more esmen and get him some assistance in the form of other pseudos. Eventually females will be sent down, and uncontrolled males, to be educated by the puppets. A new generation will be born normally—well, anyhow, the ultimate aim is a small civilization of Jovians. There will be hunters, miners, artisans, farmers, housewives, the works. They will support a few key members, a kind of priesthood. And that priesthood will be esp-controlled, as Joe is. It will exist solely to make instruments, take readings, perform experiments, and tell us what we want to know!"

Cornelius nodded. In a general way, this was the Jovian project as he had understood it. He could appreciate the importance of his own assignment.

Only, he still had no clue to the cause of that positive feedback in the K tubes.

And what could he do about it?

His hands were still bruised. *Oh God,* he thought with a groan, for the hundredth time, *does it affect me that much? While Joe was fighting down there, did I really hammer my fists on metal up here?*

His eyes smoldered across the room, to the bench where Cornelius worked. He didn't like Cornelius, fat cigar-sucking slob, interminably talking and talking. He had about given up trying to be civil to the Earthworm.

The psionicist laid down a screwdriver and flexed cramped fingers. "*Whuff!*" He smiled. "I'm going to take a break."

The half-assembled esprojector made a gaunt backdrop for his wide soft body, where it squatted toad fashion on the bench. Anglesey detested the whole idea of anyone sharing this room, even for a few hours a day. Of late he had been demanding his meals brought here, left outside the door of his adjoining bedroom-bath. He had not gone beyond for quite some time now.

And why should I?

"Couldn't you hurry it up a little?" snapped Anglesey.

Cornelius flushed. "If you'd had an assembled spare machine, instead of loose parts—" he began. Shrugging, he took out a cigar stub and relit it carefully; his supply had to last a long time. Anglesey wondered if those stinking clouds were blown from his mouth of malicious purpose. *I don't like you, Mr. Earthman Cornelius, and it is doubtless quite mutual.*

"There was no obvious need for one, until the other esmen arrive," said Anglesey in a sullen voice. "And the testing instruments report this one in perfectly good order."

"Nevertheless," said Cornelius, "at irregular intervals it goes into wild oscillations which burn out the K tube. The problem is why. I'll have you try out this new machine as soon as it is ready, but, frankly, I don't believe the trouble lies in electronic failure at all—or even in unsuspected physical effects."

"Where, then?" Anglesey felt more at ease as the discussion grew purely technical.

"Well, look. What exactly is the K tube? It's the heart of the esprojector. It amplifies your natural psionic pulses, uses them to modulate the carrier wave, and shoots the whole beam down at Joe. It also picks up Joe's resonating impulses and amplifies them for your benefit. Everything else is auxiliary to the K tube."

"Spare me the lecture," snarled Anglesey.

"I was only rehearsing the obvious," said Cornelius, "because every now and then it is the obvious answer which is hardest to see. Maybe it isn't the K tube which is misbehaving. Maybe it is you."

"What?" The white face gaped at him. A dawning rage crept across its thin bones.

"Nothing personal intended," said Cornelius hastily. "But you know what a tricky beast the subconscious is. Suppose, just as a working hypothesis, that way down underneath, you don't *want* to be on Jupiter. I imagine it is a rather terrifying environment. Or there may be some obscure Freudian element involved. Or, quite simply and naturally, your subconscious may fail to understand that Joe's death does not entail your own."

"Um-m-m." *Mirabile dictu,* Anglesey remained calm. He rubbed his chin with one skeletal hand. "Can you be more explicit?"

"Only in a rough way," replied Cornelius. "Your conscious mind sends a motor impulse along the psibeam to Joe. Simultaneously, your subconscious mind, being scared of the whole business, emits the glandular-vascular-cardiac-visceral impulses associated with fear. These react on Joe, whose tension is transmitted back along the beam. Feeling Joe's somatic fear symptoms, your subconscious gets still more worried, thereby increasing the symptoms. Get it? It's exactly similar to ordinary neurasthenia, with this exception, that since there is a powerful amplifier, the K tube, involved, the oscillations can build up uncontrollably within a second or two. You should be thankful the tube does burn out—otherwise your brain might do so!"

For a moment Anglesey was quiet. Then he laughed. It was a hard, barbaric laughter. Cornelius started as it struck his eardrums.

"Nice idea," said the esman. "But I'm afraid it won't fit all the data. You see, I like it down there. I like being Joe."

He paused for a while, then continued in a dry impersonal tone: "Don't judge the envornment from my notes. They're just idiotic things like estimates of wind velocity, temperature variations, mineral properties—insignificant. What I can't put in is how Jupiter looks through a Jovian's infrared-seeing eyes."

"Different, I should think," ventured Cornelius after a minute's clumsy silence.

"Yes and no. It's hard to put into language. Some of it I can't because man hasn't got the concepts. But . . . oh, I can't describe it. Shakespeare himself couldn't. Just remember that everything about Jupiter which is cold and poisonous and gloomy to us is *right* for Joe."

Anglesey's tone grew remote, as if he spoke to himself "Imagine walking under a glowing violet sky, where great flashing clouds sweep the earth with shadow and rain strides beneath them Imagine walking on the slopes of a mountain like polished metal with a clean red flame exploding above you and thunder laughing in the ground. Imagine a cool wild stream, and low trees with dark coppery flowers, and a waterfall—methanefall, whatever you like—leaping off a cliff, and the strong live wind shakes its mane full of rainbows! Imagine a whole forest, dark and breathing, and here and there you glimpse a pale-red wavering will-o'-the-wisp which is the life radiation of some fleet, shy animal, and . . . and . . ."

Anglesey croaked into silence. He stared down at his clenched fists, then he closed his eyes tight and tears ran out between the lids. "Imagine being *strong!*"

Suddenly he snatched up the helmet, crammed it on his head and twirled the control knobs. Joe had been sleeping, down in the night, but Joe was about to wake up and—roar under the four great moons till all the forest feared him?

Cornelius slipped quietly out of the room.

In the long brazen sunset light, beneath dusky cloud banks brooding storm, he strode up the hill slope with a sense of day's work done. Across his back, two woven baskets balanced each other, one laden with the pungent black fruit of the thorn tree and one with cable-thick creepers to be used as rope. The ax on his shoulder caught the waning sunlight and tossed it blindingly back

It had not been hard labor, but weariness dragged at his mind and he did not relish the household chores yet to be performed cooking and cleaning and all the rest. Why couldn't they hurry up and get him some helpers?

His eyes sought the sky resentfully. Moon Five was hidden

down here, at the bottom of the air ocean, you saw nothing but the sun and the four Galilean satellites. He wasn't even sure where Five was just now, in relation to himself. *Wait a minute, it's sunset here, but if I went out to the viewdome I'd see Jupiter in the last quarter, or would I, oh, hell, it only takes us half an Earth day to swing around the planet anyhow—*

Joe shook his head. After all this time, it was still damnably hard, now and then, to keep his thoughts straight. *I, the essential I, am up in heaven, riding Jupiter Five between cold stars. Remember that. Open your eyes, if you will, and see the dead control room superimposed on a living hillside.*

He didn't, though. Instead, he regarded the boulders strewn wind-blasted gray over the tough mossy vegetation of the slope. They were not much like Earth rocks, nor was the soil beneath his feet like terrestrial humus.

For a moment Anglesey speculated on the origin of the silicates, aluminates, and other stony compounds. Theoretically, all such materials should be inaccessibly locked in the Jovian core, down where the pressure got vast enough for atoms to buckle and collapse. Above the core should lie thousands of miles of allotropic ice, and then the metallic-hydrogen layer. There should not be complex minerals this far up, but there were.

Well, possibly Jupiter had formed according to theory, but had thereafter sucked enough cosmic dust, meteors, gases and vapors down its great throat of gravitation to form a crust several miles thick. Or more likely the theory was altogether wrong. What did they know, what *could* they know, the soft pale worms of Earth?

Anglesey stuck his—Joe's—fingers in his mouth and whistled. A baying sounded in the brush, and two midnight forms leaped toward him. He grinned and stroked their heads; training was progressing faster than he'd hoped, with these pups of the black caterpillar beasts he had taken. They would make guardians for him, herders, servants.

On the crest of the hill, Joe was building himself a home. He had logged off an acre of ground and erected a stockade. Within the grounds there now stood a lean-to for himself and his stores, a methane well, and the beginnings of a large, comfortable cabin.

But there was too much work for one being. Even with the half-intelligent caterpillars to help, and with cold storage for meat, most of his time would still go to hunting. The game wouldn't last forever, either; he had to start agriculture within the next year or so—Jupiter year, twelve Earth years, thought Anglesey. There was the cabin to finish and furnish; he wanted to put a waterwheel, no, methane wheel, in the river to turn any of a dozen machines he had in mind, he wanted to experiment with alloyed ice and—

And, quite apart from his need of help, why should he remain alone, the single thinking creature on an entire planet? He was a male in this body, with male instincts—in the long run, his health was bound to suffer if he remained a hermit, and right now the whole project depended on Joe's health.

It wasn't right!

But I am not alone. There are fifty men on the satellite with me. I can talk to any of them, anytime I wish. It's only that I seldom wish it, these days. I would rather be Joe.

Nevertheless . . . I, the cripple, feel all the tiredness, anger, hurt, frustration, of that wonderful biological machine called Joe. The others don't understand. When the ammonia gale flays open his skin, it is I who bleed.

Joe lay down on the ground, sighing. Fangs flashed in the mouth of the black beast which humped over to lick his face. His belly growled with hunger, but he was too tired to fix a meal. Once he had the dogs trained . . .

Another pseudo would be so much more rewarding to educate.

He could almost see it, in the weary darkening of his brain. Down there, in the valley below the hill, fire and thunder as the ship came to rest. And the steel egg would crack open, the steel arms—already crumbling, puny work of worms!—lift out the shape within and lay it on the earth.

She would stir, shrieking in her first lungful of air, looking about with blank mindless eyes. And Joe would come and carry her home. And he would feed her, care for her, show her how to walk—it wouldn't take long, an adult body would learn those things very fast. In a few weeks she would even be talking, be an individual, a soul.

Did you ever think, Edward Anglesey, in the days when you also walked, that your wife would be a gray four-legged monster?

Never mind that. The important thing was to get others of his kind down here, female *and* male. The station's niggling little plan would have him wait two more Earth years, and then send him only another dummy like himself, a contemptible human mind looking through eyes which belonged rightfully to a Jovian. It was not to be tolerated!

If he weren't so tired...

Joe sat up. Sleep drained from him as the realization entered. *Ie* wasn't tired, not to speak of. Anglesey was. Anglesey, the uman side of him, who for months had slept only in cat naps, vhose rest had lately been interrupted by Cornelius—it was the uman body which drooped, gave up, and sent wave after soft vave of sleep down the psibeam to Joe.

Somatic tension traveled skyward; Anglesey jerked awake.

He swore. As he sat there beneath the helmet, the vividness f Jupiter faded with his scattering concentration, as if it grew ransparent; the steel prison which was his laboratory strengthened ehind it. He was losing contact. Rapidly, with the skill of experience, he brought himself back into phase with the neural curents of the other brain. He willed sleepiness on Joe, exactly as man wills it on himself.

And, like any other insomniac, he failed. The Joe body was oo hungry. It got up and walked across the compound toward its ack.

The K tube went wild and blew itself out.

The night before the ships left, Viken and Cornelius sat up ate.

It was not truly a night, of course. In twelve hours the tiny noon was hurled clear around Jupiter, from darkness back to larkness, and there might well be a pallid little sun over its crags vhen the clocks said witches were abroad in Greenwich. But most of the personnel were asleep at this hour.

Viken scowled. "I don't like it," he said. "Too sudden a hange of plans. Too big a gamble."

"You are only risking—how many?—three male and a dozen emale pseudos," Cornelius replied.

"And fifteen J ships. All we have. If Anglesey's notion doesn't vork, it will be months, a year or more, till we can have others uilt and resume aerial survey."

"But if it does work," said Cornelius, "you won't need any ships, except to carry down more pseudos. You will be too busy evaluating data from the surface to piddle around in the upper atmosphere."

"Of course. But we never expected it so soon. We were going o bring more esmen out here, to operate some more pseudos—"

"But they aren't *needed,*" said Cornelius. He struck a cig to life and took a long pull on it, while his mind sought careful for words. "Not for a while, anyhow. Joe has reached a poi where, given help, he can leap several thousand years of history- he may even have a radio of sorts operating in the fairly ne future, which would eliminate the necessity of much of your es ing. But without help, he'll just have to mark time. And it's stup to make a highly trained human esman perform manual labo which is all that the other pseudos are needed for at this momen Once the Jovian settlement is well established, certainly, then yc can send down more puppets."

"The question is, though," persisted Viken, "can Anglese himself educate all those pseudos at once? They'll be helpless infants for days. It will be weeks before they really start thinkir and acting for themselves. Can Joe take care of them meanwhile?"

"He has food and fuel stored for months ahead," said Co nelius. "As for what Joe's capabitilities are—well, hm-m-m, w just have to take Anglesey's judgment. He has the only insi information."

"And once those Jovians do become personalities," worrie Viken, "are they necessarily going to string along with Joe? Don forget, the pseudos are not carbon copies of each other. Th uncertainty principle assures each one a unique set of genes. there is only one human mind on Jupiter, among all those aliens—

"One *human* mind?" It was barely audible. Viken opened h mouth inquiringly. The other man hurried on.

"Oh, I'm sure Anglesey can continue to dominate them," sa Cornelius. "His own personality is rather—tremendous."

Viken looked startled. "You really think so?"

The psionicist nodded. "Yes. I've seen more of him in th past weeks than anyone else. And my profession naturally orien me more toward a man's psychology than his body or his habit You see a waspish cripple. I see a mind which has reacted to i physical handicaps by developing such a hellish energy, such a inhuman power of concentration, that it almost frightens m Give that mind a sound body for its use and nothing is impossib to it."

"You may be right, at that," murmured Viken after a paus "Not that it matters. The decision is taken, the rockets go dow tomorrow. I hope it all works out."

He waited for another while. The whirring of ventilators in h little room seemed unnaturally loud, the colors of a girlie picture on the wall shockingly garish. Then he said slowly, "You've been rather close-mouthed yourself, Jan. When do you expect to finish your own esprojector and start making the tests?"

Cornelius looked around. The door stood open to an empty hallway, but he reached out and closed it before he answered with a slight grin, "It's been ready for the past few days. But don't tell anyone."

"How's that?" Viken started. The movement, in low gee, took him out of his chair and halfway across the table between the men. He shoved himself back and waited.

"I have been making meaningless tinkering motions," said Cornelius, "but what I waited for was a highly emotional moment, a time when I can be sure Anglesey's entire attention will be focused on Joe. This business tomorrow is exactly what I need."

"Why?"

"You see, I have pretty well convinced myself that the trouble in the machine is psychological, not physical. I think that for some reason, buried in his subconscious, Anglesey doesn't want to experience Jupiter. A conflict of that type might well set a psionic-amplifier circuit oscillating."

"Hm-m-m." Viken rubbed his chin. "Could be. Lately Ed has been changing more and more. When he first came here, he was peppery enough, but he would at least play an occasional game of poker. Now he's pulled so far into his shell you can't even see him. I never thought of it before, but . . . yes, by God, Jupiter must be having some effect on him."

"Hm-m-m." Cornelius nodded. He did not elaborate—did not, for instance, mention that one altogether uncharacteristic episode when Anglesey had tried to describe what it was like to be a Jovian.

"Of course," said Viken thoughtfully, "the previous men were not affected especially. Nor was Ed at first, while he was still controlling lower-type pseudos. It's only since Joe went down to the surface that he's become so different."

"Yes, yes," said Cornelius hastily. "I've learned that much. But enough shop talk—"

"No. Wait a minute." Viken spoke in a low, hurried tone, looking past him. "For the first time, I'm starting to think clearly about this. Never really stopped to analyze it before, just accepted a bad situation. There *is* something peculiar about Joe. It can't

very well involve his physical structure, or the environment, b-
cause lower forms didn't give this trouble. Could it be the fa
that Joe is the first puppet in all history with a potentially hum
intelligence?"

"We speculate in a vacuum," said Cornelius. "Tomorro
maybe, I can tell you. Now I know nothing."

Viken sat up striaght. His pale eyes focused on the other m
and stayed there, unblinking. "One minute," he said.

"Yes?" Cornelius shifted, half rising. "Quickly, please. It
past my bedtime."

"You know a good deal more than you've admitted," sa
Viken. "Don't you?"

"What makes you think that?"

"You aren't the most gifted liar in the universe. And then, y
argued very strongly for Anglesey's scheme, this sending dow
the other pseudos. More strongly than a newcomer should."

"I told you, I want his attention focused elsewhere when—

"Do you want it that badly?" snapped Viken.

Cornelius was still for a minute. Then he sighed and lean
back.

"All right," he said. "I shall have to trust your discretion.
wasn't sure, you see, how any of you old-time station personn
would react. So I didn't want to blabber out my speculation
which may be wrong. The confirmed facts, yes, I will tell them
but I don't wish to attack a man's religion with a mere theory.

Viken scowled. "What the devil do you mean?"

Cornelius puffed hard on his cigar; its tip waxed and wane
like a miniature red demon star. "This Jupiter Five is more tha
a research station," he said gently. "It is a way of life, is it no
No one would come here for even one hitch unless the work wa
important to him. Those who re-enlist, they must find somethin
in the work, something which Earth with all her riches cann
offer them. No?"

"Yes," answered Viken. It was almost a whisper. "I didn
think you would understand so well. But what of it?"

"Well, I don't want to tell you, unless I can prove it, tha
maybe this has all gone for nothing. Maybe you have wasted you
lives and a lot of money, and will have to pack up and go home.

Viken's long face did not flicker a muscle. It seemed to hav
congealed. But he said calmly enough, "Why?"

"Consider Joe," said Cornelius. "His brain has as much ca

pacity as any adult human's. It has been recording every sense datum that came to it, from the moment of 'birth'—making a record in itself, in its own cells, not merely in Anglesey's physical memory bank up here. Also, you know, a thought is a sense datum, too. And thoughts are not separated into neat little railway tracks; they form a continuous field. Every time Anglesey is in rapport with Joe, and thinks, the thought goes through Joe's synapses as well as his own—and every thought carries its own associations, and every associated memory is recorded. Like if Joe is building a hut. the shape of the logs might remind Anglesey of some geometric figure, which in turn would remind him of the Pythagorean theorem—"

"I get the idea," said Viken in a cautious way. "Given time, Joe's brain will have stored everything that ever was in Ed's."

"Correct. Now, a functioning nervous system with an engrammatic pattern of experience, in this case a *nonhuman* nervous system—isn't that a pretty good definition of a personality?"

"I suppose so, Good Lord!" Viken jumped. "You mean Joe is—taking over?"

"In a way. A subtle, automatic, unconscious way." Cornelius drew a deep breath and plunged into it. "The pseudojovian is so nearly perfect a life-form: your biologists engineered into it all the experience gained from nature's mistakes in designing *us*. At first, Joe was only a remote-controlled biological machine. Then Anglesey and Joe became two facets of a single personality. Then, oh, very slowly, the stronger, healthier body . . . more amplitude to its thoughts . . . do you see? Joe is becoming the dominant side. Like this business of sending down the other pseudos—Anglesey only thinks he has logical reasons for wanting it done. Actually, his 'reasons' are mere rationalizations for the instinctive desires of the Joe facet.

"Anglesey's subconscious must comprehend the situation, in a dim reactive way; it must feel his human ego gradually being submerged by the steamroller force of *Joe's* instincts and *Joe's* wishes. It tries to defend its own identity, and is swatted down by the superior force of Joe's own nascent subconscious.

"I put it crudely," he finished in an apologetic tone, "but it will account for that oscillation in the K tubes."

Viken nodded, slowly, like an old man. "Yes, I see it," he answered. "The alien environment down there . . . the different brain structure. . . . Good God! Ed's being swallowed up in Joe!

The puppet master is becoming the puppet!'' He looked ill.

''Only speculation on my part,'' said Cornelius. All at onc
he felt very tired. It was not pleasant to do this to Viken, who
he liked. ''But you see the dilemma, no? If I am right, then ar
esman will gradually become a Jovian—a monster with two bo
ies, of which the human body is the unimportant auxiliary on
This means no esman will ever agree to control a pseudo—ther
fore, the end of your project.''

He stood up. ''I'm sorry, Arne. You made me tell you wh
I think, and now you will lie awake worrying, and I am mayb
quite wrong and you worry for nothing.''

''It's all right,'' mumbled Viken. ''Maybe you're not wrong.

''I don't know.'' Cornelius drifted toward the door. ''I a
going to try to find some answers tomorrow. Good night.''

The moon-shaking thunder of the rockets, crash, crash, crash
leaping from their cradles, was long past. Now the fleet glide
on metal wings, with straining secondary ram-jets, through th
rage of the Jovian sky.

As Cornelius opened the control-room door, he looked at h
telltale board. Elsewhere a voice tolled the word to all the station
One ship wrecked, two ships wrecked, but Anglesey would let n
sound enter his presence when he wore the helmet. An obligin
technician had haywired a panel of fifteen red and fifteen blu
lights above Cornelius' esprojector, to keep him informed, to
Ostensibly, of course, they were only there for Anglesey's benefi
though the esman had insisted he wouldn't be looking at them.

Four of the red bulbs were dark and thus four blue ones woul
not shine for a safe landing. A whirlwind, a thunderbolt, a floatin
ice meteor, a flock of mantalike birds with flesh as dense and har
as iron—there could be a hundred things which had crumpled fou
ships and tossed them tattered across the poison forests.

Four ships, hell! Think of four living creatures, with an ex
cellence of brain to rival your own, damned first to years i
unconscious night and then never awakening save for one un
comprehending instant, dashed in bloody splinters against an ic
mountain. The wasteful callousness of it was a cold knot in Co
nelius' belly. It had to be done, no doubt, if there was to be an
thinking life on Jupiter at all; but then let it be done quickly an
minimally, he thought, so that the next generation could be be
gotten by love and not by machines!

He closed the door behind him and waited for a breathless moment. Anglesey was a wheel chair and a coppery curve of helmet, facing the opposite wall. No movement, no awareness whatsoever. Good. It would be awkward, perhaps ruinous, if Anglesey learned of this most intimate peering. But he needn't, ever. He was blindfolded and ear-plugged by his own concentration.

Nevertheless, the psionicist moved his bulky form with care, across the room to the new esprojector. He did not much like his snooper's role, he would not have assumed it at all if he had seen any other hope. But neither did it make him feel especially guilty. If what he suspected was true, then Anglesey was all unawares being twisted into something not human; to spy on him might be to save him.

Gently, Cornelius activated the meters and started his tubes warming up. The oscilloscope built into Anglesey's machine gave him the other man's exact alpha rhythm, his basic biological clock. First you adjusted to that, then you discovered the subtler elements by feel, and when your set was fully in phase you could probe undetected and—

Find out what was wrong. Read Anglesey's tortured subconscious and see what there was on Jupiter that both drew and terrified him.

Five ships wrecked.

But it must be very nearly time for them to land. Maybe only five would be lost in all. Maybe ten would get through. Ten comrades for—Joe?

Cornelius sighed. He looked at the cripple, seated blind and deaf to the human world which had crippled him, and felt a pity and an anger. It wasn't fair, none of it was.

Not even to Joe. Joe wasn't any kind of soul-eating devil. He did not even realize, as yet, that he *was* Joe, that Anglesey was becoming a mere appendage. He hadn't asked to be created, and to withdraw his human counterpart from him would very likely be to destroy him.

Somehow, there were always penalties for everybody when men exceeded the decent limits.

Cornelius swore at himself, voicelessly. Work to do. He sat down and fitted the helmet on his own head. The carrier wave made a faint pulse, inaudible, the trembling of neurones low in his awareness. You couldn't describe it.

Reaching up, he turned to Anglesey's alpha. His own had a somewhat lower frequency, it was necessary to carry the signals through a heterodyning process. Still no reception. Well, of course he had to find the exact wave form, timbre was as basic to thought as to music. He adjusted the dials slowly, with enormous care.

Something flashed through his consciousness, a vision of clouds roiled in a violet-red sky, a wind that galloped across horizonless immensity—he lost it. His fingers shook as he turned back.

The psibeam between Joe and Anglesey broadened. It took Cornelius into the circuit. He looked through Joe's eyes, he stood on a hill and stared into the sky above the ice mountains, straining for sign of the first rocket; and simultaneously he was still Jan Cornelius, blurrily seeing the meters, probing about for emotions, symbols, any key to the locked terror in Anglesey's soul.

The terror rose up and struck him in the face.

Psionic detection is not a matter of passive listening in. Much as a radio receiver is necessarily also a weak transmitter, the nervous system in resonance with a source of psionic-spectrum energy is itself emitting. Normally, of course, this effect is unimportant; but when you pass the impulses, either way, through a set of heterodyning and amplifying units, with a high negative feedback . . .

In the early days, psionic psychotherapy vitiated itself because the amplified thoughts of one man, entering the brain of another, would combine with the latter's own neural cycles according to the ordinary vector laws. The result was that both men felt the new beat frequencies as a nightmarish fluttering of their very thoughts. An analyst, trained into self-control, could ignore it; his patient could not, and reacted violently.

But eventually the basic human wave timbres were measured, and psionic therapy resumed. The modern esprojector analyzed an incoming signal and shifted its characteristics over to the "listener's" pattern. The *really* different pulses of the transmitting brain, those which could not possibly be mapped onto the pattern of the receiving neurones—as an exponential signal cannot very practicably be mapped onto a sinusoid—those were filtered out.

Thus compensated, the other thought could be apprehended as comfortably as one's own. If the patient were on a psibeam circuit, a skilled operator could tune in without the patient being necessarily aware of it. The operator could either probe the other man's thoughts or implant thoughts of his own.

Cornelius' plan, an obvious one to any psionicist, had depended on this. He would receive from an unwitting Anglesey-Joe. If his theory was right and the esman's personality was being distorted into that of a monster, his thinking would be too alien to come through the filters. Cornelius would receive spottily or not at all. If his theory was wrong, and Anglesey was still Anglesey, he would receive only a normal human stream of consciousness and could probe for other troublemaking factors.

His brain roared!

What's happening to me?

For a moment, the interference which turned his thoughts to saw-toothed gibberish struck him down with panic. He gulped for breath, there in the Jovian wind, and his dreadful dogs sensed the alienness in him and whined.

Then, recognition, remembrance, and a blaze of anger so great that it left no room for fear. Joe filled his lungs and shouted it aloud, the hillside boomed with echoes:

"Get out of my mind!"

He felt Cornelius spiral down toward unconsciousness. The overwhelming force of his own mental blow had been too much. He laughed, it was more like a snarl, and eased the pressure.

Above him, between thunderous clouds, winked the first thin descending rocket flare.

Cornelius' mind groped back toward the light. It broke a watery surface, the man's mouth snapped after air and his hands reached for the dials, to turn his machine off and escape.

"Not so fast, you." Grimly, Joe drove home a command that locked Cornelius' muscles rigid. "I want to know the meaning of this. Hold still and let me look." He smashed home an impulse which could be rendered, perhaps, as an incandescent question mark. Remembrance exploded in shards through the psionicist's forebrain.

"So. That's all there is? You thought I was afraid to come down here and be Joe, and wanted to know why? But I *told* you I wasn't!"

I should have believed, whispered Cornelius.

"Well, get out of the circuit, then." Joe continued growling it vocally. "And don't ever come back in the control room, understand? K tubes or no, I don't want to see you again. And I may be a cripple, but I can still take you apart cell by cell. Now sign off—leave me alone. The first ship will be landing in minutes."

You a cripple—you, Joe Anglesey?

"What?" The great gray being on the hill lifted his barbaric head as if to sudden trumpets. "What do you mean?"

Don't you understand? said the weak, dragging thought. *You know how the esprojector works. You know I could have probed Anglesey's mind in Anglesey's brain without making enough interference to be noticed. And I could not have probed a wholly nonhuman mind at all, nor could it have been aware of me. The filters would not have passed such a signal. Yet you felt me in the first fractional second. It can only mean a human mind in a nonhuman brain.*

You are not the half-corpse on Jupiter Five any longer. You're Joe—Joe Anglesey.

"Well, I'll be damned," said Joe. "You're right."

He turned Anglesey off, kicked Cornelius out of his mind with a single brutal impulse, and ran down the hill to meet the spaceship.

Cornelius woke up minutes afterward. His skull felt ready to split apart. He groped for the main switch before him, clashed it down, ripped the helmet off his head and threw it clanging on the floor. But it took a little while to gather the strength to do the same for Anglesey. The other man was not able to do anything for himself.

They sat outside sick bay and waited. It was a harshly lit barrenness of metal and plastic, smelling of antiseptics—down near the heart of the satellite, with miles of rock to hide the terrible face of Jupiter.

Only Viken and Cornelius were in that cramped little room. The rest of the station went about its business mechanically, filling in the time till it could learn what had happened. Beyond the door, three biotechnicians, who were also the station's medical staff, fought with death's angel for the thing which had been Edward Anglesey.

"Nine ships got down," said Viken dully. "Two males, seven females. It's enough to start a colony."

"It would be genetically desirable to have more," pointed out Cornelius. He kept his own voice low, in spite of its underlying cheerfulness. There was a certain awesome quality to all this.

"I still don't understand," said Viken.

"Oh, it's clear enough—now. I should have guessed it before, maybe. We had all the facts, it was only that we couldn't make the simple, obvious interpretation of them. No, we had to conjure up Frankenstein's monster."

"Well," Viken's words grated, "we have played Frankenstein, haven't we? Ed is dying in there."

"It depends on how you define death." Cornelius drew hard on his cigar, needing anything that might steady him. His tone grew purposely dry of emotion.

"Look here. Consider the data. Joe, now: a creature with a brain of human capacity, but without a mind—a perfect Lockean *tabula rasa* for Anglesey's psibeam to write on. We deduced, correctly enough—if very belatedly—that when enough had been written, there would be a personality. But the question was, whose? Because, I suppose, of normal human fear of the unknown, we assumed that any personality in so alien a body had to be monstrous. Therefore it must be hostile to Anglesey, must be swamping him—"

The door opened. Both men jerked to their feet.

The chief surgeon shook his head. "No use. Typical deep-shock traumata, close to terminus now. If we had better facilities, maybe . . ."

"No," said Cornelius. "You cannot save a man who has decided not to live any more."

"I know." The doctor removed his mask. "I need a cigarette. Who's got one?" His hands shook a little as he accepted it from Viken.

"But how could he—decide—anything?" choked the physicist. "He's been unconscious ever since Jan pulled him away from that . . . that thing."

"It was decided before then," said Cornelius. "As a matter of fact, that hulk in there on the operating table no longer has a mind. I know. I was there." He shuddered a little. A stiff shot of tranquilizer was all that held nightmare away from him. Later he would have to have that memory exorcised.

The doctor took a long drag of smoke, held it in his lungs a moment, and exhaled gustily. "I guess this winds up the project," he said. "We'll never get another esman."

"I'll say we won't." Viken's tone sounded rusty, "I'm going

to smash that devil's engine myself."

"Hold on a minute!" exclaimed Cornelius. "Don't you understand? This isn't the end. It's the beginning!"

"I'd better get back," said the doctor. He stubbed out his cigarette and went through the door. It closed behind him with a deathlike quietness.

"What do you mean?" Viken said it as if erecting a barrier.

"*Won't* you understand?" roared Cornelius. "Joe has all Anglesey's habits, thoughts, memories, prejudices, interests. Oh, yes, the different body and the different environment—they do cause some changes, but no more than any man might undergo on Earth. If you were suddenly cured of a wasting disease, wouldn't you maybe get a little boisterous and rough? There is nothing abnormal in it. Nor is it abnormal to want to stay healthy—no? Do you see?"

Viken sat down. He spent a while without speaking.

Then, enormously slow and careful: "Do you mean Joe is Ed?"

"Or Ed is Joe. Whatever you like. He calls himself Joe now, I think—as a symbol of freedom—but he is still himself. What *is* the ego but continuity of existence?

"He himself did not fully understand this. He only knew—he told me, and I should have believed him—that on Jupiter he was strong and happy. Why did the K tube oscillate? A hysterical symptom! Anglesey's subconscious was not afraid to stay on Jupiter—it was afraid to come back!

"And then, today, I listened in. By now, his whole self was focused on Joe. That is, the primary source of libido was Joe's virile body, not Anglesey's sick one. This meant a different pattern of impulses—not too alien to pass the filters, but alien enough to set up interference. So he felt my presence. And he saw the truth, just as I did.

"Do you know the last emotion I felt as Joe threw me out of his mind? Not anger any more. He plays rough, him, but all he had room to feel was joy.

"I *knew* how strong a personality Anglesey has! Whatever made me think an overgrown child brain like Joe's could override it? In there, the doctors—bah! They're trying to salvage a hulk which has been shed because it is useless!"

Cornelius stopped. His throat was quite raw from talking. He paced the floor, rolled cigar smoke around his mouth but did not draw it any farther in.

When a few minutes had passed, Viken said cautiously, "All right. You should know—as you said, you were there. But what do we do now? How do we get in touch with Ed? Will he even be interested in contacting us?"

"Oh, yes, of course," said Cornelius. "He is still himself, remember. Now that he has none of the cripple's frustrations, he should be more amiable. When the novelty of his new friends wears off, he will want someone who can talk to him as an equal."

"And precisely who will operate another pseudo?" asked Viken sarcastically. "I'm quite happy with this skinny frame of mine, thank you!"

"Was Anglesey the only hopeless cripple on Earth?" asked Cornelius quietly.

Viken gaped at him.

"And there are aging men, too," went on the psionicist, half to himself. "Someday, my friend, when you and I feel the years close in, and so much we would like to learn—maybe we too would enjoy an extra lifetime in a Jovian body." He nodded at his cigar. "A hard, lusty, stormy kind of life, granted—dangerous, brawling, violent—but life as no human, perhaps, has lived it since the days of Elizabeth the First. Oh, yes, there will be small trouble finding Jovians."

He turned his head as the surgeon came out again.

"Well?" croaked Viken.

The doctor sat down. "It's finished," he said.

They waited for a moment, awkwardly.

"Odd," said the doctor. He groped after a cigarette he didn't have. Silently, Viken offered him one. "Odd. I've seen these cases before. People who simply resign from life. This is the first one I ever saw that went out smiling—smiling all the time."